MAID *to* MATCH

Books by
Deeanne Gist

A Bride Most Begrudging

The Measure of a Lady

Courting Trouble

Deep in the Heart of Trouble

A Bride in the Bargain

Beguiled

Maid to Match

MAID *to* MATCH

DEEANNE GIST

BETHANY HOUSE PUBLISHERS
Minneapolis, Minnesota

Cover design by Jennifer Parker
Cover model photography by Mike Habermann
Architectural imagery by Alamy

Scripture quotations are from the New King James Version of the Bible. Copyright © 1979, 1980, 1982 by Thomas Nelson, Inc. Used by permission. All rights reserved.

Published by Bethany House Publishers
11400 Hampshire Avenue South
Bloomington, Minnesota 55438

Bethany House Publishers is a division of
Baker Publishing Group, Grand Rapids, Michigan.

Printed in the United States of America

Library of Congress Cataloging-in-Publication Data

Gist, Deeanne.
    Maid to match / Deeanne Gist.
      p. cm.
    ISBN 978-0-7642-0806-5 (alk. paper) — ISBN 978-0-7642-0408-1 (pbk.)
    1. Biltmore Estate (Asheville, N.C.)—Fiction. I. Title.
    PS3607.I55M35   2010
    813'.6—dc22
                                       2010004415

To my PIT Crew
(Personal Intercessory Team)

Larry and Donna Drake
Gary and Carol Johnson
Pat Kane
Linda Wiltze

Who for three months prayed for me daily when
I realized it would take a miracle for me
to finish my manuscript before the deadline.

Never have the words flowed so quickly and abundantly
as when y'all stood in the gap for me.
Thank you for the incredible commitment you gave and
for seeing me through.

I love you so much,
Dee
P.S. So . . . y'all busy next summer?

DEEANNE GIST has a background in education and journalism. Her credits include *People, Parents, Parenting, Family Fun*, and the *Houston Chronicle*. She has a line of parenting products called I Did It® Productions and a degree from Texas A&M. She and her husband live in Houston, Texas, and have four grown children. Deeanne loves to hear from her readers at her Web site, *www.IWantHerBook.com*.

ACKNOWLEDGMENTS

My big sisters glommed up all the smart genes. Fortunately, there were enough creative genes to go around, but not smarts. Never was this more clearly evident to me than when it was time to research and plot this book. I had called my big sister, Gayle Evers, and asked her to go along with me on my research trip to Biltmore. We met at the airport, and while we were in the waiting area, she said, "I did some preliminary research on the Web and brought you a few articles to read."

She then proceeded to pull out this gigantic three-ring binder filled with articles on the Gilded Age, the Vanderbilts, turn-of-the-century servants, and all kinds of things. It was obvious she'd read every single page. Some were highlighted. Others had notes in the margins.

She handed it to me. "You might want to read this on the plane before we get there."

I just looked at her. There was no way. It was going to take me two months to read all that, not two hours! But I have to tell you, everything in that binder was solid gold. I think I highlighted the whole thing. Afterward, I went to her house and we plotted the book together. Her ideas were amazing.

When the manuscript was finished, she read it and critiqued

it. Meanwhile, my assistant of seven years, Paula Wolsted, found a full-time job. (Love you, Paula. We sure do miss you. They'd better be treating you right over there!) Before I started interviewing for a new assistant, I asked my sister if she'd be interested in the position. And wonder of wonders, she was. (When the middle sister, Linda, found out I was going to be the boss of Gayle, she laughed and laughed and laughed. But the truth is, Gayle's still the boss!)

I have to say, the year has been so special. The two of us have connected in ways we never had before. As I write this, I'm sitting in front of a fire in my pj's at a B&B in Asheville, North Carolina. Across from me is Gayle, also in her jammies. We are working on a Readers' Event that we are holding this fall.

I hope you will come. Not just because we're going to have a blast—info at *GetawayWithDee.com*—but because then you can meet Gayle. The woman whom I pestered constantly when we were kids. The woman who gives and gives and gives of herself to any and all. The woman whom I have been mightily blessed to have as an assistant. And doubly blessed to have as my big sister.

Thanks, Sis . . . for everything.

CHAPTER

One

BILTMORE ESTATE
NEAR ASHEVILLE, NORTH CAROLINA
AUGUST 1898

Like a butterfly breaking free from its confining cocoon, Tillie Reese emerged from the barren, tan-colored servants' hall into the opulence of Biltmore's main level. These predawn hours were her favorite. All was dark, no one stirred, and she had the entire floor—easily a half acre in size—all to herself.

She'd walked this path many times and could navigate it without candle or lamp. For just a moment, she imagined herself mistress of the chateau. Elegantly dressed, gliding across the parquet and trying to decide whether to have Chef prepare *petites bouchées* or *puits d'amour*. Whether to spend the morning reading Yeats, Browning, or Dickens. Whether to call the carriage round for a drive through the country or ride one of the thoroughbreds waiting in the stable.

Tightening her grip on her housemaid's box, she inhaled deeply. The polish she'd made of linseed oil, vinegar, turpentine, and wine tickled her nose. She allowed herself a sneeze—something strictly forbidden were anyone about.

The click of her heels echoed throughout the vast, wide-open area as she skirted the sunken atrium filled with palms, exotic plants, blooming shrubs, and a large fountain sculpture yet to be turned on. She finally reached the tapestry gallery and paused, listening to the silence, enjoying the anonymity of the dark.

Let there be light.

She pushed the familiar white button. Electric lights flared, illuminating a room so long it could hold two modest houses. Several groupings of sage brocade sofas and chairs filled the area. Huge tapestries lined one wall. Opposite them stood a wall of windows and French doors.

The soft hum of the Edison bulbs bid her good morning. The thrill and miracle of the electric lights never failed to stir her. But this morning something else warred for her attention, and suddenly, the light made her feel exposed, vulnerable, naked.

She touched the black button. Darkness slammed back down like a closing trunk lid. All was quiet again. Not a whisper of sound.

She held her breath. Felt her heart hammering in her breast. And allowed the thought she'd been hiding since last night to fully form in her head.

Bénédicte was leaving. Returning to France. Leaving the new Mrs. Vanderbilt without a lady's maid.

A lady's maid. Next to housekeeper, the highest-ranking

position for a woman. The servant who had morning tea brought to her by the first housemaid while the second house-maid made up a fire in her room.

The servant who was free to take a bath as often as she liked. Who traveled with Mrs. Vanderbilt. Who read books—*books!*—aloud to Mrs. Vanderbilt. Who was required to dress in the same fashions as Mrs. Vanderbilt. Best of all, a lady's maid earned quite a bit more money, so she could help her family and others in the community who were in need.

Tillie, as head parlormaid, would surely be considered for the position. The housekeeper had requested a private audi-ence with her before breakfast. Lord willing, it was to discuss just that.

After hugging the thought one last time, she carefully returned it to the recesses of her mind. Dawdling in fantasies when she should be setting the gallery to rights was no way to put her best foot forward.

Pushing the white button, she again flooded the room with light. If the entire first floor was to be in complete readiness before the master and his bride descended for the day, she'd best get busy.

∞

Chatter, laughter, and the clinking of plated ware filled the servants' dining hall, but Tillie participated in none of it. She avoided eye contact with the long row of liveried men sitting opposite her and the equal number of uniformed women beside her. She took particular care not to glance her brother's way. One look at Allan and he'd know something was up.

The dining hall servant, a young girl of sixteen, refilled Tillie's glass of milk. "Is everythin' to your liking, Miss Tillie? You've barely touched your liver and bacon."

"It's fine, Nell. Delicious, actually."

Nell glanced at the clock but said nothing as its minute hand jumped a step closer to the half-hour mark.

Tillie took a large bite of potatoes. She'd have to eat quickly if she was going to finish before eight-thirty. But after her meeting with the housekeeper, her stomach had lost its ability to digest.

"May I have your attention, please?" From the head of the table, Mrs. Winter made her request only once, and just that quickly, a hush fell over the room of servants. As housekeeper, she was second only to the Vanderbilts, outranking even the butler.

Her gaze briefly touched the butler's at the opposite end of the table; then she surveyed the long rows of men and women between them. "As you know, Bénédicte has decided to return to France as soon as a replacement for her can be found."

All eyes turned to Mrs. Vanderbilt's lady's maid. She sat immediately to the right of Mrs. Winter and across from the hallboy, underbutlers, and footmen. The dark green fabric of her gown strewn with pink and yellow blossoms caused her olive skin to glow.

From what Tillie had been told, between the language barrier and the isolation of Biltmore, Bénédicte could not adjust. She wanted to go home.

Next to Bénédicte was Tillie. On Tillie's right, the head chambermaid, then the first housemaid and so forth all the way down the table to the laundresses and scullery maids.

"Rather than importing someone from France or England, or even from Newport," Mrs. Winter continued, "Mrs. Vanderbilt has decided to award Bénédicte's position to one of our current staff members."

The attention immediately shifted to Tillie and the three girls to her right—the leaders of the domestic corps.

"After much consideration, she has narrowed the choice to either Tillie or Lucy."

Dixie Brown bent over her plate, capturing Tillie's attention. The excitement and delight on her friend's face was unmistakable.

Tillie offered her a slight smile, then glanced at her brother. Allan's brows had converged. His thoughts unreadable.

Mrs. Winter took a sip of coffee. "While Mrs. Vanderbilt is deciding, Tillie and Lucy will be called upon to take on a few of Bénédicte's duties. As a result, some of you will be required to take care of whatever chores they leave behind."

To Tillie's immediate right, Lucy Lewers sat tall and confident, her caramel-colored hair coiled neatly beneath a snowy cap, which was nothing more than a piece of frilly cloth resting on the crown of her head. Long lashes framed eyes the same caramel color as her hair. Her skin held no blemish, her profile no flaw. With the slightest lifting of her chin, she looked down the table at all the underlings, as if her appointment to the position was imminent.

"Finish up," Mrs. Winter admonished. "The day is calling."

∞

Allan cornered Tillie on the way to morning prayers.

"Why didn't you tell me?" Grabbing her by the arm, he propelled her into the canning pantry and closed the door. He stood a half foot taller than she, with wide shoulders and hair every bit as thick and black as her own.

"I only found out myself just before we sat down to breakfast." She rubbed the place he'd squeezed.

"What are you going to do?"

She cocked her head. "Do? I'm going to work my fingers to the bone and beg God for His favor. What do you think I'm going to do?"

He pinched the bridge of his nose. "It'll change everything. You'll be one of *them*, the swell set."

She smiled at the term referring to the butler, chef, lady's maid, and valet. "But I want to be one of them. Can you imagine all the opportunities I'll have? The pay? The clothes? The privileges? The travel?"

"Travel? You can't so much as look at a carriage without getting sick. How, exactly, do you plan to manage that?"

She stiffened. "I'm older now. I'm sure the motion won't affect me like it did when I was little. Besides, think of the freedom I'll have every single day. I'll be able to—"

"Freedom?" he scoffed. "There's no such thing as freedom with that job. You'll be at her ladyship's beck and call all hours of the day and night."

"But that's just it. I'll be confidante to *Edith Stuyvesant Dresser Vanderbilt*!"

"You won't be on the fourth floor with Dixie and all the other girls. You'll be stuck on the second floor with *her* and the high-and-mighty Mrs. Winter. You won't be able to have dessert, or tea, or gossip with the rest of us. You'll have to retire to Mrs. Winter's room with the swell set."

"And partake of the same desserts the Vanderbilts are having!" Tillie shook her head in mock sorrow. "That will certainly be a burden."

He tightened his mouth. "You won't be able to get married."

She frowned. "None of us can get married. Not unless we want to lose our jobs."

"You could get married. It would just mean you couldn't work in the house. You'd have to work on one of Mr. Vanderbilt's farms or in the dairy or something like that."

"Why would I want to do that when I can work here? Are you crazy?" She reached for the door.

He pressed his hand against it. "A lady's maid position will eat up the best years of your life, Tillie. Then the minute a gray hair pops up or a tiny wrinkle forms, out you go. Only the young and beautiful can be ladies' maids."

"Gray hairs? You're talking to me about gray hairs? I'm *eighteen.*"

"I know how old you are."

"Then what are you so worried about? I'll be careful with my earnings. And when the time comes, leaving my job won't be a concern because I'll have enough to live on for the rest of my life."

"Alone. With no one to keep you company. And not at all in the style you'll have become accustomed to."

Rolling her eyes, she crossed her arms. "I thought you'd be happy for me. If I get this position, Mama will think she's died and gone to heaven."

"Conrad's in love with you."

She stilled, then slowly lowered her arms. "Conrad? The footman?"

She pictured the gangly young man who was so skinny he stuffed his stockings in order to give himself shapely calves.

"You know any other Conrads?" Allan asked.

Anger surged through her. "Well, he'd better put me right out of his mind. I'm not caring which nor whether about him nor anybody else, and if he jeopardizes this for me, I'll have his head on a platter." She hammered a finger against her brother's chest. "You understand me?"

"You don't even like him a little? All the girls flirt with him."

"They'd better not let Mrs. Winter catch them or they'll be the ones sacked, not him." She took a deep breath. "I want this job, Bubby. I want it more than anything I've ever wanted in my life. You tell Conrad to stay clear of me. You hear?"

Sighing, he released the door. "I hear."

Two

I *will not cast up my accounts. I will not cast up my accounts.*

No matter how many times Tillie recited the mantra, the nausea would not go away. The carriage hit a rut, jostling her inside and out. Gritting her teeth, she looked out the window, but watching the trees and foliage roll past like ocean waves made it worse.

Oh, why couldn't we have ridden with the top down?

She had much more control in an open carriage. It was the enclosed ones which gave her the most trouble. Her palms began to sweat. *Think of something else.*

Edith Vanderbilt sat across from her, reading *The Prince and the Pauper*, her body swaying in rhythm with the carriage. She had brown hair and hazel eyes, was twenty-five years old, nearly six feet tall, and commanded such presence Tillie felt small by comparison—even though she herself was five foot eight.

The stale air inside the carriage thickened. Tillie's nostrils pinched together in an effort to draw in oxygen. *Think of something else.*

Mrs. Vanderbilt had met and married Mr. Vanderbilt in Paris, though she was originally from New York. So the gowns she'd brought with her were the very latest in European fashions.

Tillie's nausea crept up to chest level. She slipped a finger between her neck and collar.

You're not a child. You're a grown woman. Think of something else.

The blue serge Mrs. Vanderbilt wore was different from anything Tillie had ever seen. The skirt fastened at the side and was elaborately trimmed with graduated braids of different shades and styles. The epaulettes covering slightly puffed sleeves were pointed and trimmed in the same style.

A prickling sensation began behind Tillie's eyes. The nausea now sat at the back of her throat. Beads of moisture formed on her upper lip. *Don't do this, Tillie. Don't.*

She concentrated harder on the gown. If she were to earn the lady's maid position, would the outfit one day be hers when it was tossed aside?

Moisture collected on her neck, back, and under her arms. She opened her mouth, quietly drawing in deep breaths, then blowing them out. *Think of something else.*

She eyed her mistress more closely. Hers wasn't the lush hourglass figure so popular nowadays, but more willowy. Tillie was somewhere in between. But if she needed more fabric in the bodice, she'd be able to take a few inches from the length of the skirt.

The carriage hit another bump. Gagging, Tillie slammed her eyes shut and pressed gloved fingers to her mouth.

"Are you all right, Tillie?"

Please, Lord. Make it go away. I cannot cast up my accounts on my first assignment!

She swallowed, forcing the bile back down. "I'm fine, ma'am. Thank you."

Placing a ribbon between the pages of her book, Mrs. Vanderbilt set it to the side, then tapped on the roof of the carriage. It immediately slowed, then pulled to a stop. The vehicle rocked as the driver bounced off. The door opened.

"Is anything amiss, ma'am?"

"I think I'd like to ride the rest of the way with the top down, Earl. Would you mind?"

He held out his hand. "Not at all, ma'am."

She placed her hand in his, allowing him to guide her through the door. "Come, Tillie. Let's stretch our legs, shall we?"

The tall young coachman offered her a hand.

Tillie covered her entire mouth. Tears sprung to her eyes. Her shoulders jerked in an effort to hold the sickness inside.

Earl leaned in to see what the delay was, his eyes widening. "Take the deuce."

Grabbing her around the waist, he hauled her out of the carriage and bodily carried her to the nearest tree. Too miserable to object, she waited for him to release her, then crumpled to her knees, unable to control the waves of nausea any longer.

∞

"It's all right." Mrs. Vanderbilt smiled from across the open carriage. She'd insisted on Tillie facing forward while she rode backward. No amount of naysaying would persuade her otherwise.

And if that wasn't bad enough, after humiliating herself in front of Mrs. Vanderbilt and Earl, Tillie then succumbed to tears. Silent tears, but tears nonetheless. Tears which refused to stop. And it didn't matter anyway. Her chances of becoming a lady's maid were gone.

The thought brought a fresh bout. She made no pretense of delicately patting her eyes with her handkerchief. She wiped them, then blew her nose, knowing full well it was unlady-like. But then, so were puffy eyes, a blotched face, and a red nose.

She rubbed her head. Her mother would be heartbroken. It would have been better if Tillie had never been in the running than to have been selected as a candidate only to be withdrawn before the contest had even begun.

And not just because of her mother, but because of Tillie's own aspirations. Becoming a lady's maid was her one chance to come up in the world and see beyond the borders of Asheville, North Carolina. But now that chance was gone. Trampled. All because she couldn't ride in a vehicle for any length of time without getting sick.

Mrs. Vanderbilt cocked her head to the side. "My sister used to be afflicted with your same ailment."

Tillie sniffled.

"For her, riding backward, being enclosed, or doing stitching while in motion was what usually brought it on."

Tillie nodded. "Me too. I'm so sorry, ma'am."

"Nonsense. Don't give it another thought." She held up her book. "I found this in my husband's library. It's by a man named Mark Twain. It's quite good."

Tillie crinkled the wet handkerchief in her hands. "I've never read him before."

"You like to read?"

"I love to." Looking off into the distance, she scanned the Blue Ridge Mountains, which framed the horizon. "When I was a girl, I collected my own library. Inside the cover of each book, I'd write 'Private Library,' along with a number and my name."

Mrs. Vanderbilt leaned back. "And what books did you have in your library?"

"Let's see . . . *The Three Musketeers, Ben Hur, Macbeth, Oliver Twist.*"

"A rather adventurous list."

She dropped her gaze. "I had three older brothers and I desperately wanted to be one of them—one of the big toads, I used to say." She shrugged. "So I read books like *Pride and Prejudice* only under the cover of darkness."

Amusement played at the corners of Mrs. Vanderbilt's lips. "And did you become one of the big toads?"

"No, ma'am. They always saw me as a girl first and a pest second."

She nodded. "I only have sisters, but I can appreciate your wanting to be one of the big toads. I've felt the same way at times."

The chasm between Tillie's world and hers was insurmountable, yet the new Mrs. Vanderbilt was so approachable, so normal, it took Tillie aback. In previous wealthy homes her employers had been haughty at best, tyrannical at worst. She'd not been allowed to speak with the lady of the house unless it was to deliver a message, and then she had to do so in as few words as possible.

Yet here she sat having an actual *conversation* with Mrs. Vanderbilt. And though her mistress expressed a childhood yearning to be one of the big toads, not even her sisters would dare question her standing now.

"Where's your library?" Mrs. Vanderbilt asked. "I assume it isn't up in your room at the Estate?"

"Oh no, ma'am. It's at my parents' house. They live on the property, though. My father is a painter. He paints Mr. Vanderbilt's insignia on, well, just about anything that needs it." She gestured to the right and left. "He painted it on the doors of this carriage, for instance."

Eyes bright, Mrs. Vanderbilt raised her brows. "Did he? I'll have to take a closer look when we stop." Picking up *The Prince and the Pauper*, she gave Tillie a rundown of what had happened in the story so far. "I'd ask you to read for me, but I'm afraid that wouldn't be a very good idea under the circumstances."

"I could try, ma'am."

She chuckled. "No, no. I insist. I'll read it to you instead."

CHAPTER
Three

The day had been something straight out of a fairy tale. Other than the debacle at the side of the road, of course. But once Earl had put the top down and Mrs. Vanderbilt had begun to read aloud, Tillie's stomach settled and they reached Asheville just as the prince and the pauper decided to switch places.

Tillie had no time to ruminate about it, though. The intoxication of being in town, shopping with Mrs. Vanderbilt, and carrying her purchases had captured all of Tillie's attention. The Vanderbilts were nothing short of royalty in the area, and though everyone liked Mr. Vanderbilt, they absolutely adored his new bride.

Tillie had been told as much many times, but because most of her work was done indoors before the family rose in the morning, she hadn't had an opportunity to see it firsthand. All day long the townsfolk catered to Mrs. Vanderbilt, and then in turn to Tillie—simply because she was accompanying the lady of the manor.

Storekeepers tried to anticipate her needs. The bookshop they visited filled with customers pretending to peruse books. A young man on the boardwalk turned a startling shade of red when they passed. And children ran beside their carriage throwing flowers.

The entire experience left Tillie energized and enthralled. Arranging her skirts on the carriage seat, she savored the moments, tucking the memories deep into her heart.

As Earl turned the coach south and approached the outskirts of town, Mrs. Vanderbilt whispered, "As soon as we're out of sight, we'll switch places."

Heat sprung to Tillie's cheeks. "I'm much better, ma'am. There's no need."

"All the same. And next time, we'll be sure to bring the cabriolet so we can both face forward."

Next time? *Next time?* Was Mrs. Vanderbilt suggesting Tillie was still in the running? She couldn't possibly be. But—

"Earl?" Mrs. Vanderbilt straightened. "What's going on?"

Tillie twisted around. The old ramshackle military school sat at the end of Black Bottom Street. It had housed one failed venture after another since the Civil War until finally being converted into an asylum for indigent orphan children. If she'd received the lady's maid position, it would have topped her list of needy causes to contribute to. After helping her family, of course. But now, both were out of reach.

Barren grounds and long-deserted farm equipment surrounded the crumbling three-story brick structure with missing windowpanes and a sagging roof. In the dirt yard, a crowd of children stood shoulder to shoulder, cheering on two grown men engaged in fisticuffs. One wore a suit, the other only trousers and a shirt.

"What's happening, Earl?" Mrs. Vanderbilt repeated.

He slowed the carriage. "I'm not sure, ma'am. All I know is, my twin seems to be in the center of it."

"Your twin? You have a twin?"

"Yes, ma'am."

Tillie's attention swerved back to the two men. It didn't take long to ascertain which was the twin. The uppermost qualifications for coachmen and footmen were height and good looks. Earl had both and a good deal of brawn to go with it. So did his twin.

"Stop the carriage at once," Mrs. Vanderbilt said. "Go see if you can break them up, then bring him to me."

"Yes, ma'am."

Earl pulled into the unfenced yard, removed his hat, then jumped from the seat. Several of the children turned round, but the fighters took no notice.

Earl's tailed coat and velvet knee britches of deep maroon contrasted sharply with the simple, unadorned clothing of the orphans. And though his appearance and that of the fancy carriage distracted the children, they were unwilling to ignore the fight.

Earl's brother dodged a swing, then quickly followed with a fist to the nose of his opponent. A crack split the air.

The man's head snapped backward, eyes rolling. He slammed to the ground, flat on his back. A puff of dirt exploded around him.

Tillie barely managed to conceal her distress. The man who'd just been laid out was the new orphanage director. She gripped her hands in her lap. Mr. Sloop had done wonders with the children since taking on the directorship last year. No longer did the wards of the state race about town causing mischief in threadbare clothing and filth. They bathed, dressed respectably, and didn't stray beyond their yard—other than to attend Sunday services.

Mr. Sloop had begun to renovate the old building and was in desperate need of more funds. Funds Tillie wanted to contribute, but couldn't on her current salary.

Bending over, Earl's twin hauled Mr. Sloop back up by the collar and cocked back his fist.

Earl stepped into the circle and grabbed his brother's wrist. "He's down, Mack."

Retaining his grasp on the man, Mack whipped his head around, dirty blond hair falling into enraged eyes. A trickle of blood seeped from his mouth into an unkempt beard. Recognition cleared his eyes and his lips curled into a snarl. "Better back up, brother, or you'll soil your prissy finery."

"What's going on?" Earl made no move to release his twin's wrist.

Mack's eyes darted toward one of the children.

Earl followed his gaze, zeroing in on a girl in a brown calico with a wide sailor collar. The juvenile style of her dress did nothing to disguise her maturing form. "Ora Lou?"

Tillie caught a glimpse of a darkening bruise on the girl's cheek before the teener spun around and raced through the front door of the orphanage.

Earl returned his attention to a pair of brown eyes just like his. Only they were brimming with contempt. Whether it was contempt for Earl's livery, his station, or for Earl himself, Tillie couldn't be sure.

"You're picking a fight because he hit Ora Lou?" Earl's exasperation was clear. "She's just a girl, Mack. What does it matter?"

Mrs. Vanderbilt stiffened. Tillie sucked in her breath. She was unsure which upset her more—Earl's prejudice or his assumption the director had hit Ora Lou, which Tillie was certain he'd never do.

A low growl from the back of Mack's throat sent shivers up her arms. His muscles bulged from holding up the dead weight in his fisted hand.

As one, the children backed up.

"Take your hands off me, Earl."

Earl shook his head. "Can't do that. I've got Mrs. Vanderbilt in the coach and she wants to meet you."

"Well, I don't want to meet her."

Heat surged up Tillie's neck. Couldn't he see they were within hearing distance?

"Doesn't matter," Earl said. "She told me to bring you to her and that's exactly what I intend to do. I'd appreciate it if you'd come willingly, though. I really don't want to make a mess of my *prissy* finery."

Mack studied his brother a moment, then sighed and turned his attention to the director in his clutches. He was still out cold.

Mack drew him closer. "You ever lay a hand on my sister again, and I'll finish what I started here."

With the warning spoken to unconscious ears, he flung Mr. Sloop to the ground. Earl released Mack's wrist and swept his hand in an after-you gesture.

"This better not take long."

The children parted, too timid to approach the carriage. None of them seemed concerned for their director. Much as Tillie wanted to see to his welfare, she forced herself to stay put. Finally, an adolescent boy hurried inside. Hopefully he was fetching Mrs. Sloop for help.

As the brothers advanced, Tillie couldn't discern for certain if they were identical. They definitely had the same build, same height, and same eyes, but with Mack's beard and filth disguising all else, she couldn't be sure.

She knew what Mrs. Vanderbilt was thinking, though. Two footmen who were not only tall and handsome, but identical, would be the stuff of legends amongst her set.

"Ma'am, this is my brother, Mack Danver."

Mack looked her square in the eye. The challenge was unmistakable.

Mrs. Vanderbilt tilted her head. "I think your defense of your sister is honorable, Mack Danver, though I'm not sure about the method."

He lifted one shoulder in a disdainful shrug. "I probably overreacted. She's just a girl, after all. Little more than a domestic animal."

Tillie gasped.

Mrs. Vanderbilt lifted a brow. "A mountain highlander, I presume? What brings you to the city?"

Mack turned to leave.

Earl grabbed his arm. "Our pa's been gone awhile, but Ma just passed, so we had to break up the family. Our siblings, other than Ora Lou, were placed into homes and scattered all over the mountain. Since I live up at the Estate and Mack boards as a janitor for the Battery Park Hotel, we had to put Ora Lou here at Sloop's orphanage."

Mrs. Vanderbilt leaned into the cushions of the landau. "How would you like to work at Biltmore House, Mr. Danver?"

Tillie gaped at her mistress. She could understand wanting him on the property as a stable hand or in the dairy until he could be cleaned up and taught a few things. But in the house? Right away? Without a reference?

Mack turned his head to the side and spit. "I don't think I'd care to work there one iota."

"My husband pays his staff New York wages. Much more than what you're making at Battery Park, I'm sure. With the income you'd make at Biltmore, you'd be able to set your sister up in her own place in no time."

"She'll make do."

"In my experience, sir, orphanages rarely raise a child to adulthood. If the ward can't be placed out, she's often put onto the street."

His eyes grew cold. "She can just dress like a boy and carry a pistol, then. I'm not working for a bunch of brigetty folks who live at the back of beyond."

Mrs. Vanderbilt held his gaze for a long moment. "So you're afraid?"

Shaking off Earl's hand, Mack took a step forward. "I'm not afraid."

"Aren't you?"

He didn't answer. Nor did he need to. He looked ready to prove his point the same way he had with the unfortunate Mr. Sloop.

Finally, Mrs. Vanderbilt gave a nod. "If you change your mind, come to the house and tell them I sent you."

∞

Tillie stood in front of Mrs. Winter's desk.

"It isn't enough to pass lightly over the surface," the housekeeper was saying. Her blond hair had begun to silver and new wrinkles appeared at the corners of her eyes and mouth. "The rims and legs of the tables along with the backs and legs of the chairs and sofas need to be rubbed vigorously."

"Yes, ma'am." She'd assumed she'd been called in because of the little episode she'd had on the way to town. Never did it occur to her Alice had done shoddy work in the tapestry gallery.

"It's very unlike you, Tillie."

"Yes, ma'am. It won't happen again." She wasn't about to shift the blame to Alice. Part of her trial period was to delegate her responsibilities to others when she had need to. With the trip to Asheville, she'd needed to.

Still, as head parlormaid, those downstairs rooms were her domain. She'd see to it Alice didn't miss so much as an inch of furniture next time.

Mrs. Winter removed the glasses perched on her nose. Her blue eyes gentled. "I understand you comported yourself quite well in town today."

"Thank you, ma'am." *Here it comes.*

"Mrs. Vanderbilt was suitably impressed."

But . . .

"In a day or two she and Lucy will be going about the estate. Mrs. Vanderbilt intends to take a census of all staff members and their families."

"Yes, ma'am."

"During that time, Bénédicte will give you a tour of Mrs. Vanderbilt's bedroom, closets, and drawers. It is important you memorize everything's exact place and Mrs. Vanderbilt's preferences."

She was still in the running. A thrill shot through her. "Yes, ma'am."

Putting her glasses back on, the housekeeper made a notation on the paper in front of her. "That will be all."

Mack stepped out of the barbershop and ran a hand across his cheek, trying to adjust to the smoothness of his face. He planned to stop by the police chief's office to see what could be done about the director of the orphanage, but he knew the chief wouldn't take him seriously unless he cleaned up.

First stop had been the bathhouse. His clothes had been so filthy, they'd insisted on delivering them to the laundry while he bathed, then loaning him clean ones until his could be scoured. It wasn't that he enjoyed living in filth, it was just his employer didn't allow the nighttime janitor to make use of the hotel's wash bins or bathtubs. Not even a tin bath. And he didn't have money to spare for a bathhouse. Every cent was put toward the day he could get Ora Lou out of Sloop's orphanage.

He took a deep breath. It felt great to be clean again.

Cutting across Mule Alley and down Saloon Row, a buzzing fly pestered his ear while the smell of alcohol died on the breeze.

A squatty brick laundry house sat at the end of the road. He thought it ironic to have a place like that tucked behind the town's red light district. On second thought, maybe it was fitting. Sometimes you had to pass through the dirt before you could get yourself clean.

Of course, the city fathers hadn't meant anything profound about life. They just wanted to keep the billowing steam and drying clothes out on Asheville's edges.

He stepped through the laundry door, a blanket of wet heat immediately enveloping him. A whiff of lye and enough bleach on the air to sting his lungs momentarily cut off his oxygen. Rubbing boards, scrubbing brushes, and a big iron mangle took up most of the room. Just inside, a young woman worked tub and posser like a butter churn, her shoulders wide, her neck as thick as a man's, while her granny reached for one of the irons heating on the hob.

The washer girl paused, swiping a hand across her brow. "Earl? What're you broguin' about in the middle of the week fer? Ain't you supposed to be up at the Big House?"

Mack hesitated. It had been a long time since someone had mistaken him for Earl.

She placed a fist on her waist. "Well, come on in and set ya a cheer. I been meaning to talk to you anyways. Something's gotta be done about that sister of yourn over at Sloop's."

Frowning, he closed the door. "My sister?"

"Aw, don't act like ya don't know what I'm a'talking about."

"I'm afraid I don't, actually."

She *tsked*. "I'd think a feller who's as big on sweetheartin' as you, he wouldn't need things spelled out."

He narrowed his eyes. "What things?"

"Forbus Sloop's a regular o' Daphne Devine's. I'm surprised you hadn't bumped into him coming or going."

Mack didn't question how she knew who visited the bawdy house. She had a clear shot of Miss Daphne's place right through her side window. He glanced out at the white clapboard two-story, which had its shades drawn tight against the daylight.

He knew his brother was a regular. That and his drinking ate up every bit of money he earned. If he'd just show a little restraint, there'd be money for Ora Lou to leave Sloop's. But that wasn't going to happen.

"What do Sloop's activities have to do with my sister?" he asked.

Her red, cracked hands gripped the posser's handle. "Well, I'll tell ya. She's gettin' her womanly curves. And she's living under that sorry feller's roof while his wife turns a blind eye to his backhandin'."

His chest tightened. "Are you saying he's harmed Ora Lou?"

"I'm saying Ora Lou has a new bruise most ever' week. What do you suppose it is that has Forbus in such a swivet that he's gotta wear her out with his fists?"

Mack didn't hazard a guess. "How do you know this?"

"I pick up and deliver Sloop's laundry." She pumped the posser in and out of the water.

"How long has it been going on?"

"Couple o' months now. Though this last time the bruise was nastier 'n usual. Heard tell yer brother saw it and just about tore Forbus apart."

He scowled. "I did not."

Her churning stopped; then her eyes slowly widened. "Creation. You're not Earl. You're the brother. Land's sake, what happened to you? You look just like Earl."

"I shaved, that's all." He rubbed his jaw again. "And I'm nothing like my brother."

She resumed her chore. "Does that mean you're gonna do somethin'?"

He nodded. "I imagine so. Just as soon as you give me my clothes."

∞

Mack didn't have much occasion to go to City Hall. He had an inborn distrust of authority types, and Captain Hovious confirmed his misgivings.

The two-hundred-fifty-pound officer leaned back in his chair, his paunch swelling over his belt. "Now, that's the pot calling the kettle black, if you ask me. Forbus Sloop was in here not two hours ago, making the same complaint about you. And he was perty near black and blue all over."

"He's abusing the girls."

"I know Forbus myself. He's a happily married man."

"Who spends more time at Daphne Devine's than he does at home."

The captain grinned. "Don't we all, brother. Don't we all."

Mack tensed. "I want to talk to the chief."

Hovious picked something green from his teeth. "Well, the chief isn't here. And even if he were, he'd say the same thing. This town owes a debt to Sloop, what with the way he's taken in all those guttersnipes and cleaned them up. Before he came along, Asheville was overrun with the little beggars."

"I want someone to check on it anyway."

"Sorry, but we have more pressing matters to tend to."

Flexing his fists, Mack took a step forward.

Hovious narrowed his eyes, then slowly rose to his feet. "I wouldn't advise it, Danver."

The captain didn't carry a firearm. None of the police did. They didn't have to. They were armed with enough bulk to do what needed to be done. And if they required an edge, the clubs at their waists did the trick.

Mack kept his hands to his sides. "You tell the chief that if my sister gets any more bruises, he's gonna have trouble on his hands."

"And if she runs into a door or something?"

"Then trouble won't begin to describe it." Mack slammed out of the office. If Ora Lou was to be helped, and the police wouldn't cooperate, then he'd need to turn elsewhere. And wherever that was, it would have to involve a person of influence.

The only person like that he knew was an old friend of his late father's. A man who'd been president of the college Pa had taught at. The man who'd first brought Pa to Asheville. The man who was now Buncombe County's state representative.

Mack glanced at a giant clock on the wall of the rotunda. Maybe he could catch Leonard Vaughan before he left for the day. It had been years since he'd seen him, but he knew the man would give him an audience.

He wandered the corridors of City Hall until he finally found a door with Vaughan's name painted on the glass. He knocked, peering through the window. A man on the other side waved him in.

The office smelled of books and cigars, but the giant oak desk was clear of papers, as if Vaughan had just cleaned it off in anticipation of going home.

"May I help you, young man?" he asked, standing as he closed a drawer.

The familiar face of his father's dearest friend made Mack's chest catch. He catalogued the changes the years had wrought—a receding hairline, gray at the temples, wrinkles at his eyes. Mack tried to superimpose those changes onto the memory he had of his father, but could not.

Mack whipped off his hat. "Hello, sir. Danver, here. It's good to see you."

Vaughan stilled, lifting his brows. "Earl?"

"Mackenzie, sir."

"Well, for the love of Peter." He waved him into a seat and resumed his own. "I see you've exceeded even your father's height. Is Earl the same?"

"To the inch."

"Imagine that." After a moment, his facial muscles sobered. "I'm sorry about your mother. I went to your homeplace the moment I returned from Europe and heard of her death, but it was abandoned. All I could find out was the family had been split up."

"I tried to keep us together, but Earl wouldn't give up his job at Biltmore and come home. He'd acquired a taste for women and spirits. So the children were left to me."

"How old are they now?"

"Ora Lou's thirteen. The boys are nine, eight, and seven, respectively." He sighed. "Not so little anymore, now that I think on it."

"So what happened?" Vaughan opened a drawer and offered Mack a cigar.

Waving it off, he settled back in his chair. "Nothing changed for me, of course. Ever since Pa died I'd been using what I made at the hotel to put food on the table for Ma and the children. But with her gone, it was hard on Ora Lou."

"I guess she felt she should step into your mother's shoes?"

Mack nodded. "I couldn't bring the boys with me to work, nor could I quit and help Ora Lou."

"What'd you do?"

"I decided to start working as many double shifts as I could. By the time I made it back up the mountain, Grandpa had moved into the cabin and told the boys they didn't have to do any work. That's what Ora Lou was for. And if she didn't comply, he'd raise a hand to her."

"The devil you say." Cutting the cap off his cigar, Vaughan clucked his tongue. "I suppose I shouldn't be surprised. It was always his way."

Mack tightened his jaw. "Even still, Pa spent years training us to respect the womenfolk. I can remember Earl and me laughing about it behind his back, thinking how ridiculous it all was. But when I came home and saw those boys doing nothing while Ora Lou planted, hoed, gathered fodder, split rails, cooked, washed, and everything else, something just snapped in me."

"I can imagine."

Mack ran a hand through his hair. "I realized then, I couldn't provide for them and simultaneously protect Ora Lou and the boys from Grandpa's influence. So I took Ikey, Otis, and John-John to families on the other side of the mountain, where folks school their children. But Ora Lou was different. Even though most clans treat their women well, I couldn't quite bring myself to leave her so far out of my sphere. So I put her in Sloop's orphanage."

Vaughan lit the edges of his cigar. "Well, I daresay she'll do well there. That Sloop is a fine fellow."

"What makes you say that?"

Blowing out the match, he tossed it in a tray. "All you have to do is look at what he's done for those children. They were in the streets one day with barely enough clothing to cover their backs. The next, he had them beneath a warm roof with full bellies. Have you seen what he's done with the parlor? He's methodically renovating the whole place. He just finished his office and—"

"He beats the girls."

Vaughan stopped, the cigar halfway to his mouth.

"I've suspected for a while, but when I saw Ora Lou's face yesterday, well . . ." He gripped the arms of the chair.

"Are you sure? She didn't run into something?"

"I'm sure. And it's been going on for a while."

Vaughan fell back in his chair. "Is it just Ora Lou, or are there others?"

"I don't know, but I suspect there are others."

"Have you gone to Chief Pilkerton?"

"Just came from there. They threw me out and told me not to come back."

Vaughan rubbed his head. "Doesn't surprise me. Pilkerton and Sloop go way back."

"Well, I'm not going to put up with it. I made it clear to Sloop that Ora Lou was off-limits, but all the same, I don't like leaving her there."

Staring into the distance, Vaughan shook his head. "I just can't believe it."

"That's why I'm here."

Vaughan looked at him. "Whatever amount you need, I can have it for you by tomorrow."

Mack stiffened. "I didn't come for a handout."

"Your father was like family to me, son. I'd be honored if you'd let me do this."

"No, sir."

Sighing, Vaughan shook his head. "That confounded mountain pride. As quick to resent alms as you are to return a blow. I can't even remember how many times I asked your mother to accept my help, but she absolutely refused."

Mack leaned forward, settled his elbows on his knees, and clasped his hands between them. "Actually, I do have a favor to ask."

Vaughan took a puff of his cigar. "Name it and it's yours."

∞

Tillie sat at her parents' table soaking in the love and laughter. This was the first day off she'd had since her news had been announced, though her mother had learned of it almost as soon as Tillie had. As predicted, Mama had been over the moon.

"Did Mrs. Vanderbilt pay for her stuff with real gold coins?" little Martha asked, her blue eyes wide. "Did *you* carry her gold pieces for her?"

The Reese children had come in bunches, like radishes. Tillie and Allan were part of the first bunch—and the only ones still in North Carolina. The middle two boys had moved west.

The second batch had started coming when Tillie was six. One baby a year for three years straight. Then another dry spell. Gussie and Ricky, the oldest of that bunch, had shouldered much of the burden for the youngers.

When Tillie had left home at twelve to be a step-girl for

a well-to-do family in Asheville, another bunch had begun arriving. Five-year-old Martha was part of it.

"Nobody carries their money with them," Gussie told Martha. "It's vulgar. They have their bills sent to the steward."

Tillie and Allan exchanged a glance. Gussie would be twelve in the spring and thus leaving home. In anticipation, Mama had her reading *The Handy Book for the Young General Servant*.

"Did she buy diamonds and dresses and a new pair of shoes?" Martha breathed, her black ringlets hovering over her food as she leaned in toward Tillie.

"She can't tell you." Gussie handed a piece of bread to her youngest brother, Ennis. "Mrs. Vanderbilt relies on the total discretion of those who serve her."

Mama carved a piece of meat off the hare, her enormous bosom rocking with the motion. For such large proportions up top and down below, she had a relatively small waist— accentuated by the cinching of her apron strings. "That may be so, Gussie, but it isn't as if we're in Newport. Here, all of Asheville would know of Mrs. Vanderbilt's purchases before she ever even left the store. So if Tillie wants to tell us, I'm sure it would be all right. We are family, after all."

Gussie snorted, but the room fell silent. Tillie could feel their ears growing as they waited for her reply. Even little Ennis looked at her, his mouth now full of bread.

She took a sip of milk, stalling. The townsfolk would discuss Mrs. Vanderbilt's every move in great detail for weeks to come, but that was them. Not the staff. Not her personal maid. If she were to blur the lines, how would she know where they started and where they stopped? Before she could formulate a response, Allan came to her rescue.

44

"I don't think the good people of Asheville were talking about Mrs. Vanderbilt so much as they were Tillie," he said.

Mama's smile was smug. "Really? What were they saying?"

He jabbed some peas with his fork. "Earl Danver made sure everybody knew it took him twice as long to get to town as usual, because after every bump Tillie had to cast her bread upon the waters."

Mama popped Allan's knuckles with her spoon. *Popped* them. Tillie hadn't seen her do that since he was twelve.

"You hush up, Allan Reese. I don't want to hear another word about that or that infernal Earl Danver."

Allan's brows shot up to his hairline as he massaged his offended hand. "I'm afraid the secret's out, Ma. It's quite the joke belowstairs, and Till's endured no small amount of ribbing because of it."

"What've they said, Allan?" Ricky's toothy grin stretched from one large ear to the other. "Does she have a nickname?"

"*Ricky!*" Mama waved her spoon, but the ten-year-old was well out of reach.

"Does she?"

Straightening his spine, Allan looked down his nose. "I'm afraid, young sir, that your sister relies on the total discretion of those who serve beside her."

The little ones giggled. They loved it when he put on his footman airs.

Thank you, she mouthed.

Mama signaled for the plates and flatware to be passed to her for washing. "Tillie's still better than that Lucy Lewers. Why, Lucy has men sniffing after her all the time. You've seen the way she carries on at the barn gatherings during parlor games and twistifications. It's downright scandalous. You won't catch our Tillie doing that."

"Nothing wrong with twistifications."

All eyes swung toward Pa. He weighed about one hundred thirty pounds and, like Ricky, had a toothy grin. He didn't talk much, but everybody in the county knew him on account of his being the best dancer these parts had ever seen.

Mama gave him a stern look. "Dancing gives the boys ideas, Herbert."

"Aw, we're just letting off a little steam." Allan pulled his napkin from his collar. "Nobody thinks anything about it."

"Just the same." She turned to Tillie. "The last thing you need now is some loafer showing some interest. You probably shouldn't go to the barn gatherings at all until your position as lady's maid is secure."

Tillie frowned. "Not go? But I haven't missed a single one since I was hired on."

"I'll watch out for her." Allan pushed back his chair. "You ready to sit on the porch, Pa?"

Pa finished off his milk, then stood. Looking down the row of children, he zeroed in on Tillie. "Some ginger cookies would help you on those carriage rides."

"Ginger cookies?" she asked.

"Ayup. And you go on to those twistifications. If King David can dance like a fool, I'm figuring a few whirls around the floor'll be all right for you."

She smiled. "Thanks, Pa."

"I still think you need to be careful," Mama warned.

"I will." Tillie rose to help with the cleanup. As soon as the table was cleared, Mama shooed the little ones out, leaving her alone with Tillie.

"I'm so excited for you, dear. And so proud." Mama dipped

the plate she'd scrubbed into the rinse bowl, then handed it to Tillie.

"I want this position so bad, Mama."

"And I think you have every chance of getting it."

"I don't know." Tillie ran a drying cloth across the plate. "Lucy has a leg up after what happened to me in the carriage."

"Perhaps. But think of all the hours, days, years, even, that we've put into preparing you for this very thing."

Tillie contemplated the number of books she'd read, the perfection her mother had demanded from her needle, the laborious hours she'd spent dressing and redressing Mama's hair, along with the lessons she'd received on concocting herbal remedies and cosmetics.

"Lucy may have a leg up," Mama continued, "but when Mrs. Vanderbilt asks for Corfe's edition of Handel, I wouldn't put it past her to go searching for a coarse dish with a handle."

Tillie snorted.

Removing her hands from the water, Mama dried them on her apron, then clasped Tillie's within both of hers. "It is a rare, rare opportunity you've been given and likely the only one you'll ever have. Don't you see? This is it, Tillie. This is your dream. Your chance. You mustn't squander it."

"I won't."

"You must be cheerful even when they expect long hours. Discreet when you overhear gossip. Tolerant when Mr. Vanderbilt invades his bride's domain. And virtuous when upper menservants come sniffing about you."

"I will."

"You must not blush or lose your composure when you

perform intimate services for Mrs. Vanderbilt that women of lesser stations would be too modest to have done for them."

Even as she spoke, her mother blushed and they both thought of the lessons Tillie had been taught by doing for her mother what she would one day do for Mrs. Vanderbilt if she were to win the position of lady's maid. Services which became so frequent as to no longer embarrass Tillie, though clearly they still discomfited her mother.

Mama's eyes teared. "When I think of all our hard work and how badly I've wanted this. Now, here you are, on the precipice of living out the dream we've been clinging to. Think of the life you'll have. So much better than mine or your father's."

Tillie squeezed her hands. "I know. And I can't thank you enough, Mama. Now, don't you worry. I won't let you down."

Swallowing, Mama withdrew her hands, swiped her eyes with the corner of her apron, then returned to the dishes.

Tillie stacked the plates inside the cabinet, her resolve solidifying. No matter what it took, she must secure the coveted position. Failure was not an option.

The sun swelled over the horizon, streaking the dawn skies with orange, pink, and purple. Mack hiked up Biltmore's approach road with nothing but a pocketknife and a three-inch money belt strapped beneath his shirt.

It wasn't full enough, though. Not nearly enough. He'd asked the steward of Battery Park Hotel for an increase in pay, but the man had scoffed.

"Then I quit," Mack had said. "I'll work at Biltmore."

"Biltmore? They'll throw you out the minute they see you."

"We'll see."

The steward had curled his lip. "You leave now and you'll never work at my hotel again or anywhere else in this town."

Mack had no doubt the man would make good on his threat. Which meant he had to make this work. At least until he could earn enough to get Ora Lou out from under Sloop's roof.

Pine, rhododendron, and hemlock opened up onto a pond dusted with fallen pink blossoms. He'd heard Vanderbilt had hired some fancy-pants fellow from New York to rearrange the landscape surrounding this three-mile carriage road. The thought was ludicrous. How could some Yankee improve upon what God had already put in place? But despite himself, Mack was impressed. Around every bend the countryside offered a view which was nothing short of stunning.

Crossing a rustic bridge, he scanned the orange skies and his native mountains in the distance, trying to pinpoint the spot which cradled a cabin on Hazel Creek. That one-room dwelling had housed the first generation of Danvers to ever live in the Unakas. It had offered solitude with unhampered growth of forest on every side. It was the one place he was lord of himself and his surroundings. And the only place which gave his eagle heart the wing room it craved.

A thrush landed on a persimmon branch, whistling a soft, fluty *ah-ee-oo-lay*. Mack stopped, watching it ascend high into the tree as it embellished its song with a variety of flourishes.

This would be his last taste of freedom, of the outdoors, of everything he loved. The thought of being cooped up in some dark, dank basement for several months made his hands clammy. For the hundredth time, he considered turning back. And for the hundredth time, he forced himself to go on. Ora Lou's welfare depended upon it.

He may have told Mrs. Vanderbilt women were nothing more than domestic animals, but those were his grandfather's words, not his father's and definitely not his. He'd only said it to make the lady mad, because the Vanderbilts represented everything he hated about society. Where he came from there was no servility or headship by right of birth. Their leaders—when needed—arose from their clan by virtue of ability.

Still, his pa had been an outsider—a "furriner." The Southern Unakas highlanders had not taken kindly to the teacher who'd devoted his life to bringing a decent education to them. He'd traveled from home to home in that corner of the mountain, and though he was treated with hospitality, he was never really accepted . . . until he met Ma.

What was supposed to have been a week's stay turned into a wintering. As a guest, he'd had to stand by and watch as Grandpa used his fists on the children. But the minute he saw Grandpa raise a hand to Ma, he intervened, then whisked her away.

Eventually Pa had reconciled with his father-in-law, but in no way had he adopted the highlander's attitude toward women. He doted on Ma. Catered to her. Respected her. Even chopped the wood for her. And if that weren't enough, he then saw to his children's education. He was the laughingstock of that region. But it never seemed to bother him.

A giant gatepost topped by a female centaur signaled the entrance to Biltmore House. Mack's chest tightened. It might as well have been the entrance to Central Prison in Raleigh.

Taking a deep breath, he stepped past the post, rounded the corner, then came up short. A huge carpet of green lined with saplings spread before a fawn-colored castle of such enormity, such magnificence, such height he could do no more than gawk.

Soaring spires. Octagonal towers. Medieval turrets. Sharp gables. Steep roofs. Stone pillars. Dormer windows. Multiple chimneys. Snarling gargoyles.

The sprawling structure was unlike anything he'd ever

seen. Yet somehow its grandeur fit in with the panorama of mountains flanking it. He stayed rooted to the spot trying to figure how a structure of such gigantic proportions could remain hidden until the last second. Had the Yankee planned that, too?

Finally, he placed one foot in front of the other. Counting windows would be like counting the hairs on his head. Yet he knew someone was responsible for cleaning them. Would that fall to him now? He hoped so. It would give him a chance to be out-of-doors.

He'd heard Biltmore had two hundred fifty rooms but had never given much credence to the statement. Now he wondered if that estimate had been too modest. Vanderbilt had been a bachelor until a few months ago. What did he need two hundred fifty rooms for? What did *anyone* need that many rooms for?

Dozens of chimneys graced the roofs. Chimneys which led to scores of fireplaces. It would take a lot of chopping to supply enough wood for that many fireplaces. He wondered how many hundreds of stairsteps it would take to climb from bottom to top. He pictured himself weighted down with firewood. Or a lady's trunk. Or pieces of furniture.

Stable, outbuildings, and carriage house surrounded an open court to the right of the castle. His gaze lingered on the carriage house. Earl had only been working in there for a few weeks. Vanderbilt's head coachman had broken an arm. While he recovered, Earl had been pulled from the house to act as the interim driver. To hear his brother tell it, several undercoachmen had expected to hold the coveted position.

Earl had smiled. "None are as handsome as me, though."

And in the world of service, a man's height, good looks,

and shapely calves were premium. If he also happened to be competent, he was in even more demand . . . assuming fetching for a rich man was his life's ambition.

A massive clock tower overlooked the open court. Six o'clock already. Had Mack known the house was a six-mile hike from Asheville, he'd have risen earlier. Still, before he made his way around back, he couldn't resist taking a closer look at the looming entryway.

He climbed deep steps leading to an archway wide enough to accommodate a dozen men, behind which was the grand entrance to the house. Enormous iron gates barred his way. He lifted his gaze to the extensive scrollwork carved into the limestone. Two princely gargoyles flanked each side of the archway. Both wore musketeerlike jerkins with puffy sleeves while clutching shields with prominent Vs carved onto the crests.

One of the heavy wooden doors behind the grill creaked open. Mack froze. He knew he should dart out of sight, but according to his Bible, all men were equal.

A middle-aged man in a dark navy suit stepped onto the landing. His jowls slackened. "Earl! What are you doing out here? And dressed like that?"

"I'm not Earl. I'm his brother Mack."

The blond man scurried forward, shooing Mack with his hands. He was tall and broad, but the broadness also extended to his waist. "Return to the carriage house at once."

He sighed. "I'm not Earl. I'm his twin brother, Mack. Mrs. Vanderbilt told me to come."

The man looked down his nose. "I think I'd know if you had an identical twin, Earl. I have told you before that the joke playing has grown old. Do not think working outside the house exempts you from following my directives."

Mack tightened his jaw. "Let me talk to the butler."

Puffing up, the man released the latch and pulled the gate open. "As you well know, I *am* the butler."

"You're Mr. Sterling?" Mack extended his hand. "Earl's told me about you. I'm Mack Danver. Mrs. Vanderbilt asked me to come."

Sterling slapped Mack's hand away.

Mack didn't so much as hesitate. He hated men who used their power as an excuse to bully others. He grabbed the butler by the shirtfront and propelled him backward. "Listen, mister. When I say I'm Mack Danver, I mean I'm Mack Danver. When I extend a hand in greeting, I expect it to be taken. When it's not, I take offense."

"Unhand me!"

"Apologize first."

"I'll do no such thing!"

"Mr. Sterling? Is everything—" A maid with the fairest skin he'd ever seen stood at the door, hand covering her mouth. "Earl! What's the matter with you!"

Black hair peeked out from beneath her small white cap. Her eyes widened. The eastern sun had reduced her pupils to dots, leaving eyes so blue they appeared almost lavender. She rushed out the door. "Let him go!"

He let go.

Stumbling back, the butler caught a heel on the steps. Mack grabbed his arm to keep him from falling.

Sterling recovered his footing and shoved Mack away. "Take your hands *off* me. You're done here! I don't care what—"

Mack took a swing, but the butler swerved, causing Mack to graze the man's chin.

The girl jumped in front of him, squaring off with Mack. "Stop it! Stop it right this minute." She took a step forward.

He took a step back.

"I cannot believe you would be so careless as to drink on a work night and not turn up until morning." She propped her hands on her waist. "You've done it this time, Earl Danver. And it's going to break Mrs. Vanderbilt's heart. She thinks the world of you. And what about Mr. Vanderbilt? Can you imagine how you've let him down? After all he's done for you? *This* is how you repay him?"

The butler touched his chin, then looked at his hand. He seemed perfectly willing to let a woman do his fighting for him. Mack curled his lip.

The woman jabbed Mack's chest with her finger. "I'm very angry with you. Very angry."

She was tall for a woman, but still only came to his shoulders. Did she actually believe he was frightened of her? He felt the tug of a smile on his lips. "I'm not Earl, miss. I'm his brother Mack. And I haven't been drinking."

The disapproval she'd shown before was nothing compared to the horror that filled her eyes now. She pressed a hand against her stiffly starched apron. "Oh no. You're the brother?"

He nodded.

"But, but . . . where's your beard? What happened to your hair?"

He narrowed his eyes. "Do I know you?"

She shook her head. "I was with Mrs. Vanderbilt when she saw you in town."

That couldn't possibly be true. He would never have forgotten her had he seen her before. Still, he'd been a bit distracted at the time.

"What's this?" Sterling now held a handkerchief to his chin. "You say this man isn't Earl?"

"No, sir," the girl said. "He's Earl's twin. Mrs. Vanderbilt saw him in Asheville and offered him a position in the house. Told him to come round if he was interested."

Sterling inhaled quickly through his teeth.

"You came to the *front* door?" she asked Mack. "What possessed you to come to the front door?"

"I was just looking. I didn't knock or anything. He simply opened the door and . . ." He shrugged.

Rolling her eyes, she turned to the butler. "He's a mountain man and was engaged in fisticuffs when Mrs. Vanderbilt first saw him. I'm sure he'll refrain from using his fists in the future once we explain how we do things."

Sterling looked Mack up and down. "I don't know, Tillie."

"Please, sir. I'll take him round back myself. I'll make sure he doesn't get into any more trouble."

Mack tucked his shirt into his trousers. "I can fight my own fights . . . Tillie, is it? You needn't do it for me."

She seared him with her gaze. "Do not say another word."

He bristled and opened his mouth to argue.

She lifted her index finger. "Not. Another. Word." With her finger still in the air, she turned back to the butler. "May I take him round back, sir?"

Tugging the hem of his jacket, Sterling tightened his lips. "Go ahead, then. I'll talk with Mrs. Winter and tell you what we decide to do with him."

Mack took a step forward.

Tillie steepled one hand on his chest. With the other, she pointed toward the gate. "That way, Mr. Danver. The servants' entrance is that way."

A llan Reese held a distinct family resemblance to his sister Tillie—black hair, white skin, and light eyes—but he also had a ready grin, which she'd been lacking.

He slapped a hand onto Mack's shoulder. "Seems you're to be our new useful man. Which is a nice way of saying you're the universal packhorse of the house and should be ready to throw yourself into any and every gap."

They passed through a long corridor belowstairs, bumping shoulders with liveried footmen and freshly starched chambermaids. Parlormaids and housemaids. Kitchen maids and laundry maids. Hallboys and footboys. Tweenies and step-girls. He couldn't imagine the streets of New York City being any noisier or busier than this corridor.

"Your duties will comprise window and vestibule," Allan continued. "Cleaning the terrace and balconies. The getting up of wood for all open fires over the entire house. Trunk lifting, ice breaking, boot and shoe polishing, running errands, and doing anything which might require a strong arm."

Surprisingly, the basement was built into the downward slope of a hill, allowing windows along the entire western wall. What he'd expected to be dark and confining turned out to be filled with sunshine and fresh air.

"You'll need to be an early riser, since much of your work is to be done before the mister and missus are astir."

They passed a canning pantry lined with shelves. Rows and rows of readymade food in tin containers. Mack tried to stop. Even the grocer didn't have that many cans.

Allan propelled him forward. "The main rooms are heated with a horizontal tubular return. But the bedrooms only have fireplaces."

Mack dodged a tweenie with a tray of cream, butter, and cheese. He looked to be about thirteen. Sweat matted the hair sticking out from beneath his cap. He must have run 'tween the floors several times already.

"They're heated by a horizontal what?" he asked.

Allan shrugged. "Basically the sub-basement makes a bunch of steam, which rises up the walls through a series of radiators built into shafts. Those shafts have vents in the main living areas. The bedrooms, though, will need firewood. Firewood that you will supply."

Mack stopped. "You're joking."

Allan kept walking. "You don't have to chop it. Just haul it."

"I meant the heating system. You're joking about the heating system."

When Allan realized Mack hadn't moved, he turned. "It's true. The living areas do have fireplaces, though, for the deep of winter. The winds blow from north to south, so the north wing will be the coldest. We have an elevator you can use to haul wood, so that should ease your burden some."

Mack had just begun to move when he stopped again. "An elevator?"

"Two, actually. One for the guests and one for us. It's really slow, though. I prefer the stairs. Still, it's nice when guests are in residence and we have to lug up a bunch of trunks."

Mack had never seen an elevator, much less been inside one, wasn't sure he even *wanted* to be inside one.

Allan waved him forward. "Come on. I need to show you your workroom."

The farther they went, the farther they were from the kitchens. The hubbub began to fade until it died down completely. At the juncture of yet another corridor, two doors stood side by side. Both closed.

Allan fit a key into the one on the left. "You'll find all the tools you need in here."

He pushed the door open and touched a button on the side. Light splashed into the tiny, windowless room.

Mack jerked his head up. An Edison bulb stuck out of the ceiling, glowing and humming. "The house is wired for electricity?"

"Yes. The white button turns the light on, the black one turns it off." Allan demonstrated, plunging them into darkness, then once again into light.

"The *entire* house?" Mack asked. "Including the servant areas?"

"Everything."

Mack stood flatfooted. What manner of man was George Vanderbilt that he would provide an elevator, electric lights, and banks of windows for his servants?

"When they moved your brother out to the carriage house,

we had to utilize our useful man as a footman. As a result, a lot of things have been neglected. You're going to have your hands full catching up."

The room looked as if its occupant had been called home to Jesus in the middle of a task, leaving everything in chaos. Two tall tables had been pushed against the walls. Strewn across their surfaces were filthy cloths, open bottles of polish, and brushes.

A carpenter's box held tools in sad need of cleaning. Mack stepped to the table. Sawdust, chips, and shavings crunched beneath his boots. He opened a few drawers. Most were empty, but the ones that were occupied held tools in no particular order. Not a spare cloth in sight.

Allan handed him the key. "If you lock the door behind you, then your tools will be unmolested by anyone else. Even the butler."

Mack looked at the key in his hand. No one had ever trusted him with a key before.

Leaning a shoulder against the doorframe, Allan gave him a speculative look. "You know, the best butlers are the ones who began as useful men. You're big. You're tall. You're fair of face. If you have an eye toward advancement—and if you don't have a thirst for spirits the way your brother does—then you could do quite well for yourself here."

Mack snorted. "I have no interest in being butler or anything else."

Allan pushed off the door. "Just the same, you need to be on your best behavior. That includes staying out of sight of the Vanderbilts and any guests, following orders from anyone who gives them, and keeping your fists to yourself. You hear?"

Mack nodded but refrained from actually answering.

∽

Let there be light.

Tillie pressed the white button, then squealed and jumped backward. Earl stood before a set of glass doors opening onto the terrace, his back to the tapestry gallery. He looked over his shoulder, blond hair mussed, brown eyes dark and intense.

It wasn't Earl. It was the brother, Mack.

She touched a hand to her chest. "What are you doing?"

He stiffened. "I'm allowed. Cleaning the windows and terrace are part of my responsibilities."

Letting out a deep breath, she moved toward him. "I didn't mean you weren't allowed. I meant, why are you standing there in the dark?"

He shrugged and turned back toward the terrace. "I'm listening."

She tilted her head. "To what?"

"The silence."

The rags he'd shown up in yesterday had been replaced by typical work clothes of brown trousers, white shirt, and copper vest. There was nothing typical about the way he wore them, though.

He'd rolled up his shirt sleeves, leaving the lower portion of his arms exposed. A fine dusting of blond hair stood out against skin browned by the sun. A wheat-colored neckerchief was tied around his thick neck and his vest hung open, revealing a very broad chest and flat stomach.

"Can you turn them off?" he asked.

"What?"

"The Edisons. They're disrupting the quiet."

The hum of the light bulbs grew loud in her ears. She glanced at the control buttons. "But I have work to do. I need them on."

"Just for a minute. Please, miss."

She hesitated, understanding his thirst for quiet. It was one of the reasons she rose so early. She loved having the main floor still and hushed and all to herself.

She sighed. "All right. Just for a minute. And it's Tillie. Everyone goes by their Christian name except for the house-keeper, butler, and chef."

He nodded. "Thank you."

She plunged the room into darkness, then stepped up beside him. It was four in the morning. Much too dark to see Mt. Pisgah and the miles of backyard which belonged to Mr. Vanderbilt. But she could picture it. The rolling hills, the horseback trails, the blanket of trees in every shade of green. All hedged by the Carolina mountains and a dark blue sky on the horizon.

"His property goes on and on," she said. "As far as the eye can see. Takes two whole days on horseback just to reach its edges."

"*Shhhhh*. Listen." His words were soft. Reverent. Barely audible.

She listened, and gloried in the quiet. It was as if there were no one on earth but her, him, and God Almighty.

The smell of blacking drifted on the breeze. Had he polished everyone's boots already? She glanced up but couldn't make out his silhouette. Concentrating, she tried to hear his breathing. Nothing. Was he holding his breath? Was he even still beside her?

Yes. The shoe polish. He was definitely beside her. And so very different from Earl. Earl never stood still. Never quit flirting. And never, ever, left his vest unbuttoned.

Resisting the temptation to stay and watch God light the sky—which would be hours yet—she took a step toward the control buttons.

He grasped her wrist. "One more minute."

She barely squelched a yelp of surprise. How had he been able to find her wrist in the dark? It took her a moment just to calm herself. Finally, she tugged free and turned on the light.

He still faced the mountains. His back side was every bit as appealing as his front side. Which, of course, was why he'd been hired.

Picking up her workbox, she moved to the forest green drapes, which extended from ceiling to floor. The tapestry gallery was the longest room in the house. Three Flemish tapestries separated by fireplaces of equal proportion stretched along one wall. The opposite wall held a long line of windows and glass doors that looked out onto the terrace, and ultimately, Mt. Pisgah.

She drew the sash curtains open and raised the window shades, taking great care to keep their height uniform. Mack stood frozen in place. She wondered if he would intrude on her mornings from now on. She should have resented the possibility but found she didn't. At least not yet.

After adjusting the final shade, she began to throw open the windows and doors. Fresh air with the bite of dawn rushed into the room, chasing away its stuffiness. When she reached the doors Mack had been standing between, he was gone.

She looked left and right, then heard a sound and turned around. He was moving all the heavy furniture to the center of the rugs in anticipation of her sweeping the room's corners and sides. Usually, she had to wait until some footmen were preparing the breakfast room and, after a great deal of persuasion, could drag them away. Yet this new useful man did it without being prompted.

"Why does the furniture have wheels?" he asked.

She glanced down at the tiny black rollers beneath the

green upholstered couch he pushed. "The Vanderbilts and their guests dance in here upon occasion. The wheels make it much easier to move everything out of the way."

He stopped, his expression curious. "But it's not as if Vanderbilt would be moving the furniture. His servants would do that for him. So what does he care how easy it is?"

She allowed herself a small smile. "He cares. You'll discover that quickly enough. And thank you . . . for moving the furniture, I mean."

He grunted, then put his back into the chore. Even on wheels, those couches were heavy. It usually took two men to do the task. The muscles in his arms and shoulders bunched, but the sofa did his bidding.

Turning to the windows, she removed a moist sponge from her box and began to wipe down the sills. Most maids were not in proximity of household men. A parlormaid was different, though. She not only worked around men, she worked *with* them.

As such, Tillie found it wise to regard them as useful spokes or cogwheels in the machinery of Mr. Vanderbilt's home. Otherwise, her emotions might become engaged. And that, she reminded herself, was the kiss of death.

Slipping a crowbar beneath the lid of a newly arrived express box, Mack jimmied his way around it until it opened. Wrapped in soft tissue and packed in pungent wheat were the makings of a table lamp. Piece by piece he placed base, burner, wick, tripod, chimney, and shade onto his table, wheat kernels spilling to the floor.

The first week he'd been there, he'd stayed up late and risen early in order to clean and organize his workroom. In the mountains, his entire family shared everything. At Battery Park nothing had ever been left where he put it. But here he had a sanctuary all his own, complete with lock and key.

Settling onto a hip stool, he threaded a wick through the burner channel, then dropped the loose end into a fancy blue and white lamp base. A high-pitched jangle from the wall made him jump and jostle the lamp. Grabbing it with both hands, he steadied it, then moved to the telephone and lifted the earpiece.

"Yes?" he said into the speaking tube. He was in equal parts fascinated and repelled by the contraption. If a house was so big you had to resort to telephones, then, in his mind, it was just too big.

"Wind's fast and furious up here, Mack," the voice at the other end said. "It's sending the terrace furnishings and rugs everywhere. All hands on deck!"

"Be right there."

Grabbing his cap off a hook, he locked the door, jogged to the stairs, then had to turn around. He'd forgotten to douse the Edison. He quickly extinguished the light, then took the stairs two at a time.

The scene on the terrace had even the high-muck-a-muck butler throwing off his coat to help take in the sail. When they finished, Mr. Sterling sent Mack to all corners of the house for a dozen different jobs.

Three hours later, he found his way back to his workroom. Resettling himself on the hip stool, he carefully screwed a burner onto the lamp base. With one hand on the base, he rocked the burner back and forth while pulling slightly upward. The threading held.

A high-pitched jangle sounded again. Jumping, he glared at the telephone, then rose and lifted the earpiece. "Yes?"

"The door to the Louis XV dressing room won't open. Go unstick it."

"Is anyone in it?"

"Don't be impertinent. Of course not."

He tightened his jaw. "Where's the Louis XV dressing room?"

"Second floor. Southeast corner."

Taking his boot-leg bag off the door, he tied it around his waist, double-checking the tools, nails, and screws inside each pocket. At the stairs, he turned around and went back to douse the Edison. Halfway up the stairs, he turned back to retrieve his cap.

Finally he reached the second floor and emerged into the servants' hall next to Mrs. Vanderbilt's room, coming face-to-face with Tillie. He'd only seen her in the mornings, when she wore a lavender calico the same color as her eyes and a plain white apron. Now she wore her afternoon uniform—a full black dress and starched bib apron with frilly shoulder straps. Atop mountains of hair, her small white cap had long, flowing streamers. He wondered if her hair would be that long when released from its pins.

"Hello," she whispered. "Are you lost?"

"I'm looking for the Louis XV dressing room." He lowered his tone to match hers.

"That way." She pointed south. Her lashes were thick and dark like her hair.

He didn't move.

She stepped to the side. "Well . . ."

"Are you one of the staff that has off tonight?" he asked, stalling her. "Are you going to the barn gathering?"

"I never miss it. My whole family will be there. Are you?"

He hadn't planned on it. He only received one evening off each week and every second Sunday. The last thing he intended was to spend his few leisure hours with a bunch of people he didn't know and didn't particularly like.

"Maybe," he said. "I might relax in my room, though. Do a little reading."

She shook her head. "You don't want to do that. If you're

on the premises, they'll find you and put you to work. But you'll be safe in the barn."

He nodded. "Maybe I'll see you there, then."

"Wagon leaves at six o'clock sharp." Something behind him caught her eye and she immediately scurried off.

He turned around. The housekeeper—or the *matron*, as the staff called her when out of earshot—bore down on him. Her black dress had no apron and no shape, though that was more the fault of the wearer than the style of the dress.

"What are you lollygagging about for?" she demanded. "And roll those sleeves down. Button that vest. Get rid of that silly neckerchief."

The temptation to refuse was great. Instead, he took a deep breath. "My sleeves are too short, the vest is too small, and the neckerchief keeps my shirt from being soiled."

Her back went ramrod straight. "We have a dozen laundresses that will see to your shirt and a room full of livery in the carriage house. Go out there immediately and find clothing that fits."

"I've been there already. And the only thing that fits is footman and coachman livery, which is of no good to me, unless you want your useful man dressed like a footman."

"I don't believe you. Surely there's something appropriate."

He narrowed his eyes. "I don't lie, madam."

Without another word, he headed the direction Tillie had indicated. He heard a rustling behind him.

"Do you think I've made a mistake, Mrs. Winter, in bringing him here?"

"Oh no, Mrs. Vanderbilt. Don't worry. I'll whip him into shape."

He wasn't able to catch the mistress's response, but he knew he must at least pretend to comply because he needed the job and the income it provided, if only for a while.

He skirted Mr. Vanderbilt's room, then paused. There was no way to reach the Louis XV suite without entering into the area reserved for family and guests. He yanked his vest together and fastened the lower two buttons, but that was all that would reach. The sleeves of his shirt were hopeless. With nothing left to do, he entered the guest area.

Even if there'd been no change in wall color, he'd have known immediately he'd left the servants' area. Richly upholstered furniture offered places for guests to congregate in the Second Floor Living Hall. A housemaid dusted an elaborate writing desk while another polished a table with a box of Chinese dominoes at its center.

He cut across to a narrow hallway and passed a collection of bedrooms before finally reaching the southeast corner of the house. A bit secluded from the rest, this wing was graced with carved moldings, stained wainscoting, gleaming wooden stairs, and oriental runners.

Brass plaque holders on each of the doors indicated the name of the room and the visitor residing within. The occupant's name was ostensibly for the staff's use, but Mack had heard they also served overnight guests wishing to make midnight assignations.

At the moment, though, no guests were in residence. He read each plaque. *Damask Room. Claude Room. Tyrolean Chimney*. And finally, *Louis XV*.

He knocked and waited. No sound. Opening the door, he stepped inside. The entire room had been spun in gold. Golden draperies. Golden furniture. Golden walls stamped with dark velvet.

An upholstered chair shaped like a small sleigh sat in front of glass balcony doors offering a spectacular view of his mountains. The bed looked small within the vast room, yet it would hold two people plus a few children. To its side were two buttons. Both were white and had letters engraved onto them.

Edging closer, he bent over. *Butler's Pantry. Maid.*

He shook his head. He'd seen the giant annunciator box in the butler's pantry with arrows which pointed to the name of the room that was calling, but he'd not realized they were activated by the mere push of a button.

On either side of the bed were heavily molded doors. He assumed one led to the dressing room. He tried the one on the left, the tools in his boot-leg bag jingling. It opened with ease. Inside the white-tiled room stood a pitcher and basin, a commode chair with a flush handle, a tub with faucets that released heated water at the mere turn of a knob, and a bureau with soft, fluffy towels.

Beside the tub were two more call buttons. *Butler's Pantry. Scrub Back.*

Lifting his brows, he thought of his little brothers living in homes smaller than the bedroom he stood beside. Of Ora Lou in the orphanage. The water they heated over the fire. The tin hip-tub they bathed in. Yet here was a home with two hundred fifty rooms and forty-three bathrooms. All unoccupied, except for the master's, the mistress's, and the servants'.

A knot of resentment tightened his stomach. Whirling around, he left the bathroom and clomped to the opposite door. It stuck along the latch side. With several firm jerks, he managed to open it. Behind it was a lavish dressing area.

Digging in his boot-leg bag, he found a couple of screws a tad larger than the ones currently in the hinge plate, then used them to replace the loose ones. After testing the door several times, he cleaned up his mess and started to slam out of the bedroom when raised voices made him pause.

It couldn't be guests. There weren't any in attendance. Was it the Vanderbilts? He had no idea. Easing the door open just a crack, he listened.

"Floor polish? You're using *floor* polish to clean my boots?"

"I been running from pillar to post all day and still ain't close to finishin'." The youthful voice cracked, jumping an octave before returning back to normal. "I was just thinkin' to save a little elbow grease, is all."

Mack slowly widened the door and peered out. A liveried footman he'd seen during meals but had never met hovered over a tweenie by the name of Harvey.

The footman held up a pair of reddish brown boots. "They're ruined. *Ruined*. What am I to tell the head footman?"

"I don't care whatcha tell him." Harvey's cheeks had turned as red as his hair. "I ain't supposed to be polishin' yer boots anyways."

The footman shoved Harvey, pressing him against the wall with his forearm.

Mack didn't even remember moving, yet suddenly he was lifting the footman in the air and tossing him backward.

The boy's eyes widened.

"You all right?" Mack asked.

"Look out!" He pointed.

Whirling, Mack thrust one arm up in protection, blocking the footman's attempt to strike him from behind with the boots. With his other arm, Mack fisted his hand and made a solid connection with the man's jaw.

The footman dropped to the ground.

"Land o' Goshen," Harvey gasped. "You done laid him out flat."

Mack didn't even spare the fellow a glance. "You all right?"

"I am now."

"This fellow been bothering you?"

The boy gave a noncommittal shrug.

"If he or anybody else gives you any more trouble, you let me know." Mack scanned the gleaming floor, stepped over the footman, and picked up one of the boots for a closer look. "You used floor polish?"

Harvey bristled. "So?"

"Pretty industrious, I'd say."

The boy narrowed his eyes. "I ain't neither. I'm smart. Ever'body says so."

Mack suppressed a smile. "Nevertheless, you better get going. I'll make sure this fellow is taken care of."

With a quick nod and a thanks, the boy grabbed the boots and shot across the hall toward the servants' corridor.

Bending over, Mack tapped the footman's cheek. Still out cold.

Mack rolled his eyes. He'd barely touched him, but he doubted Mr. Sterling would believe that. Even so, he'd been taught to defend the afflicted. He just hoped it wouldn't cost him his job.

Returning to the Louis XV room, he pushed *Butler's Pantry*, then headed to the servants' area. Help would arrive soon enough for the bully he'd left behind.

Back in his workroom, he hung up his boot-leg bag and settled on the hip stool. Picking up the lampshade holder, he slipped the ring portion inside the burner tines and squeezed the edges.

A high-pitched jangle sounded in the room. He didn't jump this time, nor did he answer its call.

It sounded again. He placed both hands flat on the table. It sounded again.

Lurching to his feet, he grabbed the earpiece. "What!"

A pause. "Mr. Sterling wants to see you in his office."

"I'm busy." He slammed down the receiver and returned to his project, resolutely ignoring the rings which followed. Finally, they ceased.

He'd finished all assembly other than the actual shade when footsteps sounded in the corridor. Reaching over, he swung his door shut.

Seconds later, someone knocked, then opened the door without waiting for permission.

Allan Reese surveyed the room. "Looks great in here. How'd you manage to get it in order so quickly?"

Mack picked up the white globe that would serve as the lamp's shade.

Slipping his hands into his pockets, Allan leaned against the doorframe. "Mr. Sterling is second only to Mrs. Winter, who is second only to the Vanderbilts. When any one of them ring, you're expected to jump to do their bidding."

"I don't jump to do anyone's bidding."

"You do now."

Mack allowed the chimney to pass through the middle of the shade, making sure the edge of the globe rode down to the fitter.

"You also need to keep your fists to yourself. Mr. Sterling wants to cut you loose, but Mrs. Winter said no. Says she's willing to make an allowance—just this once—for your backwoods roots. Personally, I think it's more likely she's keeping you on because you have a twin. A tall, fair-of-face identical twin she thinks would look nice standing next to you in the banquet hall, assuming you can be brought up to snuff. But one more day like today, and twin or no, they'll send you packing."

Mack scrutinized the completed lamp. It should've taken him twenty or thirty minutes to assemble. Instead, it had taken all day.

It made him want to quit. To go back to the beloved mountains where he'd grown up. All he ever wanted was to build himself a workshop in the mountains, fashion some furniture, sell it to Asheville's mercantile, and live in peace.

He'd just begun to build a nest egg when Pa had died, leaving the responsibility of the family's welfare on Mack's shoulders. Everything he'd saved had slowly eroded until it was finally gone.

And after Ma's death, he was in even worse shape. So he'd farmed the boys out and put Ora Lou in the orphanage. Things settled down for a while—until the rumors about Sloop began to reach his ears.

Once he'd confirmed them, there was no question of leaving Ora Lou there. But that would mean finding a place for her to live in town.

He'd looked around for rooms to rent, but the ones he could afford were completely unsuitable for a thirteen-year-old girl. So he'd best do what he needed to keep his job here until he could afford a place for his sister.

Stepping into the room, Allan picked up the lid of the express box and leaned it against the wall. "They've put you in my charge."

Mack looked up. "Why?"

Allan straightened. "Because nobody else wants to deal with you."

"But you do?"

He shrugged. "You've accomplished more this week alone than Kirk did in a month, and that lightens everyone's load, including mine."

"Who's Kirk?"

"Our previous useful man." He ran a hand across his mouth. "He also happens to be the fellow you clocked on the second floor."

Mack lifted a brow. "He was bullying a child."

Allan drew his lips into a tight line. "Yes. Kirk's been needing a setdown for a while now."

Crossing his arms, Mack leaned back against the table. "What happens if I catch him doing the same thing again?"

"You keep your hands to yourself. If you don't, you'll not only lose your job, you'll take me down with you." Allan clapped him on the shoulder. "And that, my friend, isn't going to happen. Now, let's close it up in here, go to the carriage house, find you some clothes that fit, and then catch a wagon to the barn."

"There are no work clothes that fit. Only the fancy stuff Earl wears."

"Then we'll find us a seamstress. Now, come on. I get the evening off and I don't want to miss even a minute of it."

Eight

Singing "Ta-ra-ra-boom-de-ay" as loudly as he could, Aaron James galloped across the barn's wooden floor, his arm tight about Tillie's waist. The footman had a big smile and a handsome set of shoulders, but was a little on the short side.

Laughing, she allowed him to spin her until she was dizzy. When the song ended, she clung to his arm in an effort to steady her course. No sooner had he deposited her at the table with her family than he swept up the next girl passing by.

Though this barn no longer housed animals, evidence of their habitation touched the hay-scented air. Drinking deeply of apple cider, she tried to hear Allan and Pa over the noise.

"Are you sure it was wise to take on a contrary, unlettered yokel like that, son?" Pa asked him.

"I'll admit, he's rougher around the edges than Earl." Allan looked toward the corner of the building.

Tillie followed his gaze. Mack stood in the shadows watching the dancers, but had yet to participate himself.

"Underneath, though," Allan continued, "he's not your typical backwoods mountain man. He's well-spoken and educated and better read than you and me put together."

"How do you know?"

"When we polish silver we debate everything from Socrates to Oscar Wilde's new aesthetic views about art. And try as I might, I can never stump him."

Tillie looked again at Mack and caught him studying her. She quickly turned away.

"Strange that Earl's not like that," Pa said.

Allan nodded. "I think it's likely Earl has the intellect, but he's just more interested in other things."

Dixie Brown sank down beside Tillie, blond tendrils escaping her Gibson Girl hairstyle. "He's such a *dream*!"

Tillie smiled. The two of them had spent many a candlelit evening dressing each other's hair. Tonight Tillie had done both of them up in the soft, wide pompadours she'd seen in a Charles Gibson illustration. "Who's the dream this time?"

"Mack Danver. Who do you think?"

She stilled. "Mack? I thought it was Earl you had your eye on."

The two of them quickly located Earl. He'd backed one of the scullery maids against a bale of hay. She didn't seem to be putting up much of a fight.

"Every girl on the estate has her eye on Earl," Dixie said. "But to think, all this time, he had a *twin*!"

Dixie moved her gaze toward the corner of the room.

Tillie grabbed her wrist. "Don't look!"

But it was too late. Not only did Dixie look, she grabbed

Tillie back, her eyes widening. "He's coming and he's looking right at . . . at *you*!"

Tillie lurched to her feet. "I have to go."

Dixie yanked her back down into the chair. "Introduce him to me first."

"I can't. I have to go."

She squeezed Tillie's arm with surprising strength. "Please."

"No. Now, let—"

"Evening, Allan. Tillie." His voice poured out like warm molasses. Sweet, thick, and rich.

"Pull up a chair, Mack," Allan said. "This is my pa, Herbert Reese. My ma was here earlier, but she had to take the youngsters home. The rest of the family is around, though. Somewhere."

Pa stood and shook hands. "Mack."

"Mr. Reese."

"Call me Herbert."

Instead of joining them, Mack singled Tillie out. "Would you like to dance?"

No. "Have you met my friend Dixie? She's a third-floor chambermaid."

He nodded. "Evening, Dixie. I'm still trying to learn who's who." He turned back to Tillie. "Would you like to dance?"

She hesitated. Her mama had been right. She shouldn't have come. She should stay away from the barn gatherings until her position was secure.

Allan shoved back his chair and gave Dixie a broad wink. "How about you and me doing some twistificatin'?"

An adorable dimple bloomed on Dixie's left cheek. "I'm not sure you're quite the man your father is out there on the floor."

"Oh yeah?" Tweaking her nose, he hooked an arm around her waist and swept her to the center of the room.

Pa offered an arm to Tillie's little sister Gussie, who'd come to claim the final dance of the evening. Tillie and Mack were the only ones left at the table. Refusing him would be unthinkably rude. She slowly rose.

Without a word, he grasped her hand, pulling her behind him. She resisted. Surely he knew he should be guiding her by the elbow.

Yet Allan wasn't guiding Dixie by the elbow, and Earl wasn't guiding his scullery maid by the elbow. But that didn't mean Tillie had to put up with such familiarity.

She yanked back.

He looked over his shoulder, grasp firm and unyielding. "What's the matter?"

"I don't like being dragged along like so much baggage."

He quirked a brow, a teasing spark in his eyes. "At home we toss our women over a shoulder."

And that was that, though he did slow his pace a bit. Still, his legs were long and his strides deep.

Heat filled her cheeks. The moment he let go, she would leave him partnerless in the middle of the floor. She savored the moment.

But when they reached the dancers, he never let go. Simply swung her around and swept her up into his arms. The song was a favorite, and the tables had emptied as everyone not only joined the dancing, but sang along with improvised words to "Mrs. Murphy's Chowder."

```
"When Mrs. Winter dished the chowder out,
   she fainted on the spot;
She found a pair of overalls at the bottom
   of the pot.
Mr. Sterling, he got ripping mad, his eyes
   were bulging out,
He jumped on the piano and loudly he did
   shout. . ."
```

Mack whisked her across the floor, his steps sure, his lead strong.

```
"Who threw the overalls in Mistress Vandy's
   chowder?
No-body spoke, so he shouted all the
   louder.
It's an Irish trick that's true, but I can
   lick the Mick that threw,
The o-ver-alls innnnnn Mistress Vandy's
   chowder!"
```

Mack quickly caught on to the lyric substitutions and sang in harmony, of all things. She refused to look at him. Refused to smile. Refused to sing along.

He didn't miss a beat. Round and round they went through every single verse and two more choruses. When the song finally ended, he retained his hold. The other dancers emptied the floor, stranding her with him.

"What's the matter?" he asked.

"Let me go."

"You mad about me pulling you out here by the hand?"

"Yes."

"Well then, next time I'll sling you across my shoulder. Bet you won't object to being escorted by the hand after that." The corner of his mouth twitched with a hint of amusement.

"I wouldn't try it if I were you."

He shook his head. "You're so serious all the time."

She released a huff of air. "This from the man who uses his fists at the slightest provocation yet cowers in the corner until the last dance."

The smile he'd been withholding fully formed. Straight white teeth. Two deep dimples. Crinkles at the corners of his eyes. "You've been watching me."

"I certainly have not."

"Then how did you know I hadn't danced with anyone yet?"

She could think of no plausible reply.

His smile deepened. "This was the last dance?"

"'Mrs. Murphy's Chowder' is always the last dance."

"But it's so early."

"Parlor games are next."

"Ah."

They still stood on the dance floor. Alone. He had one hand on her back, the other beneath her hand, as if they were waiting for the next song to begin. Except there was no next song.

She jumped back, breaking contact. "I have to . . . I need to . . ."

Whirling around, she rushed to the women placing chairs in a large circle while the men stored the tables. It wasn't until all was arranged that she realized she'd chattered without ceasing during the task, laughing too often and too loud. Picking a seat, she pressed her hands onto her lap. Hopefully no one had noticed.

Dixie dropped down beside her. "What has you in such a dither all of a sudden?"

Tillie slid her eyes closed. "I'm not in a dither."

The older set with their families in tow headed out, leaving the parlor games to the twenty unmarried members of the house staff who had the night off.

Mack sat down directly across from her. His eyes connected with hers. Fifteen feet of nothingness separated them.

He released the top two buttons of his white shirt, then stretched out his legs, crossing them at the ankles. No vest. No neckerchief. No collar.

Allan clapped his hands together. "We have a new staff member with us for the first time. So, in keeping with tradition, he'll participate in the first game of the night."

Everyone looked at Mack. Fortunately, he'd moved his focus to Allan.

"Considering the fact that he has a twin brother," Allan continued, "I thought it appropriate for his initiation game to be Brother, I'm Bobbed."

A ripple of chuckles circulated about the room. Two chairs were quickly placed side by side in the center of the circle. One faced Tillie; the other faced Mack.

"Earl? Mack?" Allan indicated the two chairs. "Please take your seats."

The twins stood. Mack chose the chair facing Tillie.

"Blindfolds, please," Allan said.

Lucy Lewers entered the ring with two scarves. Eyes hooded, she circled the men, slowly running the blindfolds through her hands. She'd piled her abundance of caramel hair high on her head, but not as expertly as Tillie, giving it a kind of mussed look. Her long neck led to a figure which was the envy of every girl. A figure which drew attention to itself on any day, but particularly when she exaggerated her movements as she did now.

Tillie swallowed. If Lucy had been in the Garden of Eden, she'd have been the forbidden fruit.

Earl followed her every move, an appreciative gleam in his eyes.

Lucy slithered to him, then hooked the scarves behind his neck while keeping hold of each end. "Are you Earl or Mack?"

"Earl," he growled.

She smiled. "Close your eyes, Mr. Earl."

Grabbing her waist, he plunked her onto his lap.

Tillie stiffened, heat flooding her cheeks. No one moved. No one said a word.

Instead of jumping up, Lucy fit a blindfold over his eyes, then looped her arms around him to tie the knot. He made circles on her waist with his thumbs.

Squirming, Tillie looked at her brother to see if he would intervene. But Allan simply stood, one hip cocked, an indulgent half smile on his face.

She returned her attention to the center, her gaze colliding with Mack's. His chest lifted with deep breaths.

Lucy extracted herself from Earl's grasp, then slinked toward Mack. "Your turn."

Tillie held her breath. The moment Lucy was within reach, Mack whipped the scarf from her hands and tied it around his eyes.

With a throaty laugh, she slipped a finger beneath the scarf and ran it along the edge, mussing his thick blond hair. "You sure it's tight enough? We wouldn't want you to peek, now."

Tillie clasped her hands together in her lap, squeezing them.

He grabbed Lucy's wrist and thrust it back toward her.

Allan shook out of his stupor. "Thank you, Lucy. I'm sure that will do just fine. Now for the rules."

Lucy returned to her seat while Allan explained the game. But, of course, everyone but Mack already knew how it was played.

While Allan spoke, Earl quietly removed his blindfold. One by one the rest of the group began to grin. Tillie bit her lip.

Finally, Allan finished speaking and handed the laundress next to him a rolled-up newspaper. She tiptoed forward and handed it to Earl.

Winking, he slapped the newspaper against his palm and yelled, "Brother, I'm bobbed!"

"Brother, who bobbed you?" Mack asked.

"I believe Lucy Lewers bobbed me," Earl replied, sending her a lascivious glance.

The rest of the company simultaneously shouted, "Wrong!"

When all murmuring had settled down, Earl raised his arm and whacked Mack on the head with the newspaper. Hard.

Mack jumped. "Brother, I'm bobbed!"

"Brother, who bobbed you?" Earl asked.

"Allan Reese bobbed me."

"Wrong!" the crowd shouted, snickering.

Earl waited a moment, then slapped his palm again. "Brother, I'm bobbed!"

The game continued, but Earl was merciless. He smacked Mack on the side of his head, the back of his head, and again on top of his head.

"Brother, I'm bobbed!" Mack hollered for the fifth time.

The hilarity within the group could no longer be contained, and many laughed openly. Tillie covered her mouth, the amusement infectious.

"Brother, who bobbed you?" Earl asked.

Mack whipped off his blindfold. "You did!"

Earl surged from his chair but not fast enough. Mack was on him and the two rolled on the ground, knocking over chairs. Squealing, the women scattered.

Several men jumped in to pull the twins apart. Though the scuffle looked serious enough, the brothers came up laughing and clapping each other on the shoulders.

Tillie let out a quiet breath.

With a wide smile, Mack shook his finger at Allan. "You just wait. Your turn is coming."

Amidst chuckles, the group returned to their seats and played Jack's Alive, the Rejected Address, and the Sculptor. But Mack's initiation had been completed, the ice broken, and he was welcomed as one of the family.

When it was time for forfeits, so many had to be redeemed that those left to do penance were told to don blindfolds and dance the minuet. Tillie was no exception. Before she could obtain a scarf, however, Mack stood before her with two. He said nothing, just held one out.

She looked around for a different partner, but the others were already pairing up. Careful not to touch him, she took the proffered blindfold and tied it on.

The unrelieved cacophony of voices and laughter increased in volume, but the heavy pulse in her breast overpowered all else.

She stood very still, every nerve trying to sense where he was. "Is your blindfold on?"

"Not just yet." His voice was soft, deep.

"Why not?"

"Because I can look at you at my leisure without you catching me."

Goose bumps skittered across her skin. "Cover your eyes, please."

He said nothing.

Finally, she could stand it no longer. "Are they covered?"

"Yes."

"How do I know?"

He took her hand and brought it to his face, placing it against the band around his eyes. "I don't lie. Ever."

Her fingers grazed his thick hair. Her palm scraped against his whiskers. She jerked her hand back, covering it with her other hand as she pressed it against her waist.

The minuet started. At the end of the prelude, she slowly stretched her right hand in front of her. Like a homing pigeon, he found it, capturing her fingertips. She advanced a step, retired a step, walked in a half circle, then was freed to curtsy.

Had he bowed?

Soft sniggers sprinkled about the room as partners couldn't find each other, and others bumped into partners not their own, and yet others not paying a forfeit watched the activity.

Ordinarily she would have joined in with the gaiety. But not this time. This time she only wanted to complete the dance and leave.

She stretched out her other hand. He cupped it, grazing his thumb over her fingers.

She missed a step, then quickly advanced and retired until she caught up with the music. They walked in a half circle, releasing hands once again to bow and curtsy.

With the introduction finished, she slowly lifted both arms and leaned back on one foot. For a beat she stood with arms wide, body open, completely vulnerable.

Then he was there, slipping one hand just below her

shoulder blade, closing his other on her waiting hand and pulling her forward into a one-two-three beat.

His arms were so long that as she rested her elbow against his, her hand only reached his bicep. It was hard and unyielding and shifted beneath her palm. She found herself curious, wanting to discover where the hill descended into valley.

She concentrated instead on the dance and the circle they made as they waltzed. The farther they went into the turn, the farther his hand slid round her back, fingers splayed wide to indicate the direction he wanted her to go.

They made it through the first round without stepping on each other's feet or bumping into someone else. But during the second, she was struck from behind and slammed forward. Instinctively, he encircled her with both arms, pulling her flush against him.

He continued to lead her with tiny steps and bent his mouth to her ear. "Are you all right?"

Fire shot down her neck and torso. "Please. You can let go now."

Around them, laughter and sharp cries of surprise rose with each measure of music. He relaxed his grip and took her hand again, but kept her far closer than was proper. Her leg brushed his through the thickness of her skirts. As quickly as it occurred, they were on to the next step, only to have it happen again. And again.

Finally, the song ended.

He released her immediately. She ripped off her blindfold, making havoc of her pompadour.

He pulled his scarf down, leaving it around his neck.

They stood in a sea of mirth and joviality. Neither smiled. Neither looked away.

His eyes darkened. His chest rose and fell. He took a step forward.

Spinning around, she wove through the crowd, out the door, and to the wagon. She wanted to go home.

He waited for her, as he always did, in the doorway of the terrace. Only this time, instead of facing his mountains, he faced the tapestry gallery. In the dark. In the silence.

After a few minutes the feminine tap of her heels against parquet floors echoed throughout the first floor and kept time with his thumping heart.

He'd not been looking for a woman. Hadn't been entertaining thoughts of settling down. Hadn't even been tempted to dance last night. Until he saw Tillie in the arms of another man.

The urge to flatten her partners—from dairyman to groom to footman—had taken him by surprise. So he'd forced himself to stay in the corner of the barn and watch. From what he could tell, she didn't favor any one over the other, though plenty had tried to monopolize her attention.

When Mack had seen Aaron James head Tillie's direction for the fourth time, he could stand it no more. He'd stepped in the footman's path, cutting him off, and then presented himself to Tillie.

For a moment, he thought she'd refuse him. And that one action told him more than any word she could have spoken, for she'd not had any hesitation in partnering anyone else. Which meant she felt the pull between them.

The heaviness of the limbs. The tightening of the chest. The squeezing of the throat.

Every morning since that first one, the two of them would stand side by side listening to the silence before beginning their chores. And with each passing day, the less they listened and the more they whispered in the dark.

She told him about sledding down snowy hills as a child in a shovel. About trimming paper dolls with lace from her mother's old petticoats. About her father lining his pocket with sweets and painting pictures on their walls with berry juice.

He told her about running wild on his mountain in nothing but shirttails. About downing his first bear. About hiking thirteen miles to the mill carrying a two-bushel sack of corn. And the way frozen trees crack like rifle shots when their limbs get heavy.

When they could no longer put off their duties, he'd move the furniture, she'd follow behind with broom and mop. She'd open the shades, he'd follow behind with window cloths. Eventually footmen would intrude, making a ruckus in the breakfast room. Under-parlormaids would trickle in to help Tillie finish what she'd started.

The mood would be broken. But not the constant awareness he had of exactly where she was. What she was doing. Whom she was speaking to.

The tapping of her heels stopped. He heard her set her cleaning box on the floor by the light controls. Then, nothing.

She didn't join him. Didn't move. Didn't breathe.

He couldn't see her. Even though his eyes had adjusted to the dark, it was impenetrable. Flaring his nostrils, he took in a deep breath. But instead of smelling her unique scent, he smelt linseed oil and turpentine.

"Come here," he whispered.

Not a sound.

He headed toward her, his footsteps loud and sure.

Light flooded the room.

He pulled up short, shielding his eyes for a moment, before slowly lowering his arm. "What did you do that for?"

She wore the lavender calico. His favorite. The fancy puff she'd made with her hair last night was nowhere to be seen. Instead, she'd somehow twisted that glorious mane into a knot, pulling her hair back so tightly it had to hurt.

The severe style brought her graceful jaw and high cheekbones into prominence. He followed the long curve of her ivory neck.

She took a step back. "I don't have time to dawdle this morning. I need to start my work."

"Why?"

Clasping her hands in front of her, she looked at the floor. "The Vanderbilts are having a party of guests in two weeks' time. There's much to do in preparation."

He waited until she lifted her gaze. Their eyes locked. His determined, hers confused.

"Turn off the light and come here," he repeated.

She backed up another step. A massive column halted her progress.

He closed the distance between them.

Scrambling around the column, she backpedaled into the main hall, holding her arm out in an effort to ward him off.

He stopped at the column. The marble entryway was almost

as big as the barn they'd been in last night and much more open.

He pushed the black button, plunging them into darkness. "Dance with me."

Before she could answer, he captured the hand she still held in front of her and began to hum the minuet. Whether she went through the motions of the dance out of reflex or a desire to acquiesce, he wasn't sure. But they made it through the introductory steps and then he had her in his arms—though not quite the way he'd imagined.

Still, he took full advantage of the moment and spun her around the large space in a series of waltz turns. *One-two-three. One-two-three.*

He threw a quick message of thanksgiving up to his pa for insisting he and Earl learn to dance when they'd reached that age between boyhood and manhood. The two of them had chafed at the lessons. What good would such foolishness do a mountain man?

But Pa had been adamant. Just as he'd been adamant about their reading, writing, numbers, geography, and languages. Just as he'd been adamant about using proper grammar within the walls of their home. Just as he'd been adamant about protecting women and children.

When Mack finished humming the song, they were exactly where they'd started. Steps away from the column and the tapestry gallery. And like the night before, he did not release her.

Nor did she pull away.

Silence.

He felt her shallow breaths with the hand he pressed between her shoulder blades. He pictured the rising and falling of her chest. The apron bib covering her bodice.

He slid his hand down her spine, slipping his little finger beneath the knot of her apron bow.

A shudder ran through her frame.

Slowly, he brought her palm to his mouth and took his first taste. Buttermilk and something indefinably sweet.

Sucking in her breath, she tugged at her hand. "Please."

Reluctantly, he freed her. She brushed past him and turned on the lights, then whirled to face him. Her eyes were wide. Her face flushed. Her chest pumped like bellows. "You mustn't do that. We'll lose our jobs."

"I don't plan on being here long."

"I do."

"Why?"

She looked at him as if he were addled. "I'm up for lady's maid. *Lady's maid*. Do you know what that means?"

"Yes. It means you'll be at the beck and call of somebody else twenty-four hours a day. It means you'll, more or less, have an electric wire attached to you at all times. It means you must be in attendance whether you want to or not, while simultaneously pretending to be deaf, dumb, and blind. It means giving up every ounce of independence and freedom you have."

She whipped herself straight, squaring her shoulders. "It *means* I'll travel the world. It *means* I won't have to rise at four in the morning. It *means* I'll make in one month what you'll make in three and what the scullery makes in six. It *means* I can help support my family and give to those in need."

"At what cost to you, Tillie?"

She looked him up and down. "I don't think it will cost me much at all. Now, if you'll excuse me, I have work to do and so do you."

∽

Sloop opened the door to the orphanage. Mack winced at the sight of him. The man's nose and jaw were bruised, and his left eye still didn't open completely. Had he done all that? It'd been two weeks since their fight.

"What do you want?" Sloop growled.

"I'm here to see my sister."

"You're not welcome in this building or on this property."

"It's visiting hours."

"I couldn't care less." Sloop started to close the door.

Mack reached out to block it. Sloop jumped back in fear.

A twinge of guilt pricked at Mack, but he reminded himself Sloop had hit Ora Lou—no telling how many times—and his anger swelled all over again. "Get her or I'll come in and fetch her myself."

"I've talked with the police chief. He's promised to throw you in jail if you so much as touch me again."

"In that case, I'll make sure I do a lot more damage next time. Maybe something permanent. Now, unless you have something to hide, I suggest you go and get her."

Seconds ticked by as they stared at each other. Without inviting Mack in, Sloop spun and stalked through a door at the end of the corridor. But he left the front door open.

Mack stepped inside, then made his way to the parlor, where visitors waited. Alone in the room, he paced beside a stiff couch and fragile chairs, the thick rug cushioning his boots. Pausing, he picked up a marble dove, speculating on what kind of tools the craftsman had used to sculpt it.

Ora Lou and another girl of about the same age entered, closing the door behind them.

"You look like Earl again," his sister said. "It's creepy. Doesn't that bother you?"

The bruise on her round face had faded to a sickly yellow.

He wondered if there were any new ones. "Has Sloop touched you again?"

She shook her head, thick blond braids swinging. "He hasn't so much as looked at me. It's as if I'm a ghost and not even here."

"What about his missus?"

"She doesn't ignore me like he does, but I'd rather she would."

He narrowed his eyes. "Why? Does she beat you, too? Harm you in any way?"

"No. She's just a grouch and a very difficult person to like."

Some of the tension left his shoulders. He glanced at the other girl. "Who's this?"

Ora Lou grasped the hand of her companion. "This is Irene, my new chum that I've been telling you about."

Had it not been for the telltale evidence of a blossoming figure, he'd have guessed the girl was about eight. She was a fraction of the size of his sister. Her petite frame and features looked as if they'd break in two at the slightest touch. Limp honey-colored hair had been twisted into thin braids.

He nodded. "I'm Mack."

She cast her gaze to the floor.

"She's a bit shy," Ora Lou said, her blond braids three times as thick as her friend's. "Where have you been? You haven't been at church or to see me in two weeks."

"I got a job up at Biltmore."

Eyes widening with surprise, she clapped her hand over her mouth to suppress a giggle. "You? You wear that stuff Earl does?"

He scowled. "Of course not. I'm a useful man. Not a footman."

She squelched her smile. "I see. Do you make lots of money, then?"

"I do."

All teasing dissipated. She released her friend's hand and took a step forward, eyes alighting with hope. "Have you come to take me with you?"

"Not yet. I don't make *that* much money. But if I'm careful and if I don't lose my job, then in a couple of months I should have enough put aside to pay for your room and board somewhere."

She shook her head. "Don't worry about the board, Mack. I can get a job and earn enough to feed myself. It's just the room I'll need help with."

"All the same, it'll probably take at least two months."

"What makes you think you might lose your job?"

He hesitated. "I've gotten into a couple of scuffles."

"With who?"

"The butler and an underfootman."

"The *butler*!" Her jaw dropped. "Well, that was a really stupid thing to do."

He bristled. "He was using his position to push around someone he considered beneath him."

She shook her head again, her brown eyes softening. "That's my big brother. Fight first. Think later."

He sighed. "I'm trying to do better."

"Anything else?" she asked. "Anything else that might cause you to lose your job?"

An image of Tillie flashed through his mind. He decided not to answer. His sister was only thirteen. What was she doing grilling him, anyway? Those months she'd been in charge of the boys had clearly gone straight to her head.

He glanced at Irene. During their conversation, she had inspected every square inch of the room with awestruck eyes.

"Have you not seen the parlor before?" he asked the girl.

She turned her gaze to his. "It's lovely. So different than the back o' the place."

He frowned. "What does the back look like?"

She immediately averted her attention to the floor.

He turned to Ora Lou. "What does the back look like?"

"Nothing like this, I can tell you that." Striding forward, she grabbed his shirt front and pulled him down for a peck on the cheek. "Thank you for taking the Biltmore job. When will you come back?"

"I have every second Sunday off from now on. You can count on my being here. Is there anything you need me to bring you?"

She gave a quick shake of her head. "They'd just take it away from me."

"What do you mean?"

But instead of answering, she clasped Irene's hand and pulled her back out the door. "Bye, Mack. Try to keep your fists to yourself and I'll see you in a couple of weeks."

∞

Tillie knocked on the door of the storage room.

"Come in," her brother's voice answered.

She opened the door, then froze. Mack stood stiff and scowling behind an old table wearing his typical workaday clothes, but with pristine white gloves sheathing his large hands.

An empty place setting, complete with glassware, lay before him on the bare table. Beside it were a variety of serving dishes and trays. Allan looked at her, a harassed expression on his face.

"Excuse me. I didn't mean to intrude." She glanced about the room. Cleaning supplies, old lanterns, china chamber pots—the gold-rimmed for guests, the plain for staff—and sundry items clogged the shelves lining the walls. Still, not a speck of dust had collected. "I was told Mrs. Winter wanted to see me in here."

Allan waved her in. "No, I'm the one who needed you."

After a slight hesitation, she entered, closing the door behind her. She didn't want to be anywhere near Mack. The sharp words they'd exchanged last week had strained the easy camaraderie they'd had before. Still, she'd felt his gaze follow her every time they were in proximity of one another.

She might've had trouble ignoring the attraction she felt growing between them if she were the only one affected, but she wasn't. Much more was at stake. This was likely her only opportunity to make more of her life. To help her family and those little ones at the orphanage. To fulfill her mother's dreams for her. Her own dreams.

"What's going on?" she asked.

Allan ran a hand through his hair. "Mrs. Vanderbilt wants to train Mack to serve."

She gaped at him. "Serve? *Mack?* But he's barely been here two weeks."

"Two and a half," Mack corrected.

"But we have guests coming," she continued, ignoring him. "A thousand things to do. You don't have time to train him right now."

Allan nodded. "I know. That's why I sent for you. I need your help."

She balked. "My help? Why me? I'm already juggling my normal duties along with the new lady's maid duties I've been assigned. I don't have time, either."

"You have more time than I do. Especially in the afternoons." He sent her a pleading look. "Please, Till."

"What's wrong with Aaron or Conrad or Kirk? Why can't one of them train him?"

"Because when Mack thinks he's being bullied, he uses his fists and I'll be accountable for it. But he won't hit a woman. At least, I don't think he will." Allan turned to Mack. "Do you hit women?"

A tick began to beat at the back of Mack's jaw. "I do not."

Allan gave her a triumphant look. "See. You're safe."

She swallowed. It wasn't Mack's fists that concerned her. "Bubby, please. There must be someone else."

Her brother was already heading to the door. "There's no one. Besides, I had to get special permission from the matron to pull you away. So it's all decided." He pinched her chin. "Thanks, brat."

Then he was gone.

The hiss of the lantern sounded loud in the room.

"This is a waste of time," Mack said. "I'm not doing it."

She sighed. "How far have you gotten in your lesson?"

He tightened his lips. "I'm *not* doing this."

"Then you'll be dismissed and asked to leave the estate. Do you want to keep your job, Mack?"

"For now, yes."

"Then you do whatever Mrs. Winter assigns you to do. At the moment, it seems she wants you to have a lesson on table waiting. Now, what have you learned so far?"

The tick grew more pronounced. "Serve from the right, remove from the left."

She blinked. "That's it? That's all you've covered?"

"Hold the plate with my thumb on the rim of the plate and two fingers extended under the bottom."

She nodded. "What else?"

He explained which linen-covered trays were for knives, which were for glasses, and which were for plates.

Nothing. They'd done absolutely nothing.

"How long have you been down here?"

"A while."

"What's taking so long?"

"I've been uncooperative."

She lifted a brow. "Well, I have a million things to do, and training you isn't one of them. So look sharp and pay attention."

She rounded the table, sat down, and placed a covered soup dish in front of her. "When the guests first come to the table, their soup or fish will already be waiting for them. You must remove the cover. If it's fish, you'll need to remove the cover from the sauce as well." She gave him a nod. "Go ahead."

He approached her left side and removed the cover.

"No, no. You have to take care that you don't dirty the cloth with drops of steam. Turn the cover up quickly. Try again."

He did it again.

"Much better. Set it on the dinner tray until you have time to take it out of the room."

He placed it on a tray behind them.

She frowned. "Next time we practice, you need to be wearing some tight shoes or thin pumps."

"No."

She lifted her gaze. "You can't move quickly or lightly in those big boots, Mack."

"No."

Leaning back in the chair, she tilted her head. "Have you not realized why Mrs. Vanderbilt hired you?"

"She needed a useful man."

Tillie shook her head. "You're Earl's twin. And Earl looks absolutely stunning in his livery. Mrs. Vanderbilt wants to, at some point, have you and Earl serving her guests. On the first floor. In the parlor. And eventually in the banquet hall. I can't even imagine the sight the two of you would make side by side."

He paled. "I figured all that, but I thought it took months and months, years even, to work your way up to footman."

"Ordinarily it takes a great deal of time, experience, and references. But because of your height, your looks, and your twin brother, well . . ." She shrugged.

"What if I sabotage my chances? What if I dribble the gravy, drop a plate, knock over a glass?"

"They'll send you packing."

He pinched the bridge of his nose, the white gloves completely out of place with his rolled-up sleeves and chambray shirt. "Why wasn't I warned about this earlier?"

"Probably because it never occurred to anyone you wouldn't want to be a footman. It's more pay. More prestige. Less heavy lifting. For mercy's sake, there's a long line of men in town who'd jump at the chance you're being given."

He scowled. "Well, they can have it. I am not wearing those, those . . . fancy clothes."

"Why not?"

"They look ridiculous!"

She lifted a corner of her mouth. "Not from where I've been standing."

He paused a second, then headed toward the door. "I'm not doing it."

Scrambling from the chair, she grabbed his arm. "If you walk out, it will be Allan who suffers."

"That's not my fault."

"It is. You're being stubborn and muleheaded and down-right silly. It's just a uniform."

His eyes were dark. Fierce.

"Is it really worth your job, Mack? Worth Allan's?"

He slammed his eyes shut.

She slowly released his arm, then returned to her seat. "Drinks are next."

He stared at her for a long moment before returning to her side and all but slamming a glass down beside her.

"Be careful. That's crystal. And you're supposed to hand it to me."

He picked it up and shoved it toward her.

"It's improper to give anything with the naked hand."

"I'm wearing gloves. Female-looking gloves. Which I hate and resent and—"

"The tray, Mack. Go get the hand-waiter and put the crystal on it."

Flexing a fist, he spun around, retrieved the cloth-covered hand-waiter, and placed the goblet on it.

After they'd covered countless procedures for the first course, he looked ready to explode.

"I think we'll stop for now," she said. "I really do have some things I need to attend to. Meet me here tomorrow, same time. We'll review what you've learned, then start on the second course."

Peeling off his gloves, he threw them on the table and slammed out of the room without so much as a word.

She stared at the door, trying to comprehend how he could get so upset about the possibility of a promotion simply because he didn't care for the uniform.

Ridiculous. But truth be told, she preferred an angry Mack

to the one who had swept her about the entry hall last week. Yes, an angry Mack was by far the safer.

She pushed back her chair. As long as she demanded perfection during these lessons, she should be all right.

Ten

When Mack stepped into the storage room the next day, his eyes went straight to the pair of large but thin shoes in Tillie's hands. She smiled to herself. Nothing like landing the first punch.

"Put these on, please." She set them on a chair next to his gloves. "I'll ready the dinnerware."

He didn't move.

She busied herself with the trays, gravy bowls, and tureens. "Step lively, now. We've a lot to cover and not much time to do it in."

The door clicked shut. For a moment she thought he'd left. Then she heard him cross the floor and move the shoes and gloves to the table.

She peeked over her shoulder. The spindle chair faced away from her, creaking as he settled into it. Its back barely reached his shoulder blades and in no way spanned the breadth of his upper body.

For a moment he sat, blond head hanging, before finally dipping his right shoulder and grabbing the heel of his boot. His shirt stretched taut, outlining shoulders, back, and trim waist.

The boot thudded to the floor. He repeated the ritual, dipping his left shoulder and leaning back for leverage. Muscles bulged and rippled, drawing her eye over every ridge, every vale.

She stood frozen in place. She had no idea backs even had muscles.

The boot came away in his hands. He gripped it, his knuckles white, before carefully arranging it on the floor next to the other.

Grabbing a thin pump off the table, he bent over, chest to thigh, working the shoe onto his foot. Hooking his fingers into the strings and yanking them tight like those of a corset before tying them in a swift bow. She watched as he did the second, fascinated with every nuance of movement. Quick. Sure. Efficient. And so different from her own.

Straightening, he reached for the gloves, dropping one on his leg while pulling the other onto his hand. Finally, he slapped his knees, pushed up off the chair, and caught her ogling him.

Their eyes met and locked. His immediately darkened, the pupils dilating, obscuring all but a hint of brown.

Without ever breaking eye contact, he brought his right hand to his mouth, nipped the tip of each finger with his teeth, loosening the glove. Then, giving his head a shake like a dog with a dish towel, he tugged it off entirely.

Something leapt within her abdomen. Something not

totally pleasant, but not totally unpleasant. Whatever it was, it began to spread from her stomach to every extremity to every nerve.

She needed to make him mad. Distract him. But she couldn't move, couldn't formulate a single sentence.

The glove hung limp from between his teeth. He drove a single burst of air from his lungs, sending the glove to the ground beside him. Then quickly removed the other one, crinkling it in those large hands before slinging it to the side.

She tried to back up, but the shelves were behind her. She had nowhere to go.

His attention moved to her lips. "Your mouth drives me crazy. Did you know that?"

Her throat closed. She tried to suck in air but couldn't. The room began to fuzz. She felt a bit like she did when she rode in a carriage.

His gaze lifted. "I've been wanting to kiss you since the moment I saw you."

She closed her eyes but could still picture his gentle expression. Hear the earnestness in his voice. Feel the spot on her palm he'd kissed last week.

He stepped close, hooking a finger beneath her chin, raising it. A quivery sensation raced along her neck and arms. Her hands fluttered to his chest in one last effort to stave him off. The thudding of his heart pounded against her fingers, transferring its rhythm from her hand, to her arm, then straight to her heart. *We cannot.*

But the thought never made it from her brain to her lips. He cupped her face, drawing her up, almost to her toes.

Voices just outside the door shattered her stupor. Snapping herself straight, she shoved him back, scrabbled away from the bookshelves, and flew to the opposite end of the table.

"Put on your gloves, please." It was her voice. Calm. Collected. No one entering now would suspect every nerve in her body trembled with need.

And need it was. She wanted that kiss. She wanted it like nothing she'd ever wanted before . . . except for a position as lady's maid.

The voices passed by, never knowing she and Mack were even in here. But they could have. Could have opened the door and caught the two of them, and that would have been the end of it. Just like that.

No lady's maid position. No Biltmore position. No references. What would her mother say?

She gripped the chair in front of her. Her mother would be devastated.

Mack took a step toward her.

She scurried to the left, keeping the table between them. He reversed directions. So did she. He eyed the table.

Good heavens. He was going to vault over it.

"Don't!" she cried. "You'll take out everything on the table."

"Then come back here."

She shook her head. "I can't, Mack. Don't you see? I *can't.*"

"You mean you won't."

"That too."

"I don't understand. Is it me?"

She crinkled her apron in her hand. "No. I already told you. It's our jobs."

"If it weren't for our jobs, would you have kissed me just then?"

Yes. Oh, most definitely, yes.

She didn't answer out loud, but he must have read it in her expression. They both leapt toward the door. In his hurry, his leg rammed the table, sending several glasses and a tureen flying.

The crash of glassware and silver rang in her ears. Not staying to investigate the damage, she scurried into the hall.

"Tillie!" His swift, long strides caught up to her at once. "How much longer are you going to deny what's happening?"

"Keep your voice down," she whispered, her eye on the end of the corridor, where the servants' stairs and elevator were. "And nothing's happening."

"It is." He dropped his tone to match hers.

A second-floor chambermaid carrying a wad of soiled linens eyed them with interest. Tillie gave her a brief nod as they passed, then increased her pace.

Mack matched her step for step.

"I thought you wanted to keep your job," she hissed.

"I do. But only for as long as it takes to earn what I need to secure Ora Lou a decent place to live."

"Well, I intend to stay here the rest of my life."

He grabbed her arm and swung her around to face him, halting all forward progress. She expected to see fury in his eyes, but what she saw was hurt. Confusion. "I don't understand."

Her stomach dropped. "I'm sorry, Mack, but I'm not leaving Biltmore. Not for anyone or anything."

The servants' elevator opened. Dixie opened the gate from inside, balancing a tray with a used teacup, teapot, and linen. Her eyes widened slightly as Tillie shook loose of Mack's hold and stepped into the elevator while she stepped out.

He made no effort to follow, nor did he make an effort to mask his feelings.

She slid the gate shut and pushed a button. For several seconds they stood, a mere foot apart, yet miles away until the elevator doors cut him from view.

∞

"How you managed to break the crystal and knock a handle off the tureen, I cannot conceive." Mrs. Winter pinched her lips together in disapproval.

Mack stood before her desk, picturing Ora Lou and the bruise on her face and the lasciviousness of Forbus Sloop. Only that kept him from telling the housekeeper exactly what she could do with her crystal and tureen.

"Well?" Mrs. Winter looked him up and down. "What do you have to say for yourself?"

Before he could answer, a tentative knock sounded at the door.

"Enter," she said.

Tillie stepped through, her glance skittering from him to Mrs. Winter. "They said you wanted to see me?"

"I most certainly do. Come here and explain to me just how you allowed this barbarian to make such a mess in the storage room."

Head down, she approached. "It was an accident, ma'am."

"Well, of course it was an accident," she snapped. "What I'm trying to ascertain is how you could let it happen in the first place. You were the one training him. If you'd taught him proper technique when handling the crystal, it wouldn't be in pieces, now would it?"

He tightened his jaw. "It was my—"

She slammed her hand onto the desk. "Silence! I am speaking to Tillie."

"There's no excuse, ma'am." Tillie kept her gaze glued to the floor.

"There certainly is not, and replacement costs will come out of your pay. Every last penny."

Tillie jerked her head up.

Mack stiffened. "That hardly—"

"Do *not* say one more word unless you have been specifically spoken to. Do I make myself clear?"

"I'm just trying to—"

She surged to her feet, her face red with fury. But instead of pouring her wrath out onto him, she aimed it at Tillie. "I want him trained in the art of table waiting and I want it done before that house party gets here. I want him taught that he is not to speak until spoken to. I want him to wear his attire in the proper manner every moment of every day. If he does not, it will be your pay that's docked and your position that's jeopardized."

Color draining from her face, Tillie bobbed a curtsy. "Yes, ma'am. I'll take care of it."

"See that you do." She pointed to the door. "Out. Both of you."

Rage made his entire body tremble, but he managed to follow Tillie from the office. The moment he closed the door behind them, he turned to her. "I—"

"*Shhhtik.*" She chopped the air with her hand, silencing him as effectively as the housekeeper. "Just follow me and keep your mouth shut."

She stormed down the hall, around the corner, and down the stairs, black skirts rustling, the apron bow at the small of her back bouncing. Never once did she look up or speak to anyone they passed or check to see if he was following.

He wanted nothing so much as to tell that housekeeper exactly what he thought of her. Allan had said the items they were using were mismatches from sets which were old or out of style or incomplete. So why were they having to replace them?

Whatever the reason, they were. Or she was. He wondered how much the crystal would cost.

His shoulders slumped. A fortune. It had to cost a fortune. But no matter what the matron said, he'd broken it. So he'd pay for it. If he had to give the money to Allan, then have him give it to his sister, so be it. But he would pay.

Still, his frustration grew. That would mean even further delays in rescuing Ora Lou from the orphanage.

They reached the basement, and instead of slowing her pace, Tillie increased it. She made a beeline for his workroom, then pointed a finger and said, "Wait for me in there."

He stopped at his doorway, taking his time with the lock while he watched her sail into the laundry room, then come back out with a measuring tape fluttering from her hand like a writhing snake.

Opening his door, he stepped inside and slipped his key into his pocket. The sound of her clickety-click heels grew louder and his stomach jumped. He hadn't been this nervous since the last time he'd been sent to the shed for switches.

He reminded himself she was only a woman. But the fact was, she was more than that. Much more.

She zoomed around the corner, punched on the lights, slammed the door with a loud crack, and braced her feet wide like a ship captain's.

Take the deuce, but she was glorious when she was mad.

Her eyes flashed, her hair loosened, the pulse at her throat pounded. He supposed kissing her was out of the question, but it didn't keep him from wanting to.

"Don't even think about it," she bit out.

He lifted his brows. He hadn't realized he was that transparent. "I'm sorry about the crystal. I'll pay for it."

She clenched her fists, crumpling the measuring tape. "I don't want your money. I don't want your attentions. I don't want anything to do with you. But it looks like I'm stuck with you for the time being, so here are the rules."

He gave a slight nod to indicate he was listening.

"No more tête-à-têtes in the mornings on the terrace. No more dancing in the entry hall. No more looking at me like I'm your next meal. And no, I mean *no*, trying to kiss me. Is that understood?"

He gave another nod.

"Answer me, Mack Danver. Answer me out loud."

"I understand the rules."

She narrowed her eyes. "And will you follow them?"

"To the best of my ability."

"Not good enough."

"It's the most I'm willing to offer. I already told you I don't lie. So if I gave you any other response, it would be dishonest."

Her eyes teared up. "You must respect my boundaries, Mack. My job, my future, everything I've ever dreamed of is at stake. Please."

Don't cry. Don't cry.

He crammed his hands into his pockets to keep from hauling her into his arms. "I understand what's at stake. I'll do the best I can to honor every one of your wishes."

She studied him for a moment; then her shoulders relaxed.

"All right. The first thing we need is to find you some shirts that reach your wrists so you aren't going around the house with your sleeves rolled up."

"Allan and I have been through every shirt in the livery room," he said.

"So I'm told. That means I'll have to make you some." She curled her lips in disgust. "I'm going to kill Allan for getting me in the middle of this."

She was going to make him a shirt? No one but his mother had ever made him a shirt before.

Shaking out the measuring tape, she looked around his room. "Do you have anything to write with?"

He opened a drawer and placed pad and pencil on the table.

"All right, then." She took a deep breath, then strode toward him. "Bend your arm, please."

He hung his arms to the sides, slightly bending his right one. She pressed the tape against his shoulder, hooked it beneath his elbow, ran it to his wrist, then make a note on the pad.

"Turn around." She measured from neck to waist, then shoulder to shoulder. "Turn back around."

He faced her.

"Lift your arms up."

He extended his arms to the sides, and before he had time to prepare, she stepped into him, slipping her arms around him in order to feed the tape about his chest.

He sucked in his breath. And with it came the scent uniquely hers.

She stepped back, her cheeks burning, and matched the tape against his chest. He didn't so much as move.

Instead of letting go, she stayed put. Finally, she peeked

up at him. "Quit holding your breath, Mack. It makes your chest expand."

Their eyes locked and he slowly released his breath. She adjusted the tape, made a note, then turned back. Again she stepped into him, but this time she wrapped her arms around his waist. Again, he sucked in his breath.

She waited, moistening her lips, before he realized what he was doing and blew out his breath.

"Just one more," she said.

But when she reached up on tiptoe and put her hands behind his neck, he could no more keep from bracketing her waist than he could keep the sun from shining.

She was so small. His hands spanned almost her entire circumference. He'd danced with her, but only one hand had rested on her back. Never two hands. And never on her waist.

The only reaction she gave was an involuntary tremor. She wrapped the tape around his neck.

He swallowed, his Adam's apple dipping down, up, and then down again. She lifted her gaze to his.

"You'd best get out of here," he whispered, kneading her waist, scratching her apron sash with his thumbs.

She checked the measurement again, then took a step back.

He didn't let go. "Tillie?"

"No, Mack." She lowered her eyes. "I knew I should have let someone else take your measurements. I'm sorry I didn't."

She broke free of his grip, picked up her notes, and placed her hand on the doorknob.

"Tillie?"

She paused, but didn't look at him.

"Why didn't you have someone else take my measurements?"

She opened the door, and he thought she wasn't going to answer. Then just before she slipped out, she looked at him, her eyes stricken. "Because I didn't want anyone else touching you."

Then she was gone.

I'm not going to be able to take you out of here as quickly as I'd hoped," Mack said.

Ora Lou's shoulders slumped. They sat in the parlor of the orphanage, Irene at her side. The girl was still quiet and timid, but at least managed to look him in the eye occasionally. He wished some of that meekness would rub off on Ora Lou.

"What happened?" his sister asked.

"I broke some crystal and a tureen and I have to pay for it."

"I thought you were a useful man."

"I am."

"Then what were you doing with crystal and a tureen?"

He shrugged. "I polish and help store all that stuff occasionally, but this time I was training to serve at the table."

"Serve?" With a small bark of laughter, she turned to Irene. "Boy, would I love to see that."

Irene answered her smile, her face almost pretty when she let her guard down.

"How much longer, then?" his sister asked.

"Two months at the earliest," he said. "Probably more like three."

She sucked in her breath. "That long? But I told you I'd find work and pay for my own board."

"It's not just that." He reached into his pocket and handed her a letter the hotel had forwarded to him. "I got this from Ikey."

Opening it, she skimmed the note from their little brother. "He's just homesick and missing Ma. That will pass."

"That's easy for you to say. You know your situation is temporary. His is permanent."

She handed him back the letter. "So what are you saying?"

"I want to reunite us. All of us."

She slumped back on the couch, her expression falling. "Oh, Mack. How? That will take forever. I don't think I can stand it here that long. We eat this mealy kind of potage every single day for every meal. We have no bedding other than a moth-eaten blanket and no fireplace in our rooms. I'll freeze if I have to stay through winter." Brightening, she sat up straight. "What if I go to live with Ikey? Me and Irene both? That would make him feel better and then you wouldn't have to worry about finding me a place to live."

Mack shook his head. "From what this letter says, you wouldn't be much better off. Besides, none of the families I left the boys with can take on another mouth, much less two. You'll just have to wait."

She pushed a tangle of hair from her face, her brown eyes tearing.

"Sloop's not mistreating you again, is he?"

"Not really." She bit her lip. "But he hurts Irene."

"What do you mean 'not really'?" he barked.

Irene ducked her chin and grabbed the end of a thin braid.

His sister gave him a warning look. "It's all right, Irene. He's not mad at us. He's worried. You can tell him."

Panic flooded the girl's face. Before he could press them, the door opened.

"Visitation is over, girls." Sloop didn't give him so much as a glance. "Get to your rooms for prayer time."

The girls jumped to their feet and hurried past the director without even saying good-bye.

Frowning, Mack stood. He should have started the visit with questions about Sloop instead of about his delay.

Sloop widened the door, the cut of his coat every bit as fine as the well-to-do men of Asheville. "Get out."

Mack weighed the wisdom of confronting the director and decided he'd best gather all the particulars first. The cozy comfort of the parlor had led him to believe the children enjoyed the same. He wondered how much funding the orphanage received. Surely enough to provide for decent bedding and meals.

Perhaps it was time to have another visit with Leonard Vaughan. But first, when he had an opportunity, he'd have a look at what lay beyond the receiving rooms.

Placing a cap on his head, he gave Sloop a curt nod and let himself out.

∞

A brown package tied with string lay in front of Mack's workroom door. As useful man, he was responsible for opening and assembling all post deliveries. But this wasn't a delivery.

There was no address. The paper wasn't crumpled. And the contents were flimsy. Turning on the light, he sliced the string with his knife, then peeled back paper and tissue. A shirt. A brand-new blue shirt.

His throat swelled. Ever since their meeting with Mrs. Winter, Tillie had refused to be alone with him. She'd made another parlormaid, Alice, rise at four under the guise of training her. Because when the grand party arrived next week, Tillie would not be doing parlormaid duties, but lady's maid duties for one of the guests.

In the afternoons, when she gave him lessons in table waiting, she again enlisted the help of Alice. According to Tillie, Alice needed to learn the rules as well and could act as a mock guest, allowing Tillie to stand well out of reach while she instructed. But in the evenings, when all her chores were done, she'd sewn him a shirt with her own hands. He lifted it, bringing it close, trying to catch a whiff of her scent, but smelled starch instead.

He fingered the placket. Tiny perfect stitches ran down the seams like rows of white corn. He wondered where she'd sat when she sewed. In her room? The servants' hall for female staff? In a rocker? A hard chair? Or alone in her bed?

Stripping off his shirt, he slipped the new one on, then held his arms in front of him. Perfect. He buttoned it up, tucked it into his trousers, and popped his suspenders in place, wondering where she was now.

He stuck his head out the door and checked the clock in the hall. Every clock in the house was keyed to the master one over the stable in the courtyard, so what he saw, she saw.

A quarter past nine. She'd be in Vanderbilt's library. Spinning around, he looked for the pair of lanterns he'd assembled a while back. Allan told him they were to go in the library.

He wrapped his boot-leg bag around his hips, stuck a jar of kerosene into it, then grabbed the lamps.

∽

Tillie always saved the library for the last room of the morning. It was the one she'd miss the most if she was promoted to lady's maid.

As it was, she'd not be able to clean it the entire time the guests were in residence. She and Lucy had each been assigned a different woman. As a test. And much was riding on it.

Climbing a walnut library step stool, she stretched to run her cloth against a row of spines on an upper shelf and marveled anew at the thousands of books in the two-story room. Wall to wall, ceiling to floor, more books than a person could possibly read in a lifetime.

Still, she knew Mr. Vanderbilt spent many an hour with a book in hand, as did the new Mrs. Vanderbilt. She wondered where in this vast room *The Prince and the Pauper* sat. Wondered what had happened to the characters when they switched places. Wondered what it would be like if she and Mrs. Vanderbilt switched places. Wondered what it would be like to have a husband of her own.

Her hand stilled as images of Mack filled her vision. Moving the furniture. Playing parlor games. Trapping her against a storage shelf with his eyes.

"Tillie?"

She spun around, knocking a book loose and dropping her rag in order to grab for support. Mack's gaze skimmed over her and she became aware of her arched back and strained bodice as she clutched the shelf behind her.

Her throat clogged. "You scared me to death. How long have you been standing there?"

"A while. What were you thinking?"

She opened and closed her mouth, scrambling for something to say. And then she saw it. The shirt. He was wearing the shirt she'd made him. But his hands were so full, she couldn't make out the fit.

Slowly, she righted herself on the stool. "What do you want?"

Even to her own ears her voice was sharp. But she'd gone to such lengths to ensure they were never alone, she couldn't help but be frustrated.

"These lamps. Where do I put them?"

Tapping the book back in place, she climbed down the steps. "I didn't know they'd arrived. Let me see."

She took one from his arms, admiring the blue-and-white mosaic design on the base. "Oooh. It's beautiful."

"Yes." His voice was deep. Hushed.

She didn't dare look up and instead surveyed the room. They'd look smart on the mantel but not very practical. The fireplace was large enough for Mack to walk into standing up and to lie down in any direction without touching the sides. Mr. Vanderbilt would have to climb a stool just to raise or lower the wick.

That left the twin, two-tiered reading tables sitting on opposite ends of the oriental rug and bracketed by matching armchairs. Handing the lantern back to Mack, she removed a couple of books from one of the tables and laid them on the lower tier.

"We'll put one here and the other over there."

When all was arranged, he carefully lifted the shade.

"What are you doing?"

"Filling them with oil."

"You were supposed to have done that already. What if you spill it? All cleaning, trimming, and filling is done in the lamp room belowstairs."

"I won't spill it." Setting down the shade, he lifted the chimney.

She ran to retrieve her dropped cleaning cloth. "Well, for heaven's sake, don't soil the shades with oily fingers and don't spill a drop."

He filled the base, his large hands steady and true. The trickle of oil sounded loud in the quiet room. She blinked against the kerosene's pungent odor, then replaced the chimney and shade.

When he'd topped off the other, he straightened. "I'll take the lamps in the other rooms downstairs. You want to hold the shades for me while I fill them?"

Shaking her head, she replaced the second chimney and shade. "I can't. It'd put me too far behind."

He sighed. "What about tomorrow?"

"Not tomorrow, either. I'm using every spare minute to make perfumed sachets for the drawers my mistress will be using when she arrives."

"When should we do the lamps, then?"

"I'll have Alice help you on Friday."

Neither moved. The air between them hummed with feelings he didn't bother to hide and which she took pains to suppress.

"Thank you for the shirt," he said.

She braved a look. "Does it fit?"

"Perfectly." He stepped back, holding his hands slightly away from his body, and turned in a slow circle. His boot-leg bag hung low on his hips like a gunslinger's belt.

She followed the inverted triangle of his torso, which led to shoulders as wide as the icebox in Chef's pantry and arms that might have been long in inches but were in perfect proportion to the rest of his body. She remembered cutting the fabric for his shirt and double-checking her measurements to be sure they were accurate. Beholding him now, she realized they'd been dead-on.

When he came full circle, she slowly raised her gaze. It wasn't desire she saw in his, but some indefinable emotion she couldn't quite place.

He ran a hand down the front placket. "I've never had a shirt so fine in my entire life. Nor one that fit me so well. I'll take good care of it."

She tried to swallow and couldn't. Tried to tell him she'd already started on a second and couldn't. Tried to tell him she'd relished every stitch and couldn't.

"Well, I'll see you this afternoon for my lessons?"

She nodded.

"This afternoon, then." He turned and walked out, leaving the scent of kerosene in his wake.

She slid her eyes closed, once again reminding herself of the many reasons she wanted to be a lady's maid.

∞

The discordant sound of harried staff members racing every which way and talking at once, each louder than the other, reminded Tillie of an orchestra tuning up before a concert. As conductor, Mrs. Winter stood just inside the servants' entrance directing footmen and grooms, chambermaids and housemaids, visiting servants who'd traveled with their masters, and anyone else underfoot.

"Tillie," she barked. "Your mistress is finally here. Have her trunks taken to the Paris Gown-Room and see to her clothing after you check on the lady herself. . . . What are you doing out there, Earl? I told you to return to the house while the guests were in residence. Change out of that coachman livery and back into footman livery. . . . Dixie, Mrs. Whitman's lady is in the courtyard. Take care of her, will you? . . . Mack, those are Tillie's . . ."

Hunched over, Mack trudged inside with a large trunk on his back, his arms straining against the straps.

"The elevator," Tillie shouted to him over the noise.

Just outside the stairwell and elevator shaft, he dropped the trunk to the floor. "I've never seen it so crowded down here."

She nodded. "That always happens when a guest party arrives. The way we're usually spread out, it's easy to forget there are sixty-six of us."

He pointed to the trunk. "She has five more."

Tillie sucked in her breath. "*Five?* Are you sure they're all Miss DePriest's?"

He pointed to the elaborate DP monogram. "Are there any more DePriests in the house?"

"No. She's the only one."

"Then they're hers. And they're big, too."

Tillie glanced at the clogged corridor. "You go ahead and collect them. I'm going to run up and check on her. Do you know where the Paris Gown-Room is?"

He shook his head.

"Fourth floor, south end, second door to the right. Look for the plaque that says *Paris*."

He turned to go.

"Mack?"

He glanced back.

"How do I look?" She smoothed her stiffly starched apron, plucked at its frilly shoulder straps, then stood up straight to face him.

She'd only meant to receive a quick word of reassurance,

but he gave the task his complete attention. Starting with her white cap, he surveyed her coif, her collar, her apron bib, her waist, her full black skirt, and then up again.

The noises receded. She held her breath.

Stepping forward, he scooped up a long streamer hanging from her cap and moved it to her back. "Perfect."

He had ridiculously long lashes. How had she not noticed them before? A bead of moisture slid from his hairline down the side of his bronzed face, tucked up under his jaw, and then trickled beneath his collar.

"Tillie!" the butler shouted. "The call button from the South Tower Room was pushed. Get moving!"

This was it. Her chance to prove herself. But doubts began to assail her. This wasn't her mother she'd be waiting on. This was a real, genuine lady who wouldn't be offering quiet corrections or gentle suggestions. She would expect Tillie to know exactly what to do and when to do it.

What if a situation came up that Mama hadn't prepared her for? What if she committed some grave breech of etiquette? She looked up at Mack, trepidation thrumming through her veins.

His eyes softened. "You'll do fine. Now, go on. I'll have these trunks up there quick as a wink."

But some hidden force, some giant magnet hiding beneath the floor, held her rooted to the spot.

He took her by the shoulders, turned her so she faced the stairs, then gave her back end a pat. "Go."

Jerking, she swished a hand behind her as if batting away a fly, then hurried to the third floor.

∞

"Where have you been? I rang for you a good five minutes ago."

Mary Pamela DePriest sat in the large oval room, her face drawn up in a pretty pout. She couldn't have been much older than Tillie. Nineteen, perhaps. But no more than twenty. She was the cousin of one of the invited guests and had been included in the party as a courtesy.

Surrounded by pastel colors and dainty floral fabric on the draperies, she looked wilted and worn in her brown travel outfit.

Tillie bobbed a curtsy. "May I help you with your hat and driving cloak, miss?"

"Do hurry up."

Tillie quickly withdrew an eight-inch, jewel-topped pin from the delectable hat the girl wore. Its melon-shaped crown had what looked like an inverted magnolia of brown velvet held together with a long gilt buckle. Tillie clasped its rim and lifted, but it resisted.

"Ouch! Careful, you clumsy child!"

Child? Tillie kept her face void of expression. "Sorry, miss."

She searched out and found two more hatpins before finally freeing the hat. She placed it on a wire holder, then assisted the girl to her feet and quickly unbuttoned the brown serge jacket she wore. Slipping it off her shoulders, Tillie laid it carefully across a striped cotton armchair.

Miss DePriest extended her arm and fanned her hand as if she couldn't wait another minute to have her glove removed.

Tillie balked. Ladies took their own gloves off, or so Mama had said. So she wasn't exactly sure how to remove gloves from someone else's hand. She couldn't very well grab the girl's wrist and yank. Mack removing his with his teeth flashed through her mind.

Miss DePriest stomped her foot. "Well? Get on with it. The trip was a complete bore and I'm anxious to have a rest."

"Yes, miss." Grasping the hem of the glove, she quickly peeled it inside out. Then moved to the next.

Not taking the time to right them, she laid them beside the jacket and started in on the double-breasted vest. A light floral scent wafted around her.

"Must you take so long?"

Instead of answering, Tillie kept her fingers busy removing collar, cuffs, skirt, shirtwaist, petticoat, and corset.

"Would you like to sit down while I brush out your hair, miss?"

Miss DePriest presented her back to Tillie and hoisted up her chemise. "Scratch."

Deep red grooves from the corset's boning marred the girl's otherwise flawless skin.

She stomped her foot again, a hairpin falling from her coiffure. "Scratch!"

Tillie ran her fingernails over the angry marks.

"Harder!"

Tillie increased the pressure, wincing as her light scratch marks superimposed themselves over the grooves.

Miss DePriest twisted from side to side and up and down, sighing and groaning like a bear against a tree trunk. Finally she dropped her chemise, fell onto the striped cotton couch, and extended one leg.

Tillie kneeled before her and removed shoes and stockings. The smell of sweaty feet that had been encased for a long period of time slapped her in the face. She struggled to keep her expression neutral, then braved a slow, cautious breath from her mouth. After setting the last stocking and garter aside, she turned to find Miss DePriest swirling her foot.

"Rub!"

Tillie hesitated only a moment before massaging first one foot and then the other. The smell from the girl's feet filled the room. Mama's had never held an odor, nor had she expected them to be rubbed. Tillie would have to throw open the windows during dinner to air everything out.

Miss DePriest sighed, her eyes drifting shut.

Finally, Tillie rose. "Would you like me to brush your hair now?"

"Uh-huh." But she didn't budge.

Tillie moved behind her, quietly slipped a handkerchief from her own pocket, wiped her hands, then removed the pins from Miss DePriest's hair. Taking up a brush, she smoothed the hair over the back of the couch. It was long, silky, and the color of lemon chiffon pie.

Tillie smiled. It was going to be a pleasure to dress it. Tucking away the brush, she turned down the soft cotton bedding and fluffed two feather pillows against a caned headboard.

"Miss DePriest?" she whispered.

A soft snore.

She hesitated, then finally decided to wake the girl. "Come now, miss. Your bed is all cozy and waiting."

Miss DePriest fluttered her eyes, their color like the blue forget-me-nots in the breakfast room flower arrangement downstairs. Tillie helped her up, guided her to the bed, and tucked her in.

Burrowing into her pillows, she mumbled something.

"Beg your pardon, miss?" Tillie leaned close.

"To dinner I'll be wearing my brown Félix with the small check in the front and back."

"Yes, miss." Tiptoeing to the chair, she collected the discarded clothing and slipped into the hall.

As soon as she reached the servants' passage, she cradled the garments and all but flew to the upstairs gown-room. She needed to unpack, find the Félix gown, undergarments, shoes, stockings, gloves and hat, then freshen them and lay them out in Miss DePriest's dressing room. All within the next forty minutes.

Tillie burst into the Paris Gown-Room and stopped short. Lucy Lewers hooked an elaborate silk evening skirt onto a lower rod. The room of highly polished hardwood floors, ceilings, and walls were lined with nothing but tier upon tier of varnished poles—offering no place for dust to harbor.

A third of the tiers were filled with gowns. The rest were barren except for a smattering of padded skirt-supporters decorated with colorful ribbons.

"What are you doing in here?" Tillie asked.

Lucy brushed a speck of dirt from the skirt she'd hung. "I ran out of space in my gown-room, so I had to put the overflow in here."

Tillie stiffened. "You can't do that. Miss DePriest has six trunks. *Six*. I need every inch of space in here. You'll have to move them."

Lucy arched a brow. "You mean you haven't even started

unpacking? Why, I'm already finished. I'd assumed this room was extra, since nothing was hanging up."

Tillie looked at the three trunks anchored in the middle of the room. "Well, it's not. As you can see, it's filled with trunks and there's more in the hall. Now, move your clothing. And where are all my skirt-supporters? I put rods of them in here early this morning."

"Did you?" She touched three fingertips to her lips. "And here I thought they were for anyone who needed them."

Tillie widened her eyes. "You used my skirt-supporters? I went up and down four flights of stairs five different times stocking my poles."

"Well, heavens. Why didn't you use the elevator?" She shrugged. "Doesn't matter now, I suppose. Good luck with unpacking all this before dinner."

"Lucy, you have to move your lady's clothing and you need to replace the skirt-supporters you took. I need them. Right away."

She waggled her fingers. "You better get busy and find some, then."

In disbelief, Tillie stared at the now empty doorway before shaking herself. Balancing the clothing she carried, she tossed the items for laundry in the corner, draped the shirtwaist, petticoat, and corset over her arm, then hung the skirt on one of the few remaining supporters.

She'd deal with Lucy later. For now, she needed to find the Félix gown and its accessories. Opening a connecting door, she entered another wooden room with a modest fireplace flanked by closets, wardrobes, chests of drawers, and an abundance of airy space. Opening the glass-fronted chiffonier, she gasped. The shelves were empty.

Throughout the past two weeks she'd stuffed rose petals,

lavender buds, and geraniums from the Biltmore gardens into sachet sacks, then lined the chiffonier shelves and drawers. Yet none of the sachets were inside. She opened the top drawer, then the next. And the next. And the next. Nothing.

Lucy.

She arranged the shirtwaist, corset, and petticoat in the drawers, then hurried into the other room. There was nothing she could do for now. She needed to find the Félix gown.

❦

Mack returned to the fourth floor to retrieve the empty trunks he'd carried up earlier and found Tillie headfirst inside one.

Heaps of white tissue paper blanketed the Paris Gown-Room floor like newly fallen snow. Trunks with raised lids were strewn about. Silky nightgowns, lace-trimmed geegaws, and beribboned articles spilled out of their bellies like jewels in a treasure box.

But it was Tillie's delectable bottoms-up profile which captured his full attention. Muttering to herself, she leaned in farther, her skirts twitching at her precarious stance while offering him a glimpse of a well-turned ankle.

"Tillie?"

She banged her head on the side of the trunk, bit out a heartfelt expletive, then raised up like a groundhog checking for spring. A piece of white tissue tumbled off her shoulder.

"Stop doing that!" she snapped.

"Doing what?"

"Sneaking up on me."

"Sneaking? I clomped down this entire hall, but you were muttering so loud, you didn't hear me coming." He looked about the room. "Is something wrong?"

"My mistress wants to wear a brown Félix with a small

check in the front and back, but I have no idea what trunk it's in. Lucy used up a third of my space in here, most of the lower rods and all of my skirt-supporters. My sachets have vanished. And once I find this blasted dress, I still have to beat it, dust her hat, brush her shoes, arrange her dressing room, lay out her toilet table, and bring her hot water. How in the world am I going to accomplish all that in the next twenty minutes?"

He didn't have the heart to tell her she would also need to repair her appearance. Tendrils of hair escaped their pins and her hat sat askew. In the month he'd been here, he'd never seen her so mussed, and he had no defense against the panic in her voice.

"What can I do?" he asked.

Her lips parted. "Do you mean it? They aren't screaming for you belowstairs?"

He shrugged. "They can do without me for twenty minutes."

Her gaze darted about the room. "I'll find her hat, gloves, and shoes; you start on the trunks in the hall. We're looking for a brown-checked shirtwaist and skirt."

Retreating to the hall, he unlatched the nearest trunk and raised its lid. Pale blue tapes crisscrossed white tissue, holding and protecting the cargo within. He flipped open his pocketknife and cut the tapes, then tossed the shielding tissue aside.

Something green. He lifted it, then reared back. The stuffed shirtwaist looked as if a headless horsewoman had lost her bottom half along with her head. Sleeves, waist, and bust had been filled with tissue, leaving every bow and geegaw intact.

Laying her on the floor, he tried not to look at her as he flung another layer of tissue to the side. More green. Yards and yards of it. He speedily lifted it.

Her bottom half, stuffed at the waist. He jammed the skirt

beneath the shirtwaist. Better. At least all she was missing now was her head.

"Mack?"

He stopped and leaned around the doorway. In one hand Tillie held a brown hat heaped high with feminine fluff. In the other, a horse brush. Or at least, what looked like one.

"You find it?" he asked.

"No, but handle the contents of those trunks very gingerly. If you wrinkle anything, it'll add hours and hours to my workday."

He glanced at the green skirt crumpled on the floor. "Will do."

He straightened the folds in the skirt like an attendant fussing with a bridal train, reaching underneath to smooth out the net lining.

"What the devil are you doing?" Earl asked, amazement tingeing his voice.

Mack snatched his hand back. His brother stood at the top of the stairs wearing indoor livery and a wide grin.

Heat rushed to Mack's face. "Tillie's lady didn't arrive until the eleventh hour and has a particular dress she wants to wear. I was helping her look for it."

Earl raised a brow, but before he could respond, Tillie waded to the doorway.

"Earl! I thought they had you in the carriage house."

"Moved me back inside for the party. Who's your bird?"

"DePriest."

He frowned. "Never seen her here before. She giving you a hard time?"

"I'm just a bit behind, is all. Did they send you up here after Mack?"

He nodded. "Time to go, big brother."

"Not until we find that dress." He tossed Earl his pocket-knife. "You start on that end. We're looking for a brown-checkered one."

Earl caught the knife one-handed, then popped open the trunk closest to him.

Tillie bit her lip. "Thank you."

"Go on," Mack said, turning his attention back to his trunk. "We'll find it."

She scurried inside the room, the tissue on the floor rustling like autumn leaves.

Earl removed a stuffed, dark blue shirtwaist with big white swirls, gave a short bark of laughter, then looked over at Mack with a leer and squeezed the bodice's plumpest part.

Mack chuckled. "Don't wrinkle it or you'll make more work for Tillie."

The green shirtwaist and skirt, ballooned as it was, had taken up almost the entire trunk. He flung a final piece of tissue aside, releasing a burst of flower-garden smells. Rearing back, he let the aroma dissipate before peering inside. A layer of the fanciest undergarments he'd ever seen lined the bottom. Frilly corsets, silk stockings, lacy falderals, and silk drawers.

He glanced at Earl, then quickly covered the unmention-ables back up. The image of all those trappings had seared his brain, though. Thank goodness he wasn't a footman. He'd never be able to look Miss DePriest in the eye.

"Found it!" Earl raised a wood brown shirtwaist with a diagonal plaid.

Tillie exclaimed from deep inside the room, then scurried out holding dainty slippers of the same fabric. "Oh! You did it! That's it! Thank you so much."

Giving her a broad wink, he bowed. "At your service, miss."

The smile she bestowed on him sucked the breath right out of Mack.

"You better hurry, though," Earl said, straightening. "The hourglass is running short."

"I know. Thanks again."

Earl laid the garment back in the trunk and headed toward the stairwell. "You coming, Mack?"

"Right behind you." But instead, he waited until Earl had disappeared, then turned to Tillie. "What all do you have left?"

"That's it. I have everything gathered and brushed, so it's just a matter of getting it down to her dressing room."

He nodded. "Well, fix your hair. You're a mess."

She touched her head, found locks of hair straggling down her back, then shoved the shoes she held toward him. "Here."

He caught them against his gut, then watched her pull the hat combs loose. Whipping off the snowy cap, she handed it to him, too, its long streamers floating down to rest against his trouser legs.

She yanked out half a dozen hairpins, stuck them in her mouth, lifted her face to the ceiling, and shook her head like some forest sprite, sending waves of black curls to her hips.

His heart slammed against his chest. Never had he seen a woman do such things before. The grace with which she moved, the silkiness of her hair, the lashes lying along her cheeks, the white teeth clamped around celluloid pins. All of it mesmerized him.

With quick, efficient movements, she gathered her hair

into her hands, then wrung it like a mop and twisted it to her head, jamming pin after pin against her scalp.

Snatching her cap from between his fingers, she propped it on top of her head and tucked in the combs. "Thanks."

He stood tongue-tied and off-balance as if he were a youth discovering life's mysteries for the first time.

She rushed back inside and returned with hat, gloves, stockings, and who knew what all draped underneath a large ruffled petticoat.

"I guess I'll have to come back for the dress. Thanks again, Mack." Grabbing the shoes he'd forgotten he had, she rushed to the stairs, white streamers flapping behind her like wings.

It took him less than ten seconds to snatch up the brown-checkered shirtwaist and skirt, then follow her to the passage-way which led to Miss DePriest's room.

Thirteen

Miss DePriest drove her fingers into her hair and vigorously scratched her head, undoing the second coiffure Tillie had styled. "No, no, no. That was too low and the last one too high. Somewhere in the middle and be quick about it."

Picking up the hairbrush, Tillie bit her cheek. She felt as if she were in the midst of Mr. Southey's story of the three bears and Miss DePriest was the grown woman who found fault with everything. Perhaps if Tillie left the window open, Miss DePriest would jump out and break her neck the way the impudent woman in the story had.

It was an uncharitable thought and she knew she shouldn't have it, but there it was. She wasn't ready to say her prayers and repent over it, either.

Twenty minutes later, hair finally dressed, Miss DePriest tugged on her gloves. "I shall want warm milk before I retire.

And see to it that I have a proper receptacle. I don't trust that . . . *chair* in the bathing room."

"Of course, miss."

"And do air out the room, Tillie. It has a bit of an odor to it."

"Yes, miss."

"But make sure you close everything up in time to build the fire. I deplore a frigid room."

"I'll make sure, miss."

She paused at the door. "But not too hot, mind you."

"No, miss." Tillie bobbed a curtsy. "I'll make sure everything is *just* right."

Miss DePriest studied Tillie as if she sensed she'd somehow been maligned but couldn't quite ascertain how. Finally, she nodded, snapping the door shut behind her.

Tillie allowed her shoulders to slump, then glanced about the room. A disaster.

Throwing open the windows, she took in a deep breath of fresh air and looked out upon God's unblemished creation. Five miles to the west and obscured by trees and hills was the French Broad River. She remembered floating along it on a raft her brothers had built, looking at puffy white clouds and building air castles. Never in all her imaginings did she dream she'd be working for one of the wealthiest families in America in a chateau that could swallow up two or three palaces in Britain. Or so she'd been told.

Sighing, she turned around and started collecting the articles strewn about the room. Over the course of the next several hours, she scoured the bathtub and bathroom, dusted every table and chair, wiped the dressing glass, cleaned the hairbrushes, emptied the pitcher, filled it with fresh water, ironed the top sheet of bedding, turned back the covers, placed a gold-rimmed chamber pot beneath the bed, wound the clock, brought fresh flowers to the room, built a fire, and closed the windows.

She dreaded going to the Paris Gown-Room to fetch Miss DePriest's nightdress and cap. She hadn't been up there since she'd left it in such disarray. Word would surely have spread to Mrs. Winter. No telling what the housekeeper had done when she saw the condition of the room and the state of the hallway. And it would be hours yet before Tillie could finish unpacking the trunks and have everything in its proper place.

Hugging a handful of soiled garments to her chest, she trudged up the stairs to the south wing of the fourth floor.

The corridor was spotless. Her stomach dropped. *Where are the trunks?*

Scrambling to the Paris Gown-Room, she opened the door and pulled up short. Not one trunk nor sheet of tissue littered the polished hardwood floor. Instead, the space was completely clear. Along the walls, Lucy's garments had been replaced with tier after tier of Miss DePriest's elaborate skirts for every occasion imaginable.

Dropping the laundry by the door, Tillie moved to the adjoining room and turned on the light. Rows of fashionable hats perched atop individual wire stands. More shoes than she'd ever seen in her life lay amongst them.

She opened the chiffonier. The green shirtwaist Mack had unpacked lay carefully inside, still stuffed with tissue. Beside it, a navy shirtwaist. Every drawer and chest had been filled but one. Inside it were the sachets of flower petals she'd labored over all week.

Who had done this? Surely not Mrs. Winter. Definitely not Lucy. Perhaps Dixie? But no. A harassed Dixie had stuck her head into Miss DePriest's room halfway through her rounds to ask if the bedding needed to be freshened or the fire stoked. But by that time Tillie had already taken care of it.

Who, then?

Turning around, she saw a single trunk shoved into one corner. Frowning, she raised its lid and found undergarments and unmentionables inside. A fleeting thought, so preposterous Tillie dismissed it before it had fully formed, came back and took root.

Had Mack and Earl done this? But they couldn't have. Earl had been in full livery and would be attending to the functions on the main floor. Mack would be chopping ice, getting up wood, carrying garbage to the outside cans, and storing trunks.

She looked again at the hats and shoes. Noticed that though they had been placed on the shelf, they hadn't been arranged in a meticulous fashion as any woman would have done. No, they'd been tossed up in any order. At any angle.

She opened a drawer. Noted a sleeve on a shirtwaist had been trapped underneath the body of the garment. She rearranged it.

Going into the Paris Gown-Room, she looked at the skirts. Several hung off-center. Implausible as it seemed, there was no other explanation. Who other than Mack would retrieve the trunks? Who other than he knew about Lucy's garments and the missing sachets? And why would all of Miss DePriest's articles be stowed away *except* the intimates?

Shaking her head, she tried to picture that big man with his big hands grappling over loops and buttons and tiny ribbon closures. Handling hats with ostrich plumes and birds' wings. Being confronted with every variety of women's underclothing from stockings to corset to drawers. And where on earth had he found all those skirt-supporters? Had he juggled the padded hangers, with ribbons and ornaments jangling, up four flights of stairs?

He must have. No one else knew she needed them. No one else had the freedom to disappear to any corner of the house. Her heart filled. With gratitude. And pleasure. And something she didn't want to acknowledge.

The dances in the dark, she could defend against. The quiet moments in the mornings, she could defend against. The kisses, she could somewhat defend against. But this. There was no defending against this. And now that she'd had a taste of what a lady's maid position required, did she even want to?

She quickly found a silk nightdress and nightcap with matching sacque. She'd lay out her lady's nightclothes, get the milk ready to warm, and then she'd track down Mack.

∞

She hadn't been able to find him. No doubt he'd headed to bed as soon as possible. In the morning he'd have more than his share of boots to polish, logs to carry, and errands to run.

She toyed with the idea of joining him on the terrace as was their custom, but Miss DePriest had only just retired. If Tillie wanted to meet with Mack, she'd have to rise in two short hours.

A night breeze drifting through the windows of the corridor cooled the back of her neck. Her candle threw shifting shadows along the succession of sharp-pointed arches leading to her bedroom.

Stopping at the second to last door, she turned the handle, anxious to fall into bed. She wondered what the visiting domestics thought after seeing the rooms they shared tonight with Biltmore's staff. She knew many worked in wealthy homes which offered nothing but dismal unheated attic rooms with bare floorboards, lumpy flock mattresses, and ill-assorted furniture discarded by the family. That they slept two, three, and sometimes four to a room. That in the thick of winter they woke up shivering while ice crusted their water jugs.

She lifted the chimney of her lantern, touching the candle's flame to it. At Biltmore, Mr. Vanderbilt had purchased brand-new furnishings specifically for his staff. Each had a wrought-iron bed, a rush-seated rocker, oak wardrobes and dressers along with all the requisite linens. They had a bathing room down the hall with indoor plumbing and heat piped through the walls.

Blowing out the candle, she replaced the chimney. Though the room had an Edison bulb, she still preferred lantern light. Turning around, she took a sharp breath.

Across her bed lay a navy serge skirt and lovely white shirtwaist. Mrs. Winter must have decided that while Tillie was acting as lady's maid, she should hang up her apron and cap in order to don clothes befitting her temporary station.

She turned on the Edison for a better look, then crept to the edge of the bed and grazed the hem of the blouse. Silk. Not a shirtwaist, after all, but a *silk*-waist.

The weariness of the day, the petulance of Miss DePriest, and the late hour all evaporated. A resurgence of energy winged through her. She wanted desperately to pick up the clothing, hold it against her, see how it would look. But she wouldn't think of touching it without washing first.

Grabbing her pitcher, she flew down the hall to fill it. Never in her life had she readied herself for bed so quickly. Within minutes she was lifting the silk-waist and pressing its sides against her, resting its arms atop hers.

She'd never worn a silk shirt before. Moving to her chest of drawers, she cleared off its surface, placing pencil tablet, brush and comb, tooth powder, buttermilk soap, and her copy of *Rob Roy* on the floor. Then she carefully laid her silk-waist on the bureau, smoothing it.

Next she folded the navy serge skirt over the back of her rocking chair. Clasping her hands together, she brought knuckles to lips, stared at the clothing, and thanked God for her good fortune.

Reluctantly, she turned off the Edison and extinguished the lantern. Crawling into bed, she closed her eyes to thank the Lord again but fell asleep before she reached the amen.

What seemed like moments later, someone shook her shoulder. "Wake up, Miss Tillie. The call button in the South Tower rang. Y' best hurry."

Layers of black weighed against her eyes. She tried to peel them away but couldn't.

More shoulder shakes. "Come on, now. Wake up."

Light flooded the room. She covered her eyes with her arm.

"Yer lady's ringing, miss."

Cool air touched her skin and someone tugged at her arm. She opened her eyes.

The night step-girl had turned on the light, thrown back the bedsheet, and was pulling Tillie's arm.

She shook the sleep from her brain. "What is it? What's the matter?"

"The South Tower Room rang fer ya."

"What time is it?"

"Three-thirty."

Three-thirty? She'd only been in bed for little more than an hour. What could Miss DePriest possibly need at three-thirty in the morning?

Swinging her feet over the side of the bed, she stuffed on her shoes without stockings and grabbed pins from her bedside table. "All right. I'll check on her. Thank you for waking me."

Twisting her hair into a coil, she jammed hairpins into it while hurrying down the dark corridor to the maid's closet. Freshly laundered uniforms, aprons, caps, and collars hung from pegs lining the four walls of the barren, oversized closet.

Poking her arms through the sleeves of a calico, she wriggled as the body of the dress cascaded over her nightdress. No corset. No drawers.

She grabbed a starched apron and cap off a peg and put them on as she made her way down the stairs. At the entrance to Miss DePriest's room she paused, smoothed her apron, then knocked and entered. Electric light from the hallway spilled into the darkened room.

"Miss DePriest?" she whispered. "Did you ring for me?"

"It certainly took you long enough." Her voice was clipped, wide awake, and very displeased.

"I'm sorry, miss. Is there something I can do?"

"The ticking of this infernal clock is keeping me from my sleep. Take it away immediately."

"Yes, miss."

She was so used to the Edisons, she hadn't thought to bring a candle. Feeling her way around the edge of the bed, she found the offending clock and tucked it under her arm.

"Will there be anything else?"

Miss DePriest flopped over to lie on her other side. "Not right now, but if I summon you again, I expect you to respond in a more timely matter. Is that understood?"

"Yes, miss."

Backing toward the light, Tillie slipped into the hall and softly closed the door. She looked at the clock, not sure of what to do with it. For now, she'd put it in the Paris Gown-Room.

It was four-fifteen before she returned to her bed. She wondered briefly if Mack was on the terrace listening to the silence. Forty-five minutes later, she was awakened. The South Tower Room's call button had been pushed.

Tillie would not find her way back to bed for eighteen more hours.

Fourteen

"We're going to the indoor pool after breakfast," Miss DePriest exclaimed, bouncing onto the vanity stool in chemise, corset, and petticoat. "Mrs. Vanderbilt said it's heated and that they have electric lights under the water. Can you imagine?"

They'd just returned from watching the sunrise, and tired as Tillie was, she'd been only too happy to accompany Miss DePriest. They'd walked outside down the esplanade, both wearing shirtwaist and serge. Not a cap or apron in sight. Had anyone happened to glance out a window, the only indication of Tillie being a servant would have been the few steps she kept between herself and her mistress.

The brilliance of the sunrise, the cantata of the birds, and the thrill of wearing a silk-waist had refreshed Tillie as nothing else could.

"The pool is a sight to see, miss. And very deep. But there are ropes all along the edges to hang on to."

Miss DePriest flipped her thick blond hair over her shoulders and picked up a tiny silver spoon. "You must take my new bathing costume to the pool dressing rooms and remain there until I come. I can hardly wait. I had the outfit made especially for this visit. Did you see it when you unpacked? It has a delicious turkey-red sailor's collar."

"Yes, miss. It's very fetching and will look lovely with your coloring."

"I know!" she gushed, foisting the spoon onto Tillie, then sticking out her tongue as if expecting an examination of her tonsils.

Tillie hesitated, uncertain of what to do.

"Well? What are you waiting for? Scrape!" Closing her eyes, she again stuck out her tongue.

Scrape? She wants me to scrape her tongue?

Dutifully, Tillie ran the edge of the spoon from the back of the girl's tongue to the front. A thick, white mucuslike substance collected on the spoon. Tillie grabbed a handkerchief from her pocket, wiped off the spoon, then scraped again. And again. Until nothing more would collect.

"All done, miss."

Popping open her eyes, Miss DePriest scooched around to face the mirror.

Tillie picked up the brush. Before she had a chance to take one stroke, Miss DePriest gasped and leaned forward, examining a blemish on her right jaw.

"Oh dear. Look, Tillie. You must take care of this at once."

Tillie nodded. "Would you like me to make a honey potion?"

"Indeed I would. But first you must pop it."

She stared at Miss DePriest in the mirror. *Pop it?*

The girl crinkled her brow. "I'm growing extremely tired of your slothful responses. Fetch a needle and pop my pimple. Hop to it!"

Opening a vanity drawer, Tillie retrieved a needle case. Miss DePriest lifted her face and flattened her cheek against her jawbone like a man preparing to shave.

Tillie swallowed. With fingers shaking, she pierced the skin then squeezed. A dollop of white burst out onto her finger. She willed her face not to show the revulsion she felt.

The only handkerchief available was the one soiled from the tongue scraping. She wiped her finger on its very edge.

Miss DePriest reexamined her spot in the glass. "Oh, I hate those things. Quickly, go make a honey treatment. I simply must have one before breakfast."

"Yes, miss." Collecting the soiled linen and clothing, Tillie hurried from the room.

∞

Mack glanced up from his kneeling position, then sat back on his heels and stared. Tillie crossed the wooden pool deck, a stack of neatly folded towels in her arms. She wore no uniform. With each step her heels kicked back the hem of her dark blue skirt. Her hair poofed out like an oversized halo, a knotted bun anchoring its center.

Setting the towels on a stand in the corner, she pulled a long fat ribbon that hung from her neck and wrapped it around the linens like a gift. She fluffed the bow, admired her work, then turned around and saw him.

He slowly rose to his feet, scrub brush in hand. Her white top draped gently across her curves and was tucked tightly into the tiny waist of her skirt. With his neckerchief, he wiped the sweat from his face.

"Mack." Her eyes shone as a smile he'd seen her share with others now turned its full force onto him. He felt its impact as strongly as a blow to the gut.

"Why are you dressed like that?" he asked. "Did you quit?"

Her smile dimmed and she glanced down. "No. This is what a lady's maid wears."

His throat squeezed shut. "You got it, then? You're Mrs. Vanderbilt's lady's maid?"

"No, no. Her maid won't be assigned until Bénédicte returns to France. So I'll go back to being a parlormaid as soon as Miss DePriest leaves."

He took a breath. "I see."

She clasped her hands together, twisting her fingers. "I looked for you last night but couldn't find you."

"You did? You couldn't?"

"I wanted to thank you for putting away Miss DePriest's things. It was you, wasn't it?"

He nodded. It never would have occurred to him to do that for her if he hadn't heard Lucy Lewers regaling one of the footmen about the mess and relishing the comeuppance Tillie was sure to receive.

He'd walked straightaway from the task he'd been doing and headed to the Paris Gown-Room. He'd tossed what he could into drawers and onto shelves and dumped the things he had no business handling into one of the trunks.

When he'd returned Lucy's things to her designated gown-room, he found a stash of skirt-supporters along with the sachets Tillie had mentioned. He recovered both, slung Miss DePriest's skirts onto hangers, stuffed all the tissue paper into empty trunks, and hauled the luggage to storage. Took him no time at all.

The heated water in the pool gave off a musky odor and made the room muggy and humid. He wiped his mouth with the back of his hand.

Tillie's eyes softened, her lashes thick and dark. Not a drop of sweat touched her ivory skin. "I don't know what to say. How to thank you."

"Spend your next day off with me."

She frowned. "Mack, I told you—"

"You said no private conversations on the terrace, no dancing in the dark, and no kissing. I'm not asking for any of that. Just a day. One day."

Her gaze bounced about the room, touching the water, the diving platform, the long ladder into the pool, and the palm trees in the corner before finally returning to him.

"It's forbidden," she whispered.

"I promise to follow your rules."

She shook her head. "You ask too much. But I will make it up to you. Somehow."

She glanced at the white cambric shirt he wore. The blue one she'd made was being laundered. "Perhaps another shirt?" she said.

"I'd rather have a day with you."

She took a quivering breath. "We can't. But if you tell me where you'll be going and if we happen to accidentally meet or something, well, I suppose there'd be no harm in that."

A wave of satisfaction washed through him. "I'll be going to Asheville."

Her brows lifted. "All that way? But it's six miles—a good two-hour walk each way. What's wrong with Biltmore Village?"

"I need to see my sister."

"We'd never make it back by curfew."

"I guarantee I'll get you back on time."

With a wary look, she fingered the buttons at her neck. "I'm sorry. It's too far."

She took a step away from him, then hurried to the door.

Sighing, he returned to his hands and knees and took up scrubbing again. It was just as well. He needed this job for at least two more months. No sense in jeopardizing it at this juncture.

But his mind ignored his warnings and continued to call up the myriad of conversations they'd had on the terrace. The vulnerability she'd shown before meeting Miss DePriest. The desperation in her voice when she'd said she wanted no other woman to take his measurements.

His scrub brush stilled. They were in agreement on that, at least. There wasn't anyone else whose touch he wanted, either. Just hers. Only hers. And before he left Biltmore, he was determined to convince her of it.

∞

Tillie helped Miss DePriest into a seamless dinner gown the exact color of the girl's eyes. It was all one piece rather than a separate bodice and skirt and had no seam at the waist—or anywhere else in evidence. Cut on the bias, the dress clung to the upper body, then belled out at the hips.

Miss DePriest lifted her arm while Tillie secured the gown down the left side, rendering the fastenings invisible.

"You look lovely," Tillie breathed, stepping back to admire the long slit up the side of the blue gown, which revealed a gold underskirt.

"Fetch my necklace, please. I don't wish to be late."

Tillie opened a plush red jewel box and removed several rows of pearls held together with vertical bars of diamonds and sapphires. She laid them against Miss DePriest's neck and fastened the closure in the back.

Miss DePriest tugged on her gloves. "Mrs. Vanderbilt complimented me on my hair last night."

"Did she?" A thrill of pleasure shot through Tillie.

"Yes." She slipped a golden fan over her wrist. "I told her I had to make you do it three times before you got it right and that it took my constant direction."

Tillie sucked in a silent breath.

"After dinner there's to be parlor games and dancing in the tapestry gallery, so I expect to be quite late. That should give you plenty of time to prepare the room to my liking. I do *not* want a repeat of last night."

Tillie's posture went rigid. "Yes, miss."

As soon as the door clicked shut, Tillie marched to the bathing room and snatched up item after item. All the while her dislike for Miss DePriest percolated.

Opening the door, she moved with calm decorum down the hall. The moment she stepped into the servants' area, she allowed her anger to once again spill over, and she thundered down the stairs to the laundry.

Before she reached it, the loud rumble of engines running progressive new machinery obliterated all other sounds. A huge barrel washer agitated by a pulley system cleaned the substantial amount of clothing and linens generated by the family, guests, and servants.

The washer, extractor, and mangle were not only electric, but were on the same scale as what any fancy New York hotel would have in their basement. That didn't mean the work wasn't grueling, though.

Waving to a laundress bent over a deep white sink, Tillie shouted hello over the noise and dropped her load into a basket designated for Miss DePriest. The smell of bleach and ammonia made her eyes water.

The woman jerked her head toward something behind her. Tillie glanced over. Mack lay on his stomach in the drying room, oiling one of the rolling wooden frames that held wet sheets and clothing draped over a long dowel. When the frame was pushed into the wall cabinet, electric coils running along the floor of the cabinet would dry the items on the dowel—replacing the need for clotheslines.

She stepped into the room, the gently heated floor immediately warming her shoes. "What happened?" she shouted.

He looked over his shoulder. "The rack was stuck."

"Isn't the floor hot against your chest?"

Rolling to his back, he lifted himself to his feet without using his hands. "Yeah."

Sweat poured from his face and a smudge of dirt streaked across his cheek. His hair fell every which way. No hat in sight.

She glanced at his shirt to see if it had been singed but could find no evidence. She took an involuntary step forward and placed her hand against his chest. Heat and moisture immediately bathed her hand. "Did it burn you?"

Lifting her palm to his lips, he kissed its center, then released her. "I'm fine."

It happened so fast she had no time to jerk away. Still, liquid fire shot straight from her palm to her inner core.

But concern for him pushed all else aside. She couldn't believe he'd been so careless as to lie on a heated floor. "How long were you down there?"

He shrugged.

She scrutinized the edges of his button placket. "It burned you, didn't it?"

"I'm fine," he repeated, his voice soft. So soft she only saw his lips form the words. And suddenly, she couldn't draw her gaze away from them. She studied the slight fullness of his lower lip and the thin line of his upper. The shadow of blond end-of-the-day whiskers.

His eyes flicked to the laundry room over her shoulder, then he turned and rolled the drying frame into the cabinet.

"Tillie!"

Jumping, she whirled around.

Allan grabbed her hand and pulled her from the room, shouting all the while. "Kirk broke a crystal goblet and sliced open his hand. Conrad is so sick he's glued to the commode. We need you to help us serve. Quick, go change."

"What?" She had to run to keep up with him.

He dragged her down the hall and around the corner, and then pushed her toward the stairs. "Hurry. Dinner starts any minute and we need help. *Run.*"

The panic in her brother's voice had her instinctively following his orders. Lifting her skirts, she raced up the stairs.

Tillie strode down the kitchen corridor freshly scrubbed and turned out in black alpaca, white lace, and a large frilly apron. With each step the streamers from her cap flitted behind her like kite tails.

Delectable smells filled the basement. Roasted turkey from the Rotisserie Kitchen. Almond cake from the Pastry Kitchen. And a conglomeration of masterpieces from the Main Kitchen.

She peeked inside, trying to determine which delicacy the artists of the saucepan had chosen for tonight's main course. Chefs flew about in white caps, jackets, and aprons, their faces set, their eyes keen. Kitchen maids scurried to do their bidding, the intense heat flushing their cheeks.

An electric signal from abovestairs rang.

"Send the first course up!" the head chef shouted, followed by a string of French orders. And though no one understood the language, all were aware of what he required.

Mrs. Winter caught sight of Tillie and handed her fresh hand linens. "Quick, two more bottles of champagne."

"Where are they?"

"In the Brown Laundry." She hastened Tillie with a flutter of the hands.

Tillie rushed down the hall and around the corner to a small room where fine hand-washables were laundered on wooden washboards. In four of the six brown porcelain tubs cooled several bottles of champagne on ice.

The laundresses, now forced to complete mountains of delicate wash in just two sinks, eyed her with displeasure, as if she were the one who'd usurped their domain.

"I'm terribly sorry about this, girls." She lifted two bottles, dried and wrapped them in linen, then scurried up the stairs to the butler's pantry to have them opened.

A footman intercepted her at the door. "I'll take care of these. You get across the hall."

Halting in front of a massive oak door, she collected herself, raised her chin, and noiselessly entered the largest room of the house.

Seven stories high and every bit that long, the Banquet Hall always made her feel as if she were stepping back in time and had entered the Great Hall of a medieval castle, complete with armor, flags, and gilt-trimmed thrones. Footmen had painstakingly placed sixty-four padded chairs around the elongated table, then decorated it with fine linen, flowers, and twelve large porcelain figures. Each depicted one of Christ's apostles.

Tillie had cleaned and dusted every one of them more times than she could count. And with each dusting, she wondered what it would have been like to have physically walked side by side with the One and Only, the way the apostles had.

Mr. Sterling stepped down a line of footmen like a general

inspecting his troops. One row of liveried servants stood at the far end of the room. Perpendicular to them, the second line stood behind the table. Tillie joined their ranks, resting her gaze on an enormous tapestried Venus, who made eyes at her lover, Mars.

The butler stopped in front of the footman to Tillie's left, then clicked his heels and thrust out his chest. The footman immediately straightened his spine.

Taking a giant step, Mr. Sterling stood before her. She focused on a winged cherubim in the tapestry who hovered above the celestial lovers.

The butler tapped her chin up and lifted his own. Finally, he finished his assessment and gave the table one last glance. The first course of *consommé Julienne*, covered with shiny domes, waited in readiness at each place setting. Clearing his throat, he removed to the salon to announce dinner.

Moments later Mr. Vanderbilt crossed into the Banquet Hall at the head of a procession, a favored guest on his arm. His willowy build, thin mustache, and thick black hair reminded Tillie of Dumas's *Count of Monte Cristo*.

To receive the glamorous party, two bearskin rugs had been positioned on either side of the double-arched entrance, their jaws frozen in a growl.

"This way, everyone," Vanderbilt said, stretching his hand toward the sparkling table.

Along with the other servants in line, Tillie stood rigidly as the party approached. Merry voices and soft laughter accompanied the parade of women in exquisite gowns and flashing jewels. Their escorts, in immaculate cutaway coats, seated them with great aplomb. Tillie wondered what figure would be tallied if she added the accumulation of wealth among the guests.

"You are simply radiant this evening," one of the men

murmured to the woman in his charge. She smiled, the diamonds in her hair winking under the massive chandeliers.

A few seats down, another woman gestured demurely to a fortune in jewels studding her corsage. "A token from the Prince of Wales upon my last visit."

Miss DePriest tapped her fan against the gentleman ushering her in, a tilt of her head drawing attention to the lustrous pearls around her neck. Still another woman passed under Tillie's nose, a gemmed girdle encircling her waist. The spectacle dazzled her. So much beauty. So much excess.

Last of all, Mrs. Vanderbilt entered on the arm of another special guest, her *peau de soie* gown with spangled chiffon complementing her long, slender form. Tillie's heart swelled with pride. Her mistress hadn't draped herself with diamonds and gems, but wore only an exquisite bracelet with small emeralds and pearls set in platinum.

Rather than taking the traditional seats at the head and foot of the table, Mr. and Mrs. Vanderbilt always sat side by side in the middle. Her escort guided her to her husband and pulled out the chair. Mr. Vanderbilt gave her a slight smile, his eyes lighting with pleasure.

Once everyone had settled, the footmen at the far end of the room moved to stand along the length of the table opposite Tillie. She advanced with the other servants, removing the soup covers and quietly placing them on dinner trays, which were whisked away by liveried footboys waiting in the wings. She returned to her station, a few feet behind the guests in her charge and slightly to the left.

Raising her gaze to stare unseeing at the footmen directly across from her, she sucked in her breath. Mack and Earl stood side by side, resplendent in their livery. She knew immediately which was Mack. She'd know him anywhere, and not just because he was stiff and uncomfortable in his livery.

The last she'd seen him he'd been unshaven, filthy, and covered in sweat. To have him unexpectedly appear stunning and magnificent in braided coat, gold buttons, burgundy knee breeches, silk stockings, and white gloves, she had to remind herself to breathe.

She'd seen Earl in his dinner attire countless times. Always handsome and attractive. But in spite of his identical appearance, he'd never frozen her in place. Never made her heart race.

A guest with a perfect part down the center of his head lifted a glass. "I've acquired one of Edison's phonographs." He shook his head. "Amazing devices, but the cylinders only last two minutes."

The man across from him finished his soup and relaxed in his chair. "I saw George Gaskin last month. He said he had to sing the same song two hundred times in order to record enough cylinders for Edison's company to sell."

"Oh, I love George Gaskin." A woman tapped the corners of her mouth with a napkin elaborately embroidered with the golden V monogram. "Such a wonderfully tinny voice."

Mack captured Tillie's gaze. He looked horrified. At the table conversation, she wondered? Or because he was wearing the livery? Or perhaps he was petrified of making a mistake.

Picking up a hand-waiter, she gave him a "just watch me" glance, then placed the tray in her right hand. Mack moved his to his right hand.

She removed a spoon from an empty soup bowl and placed it on the waiter. A moment behind her, Mack did the same.

She remembered her first time serving. How she'd trembled and fumbled. How she'd had an unconquerable desire to laugh at a joke Mr. Vanderbilt had told at the table. How difficult it had been to project a deliberate, ineffable calm while under-neath she was a bundle of nerves.

She tried to reassure Mack with her eyes, but the truth was, she wasn't certain he'd be able to accomplish the task. He watched her and Earl without being obvious. They both sent him subtle signals of what to do next or how to correct a wrong before it occurred, then breathed a sigh of relief when he managed it.

After many courses had come and gone, after the wine and champagne began to flow, after olives and salads and pure white celery hearts had been placed before the guests, her admiration for him flowered.

He never missed a step. Never spilled a drop.

"I understand there are to be parlor games in the gallery later this evening." The gentleman with the center part leaned close to the lady beside him. "I hope I shall have an opportunity to partner with you in one of them."

She peeked at him from beneath her lashes. "And what games are we to play?"

"The Wolf and the Lambs," he replied, his voice dropping.

The woman blushed and nearly knocked her wineglass over. Mack lurched, then caught himself before making a spectacle. The guest recovered her drink without incident.

Mack and Tillie exchanged a glance. Never had she been so in tune with another. So aware of his every move.

Finally, the last of the dessert cake, cooling ices, and tropi-cal fruit were eaten. Mrs. Vanderbilt rose. The men immedi-ately stood, assisting their neighboring ladies to their feet. The women followed Mrs. Vanderbilt to the salon, leaving the men to their cigars, wine, and after-dinner talk.

Tillie, too, needed to leave. Over the heads of the gentlemen, she sent Mack a silent congratulations. And to her absolute horror, he winked.

∞

During the following two weeks, Tillie only saw Mack from afar. She never knew from one moment to the next if he would be hobnobbing with the coal heavers in his workaday clothes or standing gorgeous in livery amidst the flower-scented wealthy and fashionable set.

Mrs. Winter had an alternate shirtwaist and tweed skirt delivered to Tillie's room, allowing her to wear one while the other was laundered. Today she wore her navy serge and silk-waist while following Miss DePriest to the basement for a game of bowling.

She'd never had access to this portion of the basement, nor even seen a bowling alley. Anticipation swelled as she stepped into the long, crowded room. Excited chatter interspersed with cheers bounced off the two-story ceiling.

Young men in plaid shirts and striped jackets congregated at the foot of two maple lanes which stretched an impossibly long way toward dark fireplace-like alcoves. But instead of burning wood, each held a grouping of white pins.

All quieted as one of the men picked up a heavy black ball with two holes, took four long steps down the lane, then released the ball with a spin. Unable to see without being obvious, Tillie listened to its rumbling roll and culminating crash. One set of men roared, the other set groaned. Several women *oohed* and clapped their gloved hands.

A group of young girls hailed Miss DePriest, offering her an available chair. Tillie immediately stationed herself against the wall behind them and became "invisible."

Miss DePriest's companion whipped open her fan. "Look

there at Mr. Huffman and Miss Lowery. She had to pay him a kissing forfeit last night after Pinch Without Laughing. He's been following her around like a besotted pup ever since."

Tillie looked across the way but was unable to ascertain exactly who the ladies were gossiping about. What she did see, though, was Lucy Lewers standing calm and collected behind her lady. The advanced years of her charge surprised Tillie.

At first, a spurt of pride raced through her at how much lovelier Miss DePriest was than Lucy's lady. But it only took a moment to ascertain Lucy's woman comported herself with genuine grace and was clearly a favorite of Mrs. Vanderbilt's.

Footmen wove through the throng, blocking her view as they offered silver trays of dainties and refreshments from the kitchen. Mack was not among the men.

Miss DePriest grabbed the elbow of the woman beside her. "Look! It's *them*."

The girl craned her neck just as a liveried footman stepped from behind a wooden barrier at the far end of the bowling alley. He quickly set the pins to rights, then rolled the ball back to the players via a long wooden gutter.

When he straightened, Tillie caught her breath. Mack. She glanced at the other alley and saw Earl standing behind its barrier.

The girl and Miss DePriest dipped their heads together, giggling and murmuring. "Aren't they just the most divine things you've ever seen?"

"And here we thought bowling was going to be the main attraction!"

They broke apart in nervous sniggers.

Tillie stiffened.

"Let's sign up to play," Miss DePriest whispered.

"Are we allowed?"

"Yes, of course, see there?"

Mrs. Vanderbilt in a white serge gown with tubular braids stepped up to Earl's alley. With a much smaller, more delicate ball, she took four steps and sent the sphere whirling down the lane.

All but two of the pins skittered across the highly polished wood. Her team roared, and a footman at a chalkboard made a notation.

"Which lane should we sign up for?" Miss DePriest asked.

"Heavens, does it matter? They're identical."

Miss DePriest ran a hand up the back of her hair twist. "Perhaps, but I can tell them apart."

Her friend turned rounded eyes onto her. "Never say so. How?"

She gave a dainty shrug. "I just can, and it's *that* one, the one on the right, that I shall want arranging my pins."

With a wicked laugh, her friend swatted Miss DePriest with a fan, then glanced at her maid. "Hilda, put our names on the slate."

Tillie locked her jaw. Miss DePriest was ogling Mack. *Her* Mack.

It took every ounce of self-control she had to keep from jerking Hilda back. But there was nothing she could do. Nothing she could say.

So she stood where she was, rigid and angry and at a complete loss as to how to handle the unwelcome feelings.

∞

Tillie toed the floor, setting her chair into a gentle rock. Positioning another diamond onto the bodice of Miss DePriest's evening gown, she secured it in place with needle and thread.

The servants' hall, where female staff gathered during their breaks, was deserted. With a large house party in residence, no one had time to read the popular titles lining the bookcase or to have a cup of tea or to knit or mend their clothes.

Especially not today. The guests would be taking their leave tomorrow and as a finale Mr. Vanderbilt was holding a formal ball. It would be the first ever held with the new Mrs. Vanderbilt and would be attended not only by their house guests, but by Asheville's most wealthy and influential.

The orchestra from Asheville's Opera House had shown up en masse at the servants' entrance. The kitchens had prepared dainty after dainty since the predawn hours. The butler and head chef nearly came to blows over where to cool the endless bottles of wine and champagne. And the gardener brought in mounds of out-of-season flowers from his hothouses and conservatory.

Ordinarily, Tillie would have helped arrange the bouquets of roses, orchids, and lilies of the valley. Instead she sewed sprays of diamonds, simulating foliage, onto Miss DePriest's bodice. And when the ball was over, she'd return to this very spot in the wee hours of the morning to rip them all out before returning them to her mistress's jewelry case.

She shook her head, awed by the expensive gown and priceless gems. Surely no royal princess in all the world was more handsomely gowned than these American women of wealth.

Knotting off the last diamond, she rose on weary legs. She didn't look forward to Miss DePriest's toilet. It seemed like all she did, day after day, hour after hour, was dress, dress, dress. For breakfast, for riding, for boating, for lunch, for tea, for croquet, for . . . everything.

And after every toilet, Tillie had to clean and polish every surface. Remove all signs of cosmetics and powder. Arrange every drawer. Return every article to its proper place. Freshen the gowns. Repair any rips. Prepare the next change of clothes. And start all over again.

She gathered her sewing items, then turned as Lucy Lewers sailed into the hall with a tea tray. The sweet smell of tea filled the room, making Tillie's mouth water.

"Oh, Tillie, I'm so glad to find someone here. I was worried no one would be able to share a bit of tea with me. You aren't leaving, are you?"

She nodded. "I'm afraid so. I need to lay out Miss DePriest's articles for tonight's ball."

Lucy poured the rich amber liquid into a cup. "Isn't being a lady's maid absolutely divine? My mistress is the sweetest, loveliest lady. Do you know what she did this morning?"

Tillie offered no response. It took all the energy she had to simply stay standing.

"She told me to take the afternoon off. She knew we'd be up late with the ball and she didn't want me to tire. So I've just awoken from a nice long nap." Lucy took a sip, her eyes sparkling over the cup. "What about you? Did you have the afternoon off?"

Tillie hadn't had a single moment off since Miss DePriest's arrival. She'd worked twenty days and had been called upon at all hours of the night. Last evening she'd just crawled into bed when Miss DePriest rang for her. The summons had been so Tillie could hand her a book, which was not four feet away.

"No," she said, "I'm afraid I didn't have the afternoon off."

Lucy gave her a pretty pout. "Poor Tillie. You look awful. Rings under your eyes. Droopy shoulders. Sullen expression. Perhaps you don't have what's necessary to be a lady's maid."

Perhaps I don't. Still, she straightened, shook the fatigue from her frame, and headed to the Paris Gown-Room. "Enjoy your tea, Lucy."

Tillie gathered folds of delicate lace at the small of Miss DePriest's back while trying to secure it in place with a wide diamond pin.

Miss DePriest clutched the back of a chair to hold herself steady. "Miss Houghton and I were thinking to visit Bass Pond and look at the stars. I'd like the twin footmen to escort us."

Tillie hesitated, then continued to work the pin in. "Tonight? In your ball gown?"

"It's supposed to be a dark sky and with this being our last chance to see them and all, well . . ."

Last chance to see what? The stars or the twins?

The pin came through, but at a crooked angle. She pulled it back and started again. "I'm afraid the footmen will be busy waiting in attendance at the ball. But, if you'd like, I can escort you."

She let out a short huff of air. "Don't be ridiculous. You can't protect us from night creatures, nor drive the carriage. No, we will require the twins. One to drive, the other for protection."

Tempting as it was to jab her, Tillie refrained and secured the clasp. "I'm afraid that will be impossible. We simply don't have any footmen to spare."

Miss DePriest whipped around, her satin skirts swirling about her feet. "I will not be disappointed in this. I want to see the stars and I want to be escorted by the twin footmen. You will take care of it for me, Tillie, or there will be the devil to pay."

"I will put forth your request to the butler, miss. Perhaps he can find someone to spare, but I can't guarantee who it will be."

Miss DePriest yanked on her gloves. "You tell your butler I will have no one else. They took Miss Cuff and Miss Rappolee last evening and they . . . well, it's no business of yours what they did. You just tell the butler I *insist* it be the twins."

Tillie stared at the girl, unwilling to believe the implication. She'd heard plenty of rumors about Earl, but she didn't want to believe it of Mack.

She forced herself to curtsy. "Yes, miss. I'll give him your message."

A feline smile pulled at Miss DePriest's lips. Tillie tried to see her as a man might. Clear skin, huge blue eyes, mountains of blond hair, and an hourglass form sheathed in a low-cut bodice shimmering with diamonds.

No question, she was breathtakingly beautiful . . . on the outside. And with Earl, that's all that mattered. But not with Mack. Surely not with Mack.

At the door, Miss DePriest presented her back and held up her arms. Tillie draped a shawl over her shoulders.

Miss DePriest turned her head and gave Tillie a knowing look. "I might be out quite late. If I need help undressing, I'll ring for you." She opened the door, then paused. "And no need to come too early in the morning. You may wait for my summons."

The door clicked shut behind her. Horror and dismay stacked up at the back of Tillie's throat. There was only one reason Miss DePriest wouldn't need help undressing.

Taking a deep breath, Tillie began to clean the room and prepare it for the night. She would give Mr. Sterling the message. And as gracious as the Vanderbilts were, there was no doubt in her mind Mr. Sterling would do everything he could to accommodate any and every request.

∞

Miss DePriest hadn't rung for her at bedtime, nor once during the night, nor yet this morning. Tillie told herself to be thankful for the much-needed sleep. Instead, she was furious. With Mack. And Earl. And Miss Highfalutin' DePriest.

The temptation to cram the gowns into the trunk was great. But no matter how angry Tillie was, she couldn't bring herself to abuse the beautiful articles. Still, if she pretended she was stuffing Miss DePriest as she scrunched up tissue and poked it inside the shirtwaists, so be it.

Mack strode into the room, an empty trunk on his back. "Tillie. I didn't expect to see you up here already."

Snatching up a new piece of tissue, she crinkled it into a tight ball. "Really? Where did you expect me to be?"

"With Miss DePriest, I guess. She seems to monopolize every moment of your time these days."

"Oh, you're right about that." She crammed the tissue into

the gut of the shirtwaist. "She monopolizes my days. And my nights, too. All except last night, that is." Straightening, she propped a fist onto her waist. "Why do you suppose that is, Mack?"

A wary look entered his eyes. "She wanted you to get some sleep?"

"Ha!" She didn't even try to suppress her irritation.

He studied her. "Are you mad at me about something?"

"Mad? Why should I be mad?" She pressed the shirtwaist into the trunk. "What does it matter to me how you or Miss DePriest or anybody else spends their nights, or with whom. It's certainly none of *my* affair."

His eyes narrowed. "Just what exactly is that supposed to mean?"

"Nothing." She slammed the lid of the trunk closed with a whack. "Nothing at all."

"Oh, it was something, all right. I just can't figure out what."

"So how were the stars last night? Or did you even bother to look?"

Removing his hat, he scratched his head. "Stars? What the devil are you talking about?"

She started advancing. "Don't you play innocent with me, Mack Danver. You and I both know that you and Earl have been escorting lady after lady, night after night, out to the privacy of Bass Pond to 'gaze at the stars.' "

A spark of amusement flashed in his eyes, before he quickly suppressed it. "Oh, *those* stars."

"Yes, *those* stars. You ought to be ashamed. What were you thinking?"

He lifted one shoulder. "Well, you know the Vanderbilts. They always aim to please. I was only doing my job."

"Your job?" She jabbed his chest with a finger, punctuating her words. "Your *job*? Well, let me tell you, your job does not entail being lady's maid to my mistress or anyone else's for that matter."

The arrogant lout had the audacity to grin full out. "You're jealous."

"Jealous?" She looked him up and down. "Of what?"

He grabbed her by the arms and hauled her flush against him. "Of the ladies I've been attending and whatever it is you think I did with them at the pond."

She struggled. "Let me go. You know perfectly well what you did and so do I."

"Oh, I know what I did. And clearly you think you know what I did. But you're mistaken if you think I was anything less than honorable. I haven't so much as touched Miss DePriest or any other woman in this house other than you."

She stilled.

"*I never lie.*"

The words came back to her, repeating themselves in her mind like the chorus of a song. She studied his eyes, trying to peer into their depths. Trying to break through any barriers and confirm the truth.

"Then why didn't Miss DePriest call for me last night or this morning?" she asked.

"I don't know."

All she saw was sincerity. And genuineness. And huge, beautiful brown eyes which she liked far too much.

"Let me go." Her words were soft. "Someone will see."

He gentled his hold, rubbing the spots he'd squeezed. "Why do you fight it, Tillie?"

She stepped from his embrace. "You know why."

"You can't tell me after these three weeks that you still want to be a lady's maid?"

"Mrs. Vanderbilt is nothing like Miss DePriest."

"Maybe not, but the job still requires you to be at the beck and call of someone else at all hours of the day and night. How can you want that?"

Sighing, she returned to the trunk she'd been packing and lifted its lid. "It doesn't matter what I want. Miss DePriest has done nothing but complain about me. And she's voiced her complaints to Mrs. Vanderbilt. So it's a moot point."

The disappointment and fatigue and emotional upheaval all converged at once. Her chin quivered.

Mack took a step toward her, but the sound of hurried footfalls in the corridor forestalled him.

A tweenie stuck his head around the door. "South Tower Room rang the call button."

Glancing up, she nodded. "Thanks, Harvey. I'm on my way."

She straightened her cap, then headed to the door.

Mack grabbed her hand. "Tillie?"

She pulled away. "I have to go, Mack. Thanks for bringing up the trunks." Stopping at the doorway, she placed her hand on the frame, but didn't turn around. "And thanks for acting honorably."

Seventeen

With the guests finally gone, the Vanderbilts rewarded the entire staff with an evening off. Mr. Sterling, Mrs. Winter, and a handful of others went straight to bed, but most headed to the barn.

Three members of the orchestra, being friends with the staff, had stayed behind to provide the music. While they tuned up in the corner, Mack helped the men set up tables. Tillie and Dixie lit the lanterns. The kitchen staff set out oranges and apples. A housemaid poured cider into a large bowl.

Since the gathering was impromptu, none of the estate families were present. Only house staff. All of them young. All of them single. All of them euphoric that the visitors had left.

Mack filled a mug with cider, took a sip, then raised it to his nose. He scanned the room and found two of the younger footmen watching him with amusement. He lifted a brow, took another sip, and made a note to drink sparingly.

The music started and the dance floor filled. There was nothing wrong with the mandolin, fiddle, and piano the old-timers usually played, but the quality of tonight's music was unheard of for a barn gathering. The bass player spun his instrument and picked out notes with his finger. The violinist lunged and rocked as he sawed with his bow. And the cornet player blasted out notes from the top of the scale to the very bottom.

The dance floor stayed full, and the more the revelers danced, the thirstier they became. The thirstier they became, the more cider they drank. The more cider they drank, the more raucous they grew.

Mack stayed on the sidelines, but not so Tillie. She danced and laughed and drank, then danced and drank some more. He thought to warn her about the cider, but she had a brother who should have done that already. So Mack kept track of where she was, who she partnered with, and how many times.

Conrad, a skinny, lanky footman, had just begun to make a nuisance of himself when the musicians called for a break.

Allan whisked a chair from one of the tables and plunked it in the middle of the room. "That will allow just enough time for a game of Frincy-Francy."

Mack had never played parlor games until he'd come to Biltmore House, but the rest of the company seemed to recognize the title, and from the titters of the women and the grins of the men, it promised to be interesting.

He remained along the back wall, keeping to the shadows. Earl joined him with two cups of cider and handed him one.

Allan escorted a lovely kitchen maid to the chair. After she'd settled comfortably, Allan swept his hand in a gesture that encompassed the entire room. "Which of these fine gentlemen,

Tolene, would you like to award with a kiss? For if you don't choose one, you will pay a most embarrassing forfeit."

She turned a becoming shade of red. "Mason."

Footmen hooted as the hallboy, a lad of sixteen, stumbled to the center. When he reached his goal, the entire crowd grew silent. Rubbing his hands against his thighs, the gangly youth took a deep breath, scrunched his eyes closed, then leaned over and gave Tolene a hasty peck . . . right between her eyes.

Laughter and applause filled the barn. Tolene turned even redder than before as Allan escorted her to the side.

"Mason?" Allan called. "Which of these fine ladies would you like to award with a kiss? For if you don't choose one, you will pay a most embarrassing forfeit."

He plopped into the vacated chair. "Zenith!"

His shout was so loud, several of the girls jumped.

Mack glanced at Tolene's stricken face, then watched as Allan escorted the head housemaid to Mason's chair. She was a good five years older and five inches taller than the boy and outranked him several times over.

He grinned and lifted his chin.

She stretched out her hand. His face collapsed, but he gamely kissed her fingers—amongst more laughter and applause.

The chair had held several different occupants when it was Lucy Lewers's turn to call a name.

"Mack." She knew exactly where he was, but he noted she glanced between him and Earl.

He looked at Earl, a slow smile forming.

Returning the grin, Earl pushed himself from the wall and approached the head chambermaid. When he reached her, instead of bending over to give her a chaste kiss, he pulled her to her feet and awarded her with a long, lusty kiss.

The men roared. The women giggled behind their hands.

Mack looked at Tillie. A line of red crept up her neck and into her face as she watched the couple. She peeled her gaze away and turned it toward him, the impact of her stare as powerful as if she'd reached out and touched him.

She knew it was Earl out there. Had known all along. How could she tell them apart so easily? Even his siblings would sometimes confuse them.

In an instant it occurred to him, if he didn't get into that chair soon, someone else might call her name.

Earl and Lucy broke apart. A tremendous cheer rose. Lucy stared at him wide-eyed. Allan took her hand and tucked it into his elbow, but before he escorted her away, he looked between Earl and Mack with a speculative glare.

If they were found out, they would have to pay a forfeit for certain. Mack gave him a saucy salute and an exact replica of Earl's devil-may-care grin.

"Tillie," Earl called out.

Mack whipped his attention to his brother, all amusement fleeing. Earl stared right at him, a brow lifted in challenge.

Tillie looked to Mack, clearly horrified at the prospect of what Earl might do. But he was powerless. So help him, though, if Earl tried to kiss her the way he'd kissed Lucy . . .

Allan escorted Tillie to the center. Earl started to stand, but Allan pressed him into the seat. Chuckling, Earl settled back down, widened his knees, and grabbed her waist, pulling her forward.

She propped her hands against his shoulders in an effort to keep him back. Not to be denied, he swept an arm beneath her knees, swinging her into his lap.

She squealed and he silenced her with his mouth. Mack shoved his way through the throng, but before he could break into the circle, Tillie jumped to her feet and slapped Earl's face hard enough to twist his head clean around.

A collective gasp rose as everyone froze.

"Earl Danver, who do you think you are, kissing me like that?"

Allan jumped into the void. "Earl? *Earl?*"

Tillie dragged her sleeve across her mouth. Earl rubbed his cheek, his grin wide.

"Ladies and gentlemen," Allan said, crossing his arms. "I believe we've been had. I call for a forfeit!"

The crowd gave an answering cry as Mack was shoved into the center. Tillie tried to scurry away, but Allan grabbed her arm.

"Not so fast, sister. You're just as guilty as these two because you knew they'd switched and didn't speak up."

"Bubby," she pleaded.

"The three of you, out of the barn while we discuss your forfeits."

Mack clasped her hand and pulled her outside. The minute the door closed behind the three of them, Mack threw a punch at Earl. But his brother had been expecting it and dodged.

"Come on, Mack," he said. "It's just a game."

Mack advanced, his fists clenched, his chest puffed out. Earl backed away, still grinning. "I was only funning."

"You ever touch her again and I'll beat you to a pulp."

Holding his hands up, Earl chuckled. "All right. All right. I didn't know. You never used to get mad about stuff like that. What's the matter with you?"

"You know good and well what's the matter. You knew it before you ever called her name."

She hovered near the door, afraid to intervene, afraid not to.

Earl sighed, putting a bale of hay between himself and Mack. "I admit, I suspected. I just wanted to know for sure."

"You could've asked."

"You wouldn't have told me."

The barn door opened. "Earl, get in here."

He edged around the bale of hay, then entered the barn. The door rolled shut.

Cicadas and crickets chirped in an effort to drown out the noisy humans. Tillie hugged herself, her mouth downturned.

"You all right?" he asked.

"I hate those stupid games. I don't know why we have to play them."

"You don't."

"Allan says they're harmless. And usually they are. Only Earl and a couple of the others try to take advantage. But never with me. Never." She touched two fingers to her temple. "Goodness. My head simply won't quit buzzing."

He slipped his hands into his pockets. "How many mugs of cider have you had?"

"Cider? I don't know. A lot, I guess. Why?"

"Go easy. It's—"

The door opened. "Mack, you're next."

Before he entered, he looked at her. "You don't have to do anything you don't want to do. Ever. All right?"

Allan grabbed him by the arm. "Come on."

Inside Lucy stood in the center of the ring. Mack scanned the crowd and found Earl back against the wall, a smirk on his face.

"Since Lucy was the one tricked," Allan said, pushing Mack into the circle, "she has three questions for you. They are all yes-or-no questions."

Mack eyed the two of them, then nodded.

"Thing is," Allan continued, "you have to answer them first. So give us your answers, and she'll give you the questions."

Mack thought for a moment. "No. Yes. No."

The smug expression on Lucy's face fell a fraction. "So, Mack, would you like to be kissed by every lady in the room?"

Allan clapped him on the shoulder. "What was your first answer, my friend?"

"No."

The men chuckled.

"Would you like me to *not* to kiss you?" she asked.

"Yes."

She took a step closer and lowered her voice. "Would you like me to kiss you?"

"No."

The vehemence of his answer tickled the crowd and they laughed at Lucy's expense.

Her smile turned brittle. "Too bad for you. You lose."

He refrained from commenting.

Allan escorted her to the sidelines. "Mack, you will ask the same questions of Tillie, in the same order."

Tillie was brought in from outside and led to the center of the ring, where she faced Mack. Her face was flushed, her hair mussed, and her step a tad unsteady.

Allan explained the forfeit.

She frowned. "I don't like these games, Allan."

"Yes or no, Till."

She crossed her arms. "No. No. Yes."

The men chuckled. Allan bowed to Mack.

"Would you like to be kissed by every gentleman in the room?" he asked.

"No."

"Would you like me *not* to kiss you?"

Her eyes widened slightly. "No."

Taking her chin between his fingers, he leaned over and kissed her cheek.

The men booed and hissed. She flushed.

"Would you like me to kiss you, Tillie?"

The crowd quieted as they waited for her response.

She looked at him, then his lips. Her chest rose and fell with deep, rapid breaths. "Yes," she whispered.

His pulse began to thrum. "You don't have to do anything you don't want to."

She raised her gaze back up to his. "Just a little one." She pinched her fingers together to indicate something tiny.

Slipping one arm around her, he cradled her cheek, touched his lips to hers and felt the impact clear to his toes. Much as he wanted to lose himself in her, he was well aware of their audience and didn't prolong their embrace.

Stepping away, he took in her dazed expression. Her soft, parted lips. Her blue-violet eyes as they stared at his mouth. Swallowing, he handed her over to her brother.

"Let the dancing resume!" Allan shouted.

The musicians took up their instruments and the floor flooded with dancers. Mack leaned against the wall and watched Tillie. She laughed too easily. Danced too gaily. Drank too deeply. And pretended she wasn't aware of him.

But she was. And every time he caught her looking, she'd turn away, as if she hadn't been keeping just as close an eye on him as he was on her.

Earl approached him with a fresh mug of cider.

Mack shook his head. "No thanks. I'm done for the night."

"Suit yourself." He leaned against the wall.

"Was your forfeit the same as ours?" Mack asked.

Earl shook his head. "Mine was Kiss the Lady You Love Without Anyone Knowing It. So I have the rest of the evening to bestow a kiss on the woman of my dreams—but it has to be without anyone knowing it."

Mack glanced about the room. "So who's the lucky lady?"

"That's just it." Earl chuckled. "They all are. So long as no one knows, then, I can kiss as many as I can corner."

Mack raised a brow. "And how's that working out for you?"

"Come on, now. I never kiss and tell."

"You stay away from Tillie."

"I'll leave her be." He took a sip of cider. "So what's going on with you two?"

"Nothing." He sighed. "But I'm working on it."

"You work too hard and you'll lose your job—and so will she."

Mack ran a hand through his hair. "Maybe 'biding my time' would be a better way to put it."

"I thought you had plans to get Ora Lou out of Sloop's. You change your mind?"

He shook his head. "No, but she says she'll find work once I set her up in a place."

"And the boys?"

"I haven't figured that out yet. Either way, I'm hoping I won't be here much longer."

"And you really believe Tillie will go with you?"

"I do."

"Well, you better rescue her from Conrad, then. He's had his eye on her for over a year now."

Mack whipped his head around and found the footman panting after her like a puppy. He'd not been at the last barn gathering. If Mack wasn't mistaken, Conrad's days off were opposite of Tillie's.

The footman's pale blond hair, blond eyebrows, and blond eyelashes were a stark contrast to her dark ones.

"Excuse me, brother." Mack wove through the crowd.

She laughed at something the footman said, then saw Mack. Her smile faded. When he reached them, she tilted her head, eyes hooded. "Hello, Mack."

"How much cider have you had?"

"Why do you keep asking me that?"

Conrad puffed up his chest. "Sorry, Danver, but Tillie and I were about to dance."

"Not anymore." He took the mug out of Tillie's hand and set it on the table behind her. "Come on. Let's get you some fresh air."

Leaving a sputtering Conrad behind, Mack gripped her elbow, then moved her through the throng and out the back door.

The crisp night air felt good against Mack's skin. Tillie skipped ahead of him, then tilted her head back, flung her arms wide, and spun. Her skirt belled. A tendril of hair escaped from her pins. Her long, creamy neck lay open and bare.

"What a glorious night," she breathed. "Look at the stars, Mack."

She stopped as suddenly as she'd started, then thrust her lip out in an exaggerated pout. "But you've already seen the stars. Lots of times. Haven't you?"

Leaning to the side, she frowned at the ground as if to ascertain why it was moving, then took a step to catch her balance. "Haven't you?"

"I have."

"How many times?"

"Several."

"With how many ladies?"

"Several."

"And did they try to seduce you?"

He sighed. "We've been over this, Tillie."

But she wasn't listening. Placing her hands against her bodice, she moved them down her torso. "Were they covered in diamonds?" She took a step toward him, molding her shirtwaist into the evening gown she described. "And satin?" Another step. "And smelling of delicate perfume?"

She stood inches from him. Her eyes lazy. Her lips puckered. Her hands touching places he wanted to.

His mouth went dry.

"Was their hair just so?" She lifted her arms, bracketing her head, then made twirly motions with her fingers. "Did they brush against you, pretending it was an accident?"

She slinked around him, her arm barely grazing his. Her fingernails scraped along the back of his waist.

He jumped.

"Did they, Mack?"

When she stopped in front of him, they were as close as possible without touching. "Did they?"

He swallowed. "Some of them."

She rested her hands on his chest. "And what did you do?"

Covering her hands, he guided them up around his neck. "I picked my nose."

Gasping, her eyes widened and her body jerked stiff. "You didn't!"

He tilted her chin up, tracing her jaw with his thumb. "It's all right. I had my gloves on."

She dissolved into laughter. Deep, hearty, from-the-gut laughter. Breaking away from him, she gripped her waist, rocking so much he had to steady her.

"Oh, please. You didn't really. Did you?"

He chuckled. "Worked every time."

Tears poured from her eyes. Her guffawing turned to hiccups, which caused her to laugh all the more. When she finally wound down, she collapsed against him, exhausted.

Her forehead rested against his chest. Bits of hair tumbled about her waist. He rubbed her back, shoulders, and arms.

Occasional giggles erupted like an earthquake aftershock. "I think I'm falling in love with you, Mack."

His hands stilled. "Me too."

She lifted her face, propping her chin against him. "You think you're falling in love with you, too?"

He burrowed his fingers into her hair. "Come here."

This time, without the audience, he did what he'd been wanting to. He explored, tasted, nipped, hoping it would relieve the tension which had built inside him since he'd first seen her. Instead, it made him hunger for more. Much more.

With an effort, he dragged his mouth free.

Her eyes remained closed. "Oh, that was nice. Would you do that again, please?"

Groaning, he crushed her to him, kissing her more deeply, reveling in the feel of her. She gave back as much as she took, then something changed. She pushed against him.

He broke the kiss, but still held her close.

"Mack?"

"Hmmmm?"

"I think I'm going to be sick."

He reared back. She was as pale as her shirtwaist.

Scooping her up, he raced to the bushes, then stayed with her until she was done.

Finally, he handed her a handkerchief. "I've decided not to take this personally."

She started to laugh, then touched her head. "Please. No more. There's something terribly wrong with my head and stomach."

He sighed. "Come on. Let's get you back inside. The music has stopped, so we'll be heading home soon. Do you think you can stand?"

"Probably. Though I really like it when you carry me."

Lifting her into his arms, he stood. "Quit your job and I'll carry you all the way to Asheville."

She rested her head on his shoulder. "Don't be ridiculous. I didn't put up with Miss Persnickety DePriest for three weeks to give up now. Nobody's quitting their job."

We'll see. He took her as far as the barn, then reluctantly set her on her feet. "You go on in by yourself. Have Dixie or Allan help you if you need it. I'll circle around front." Finding a pin, he tucked her hair back up as best he could. "Tillie?"

She blinked up at him.

"No more cider." He kissed her on the forehead, then opened the barn door just enough for her to slip through.

∞

"I can't believe you didn't tell me the cider was spiked."

Mack sat beside Tillie as their train pulled out of Biltmore station. He didn't even try to hide his amusement. "They hardly put in anything at all."

"Easy for you to say—you barely touched it."

He chuckled. "You'll be all right. The worst is over."

Gripping the armrest as the train rocked around a bend, she closed her eyes. "Let's not talk about it anymore."

The countryside passed in a blur as if an artist were smearing his brush across the canvas. It was no way to travel. He couldn't hear the birds. Couldn't see the squirrels. Couldn't feel the wind or the cool mountain air.

He shook his head, still unable to believe Mrs. Winter had made them take the train to Asheville. But she had other things she wanted Earl to do and couldn't afford for him to spend the entire day driving them around.

Mack had suggested walking, but Mrs. Winter wouldn't hear of it. Not when there were parcels to tote. He'd explained he used to walk thirteen miles to the mill carrying a hundred-pound sack of corn and returning with meal the following day, but she put her foot down. They would ride the train. Period.

He sighed. At least it would give him an opportunity to spend the day with Tillie and get paid for it, too. Hopefully there'd be enough time to stop by the orphanage to see Ora Lou.

"How long's this errand of yours going to take?" he asked.

She opened her eyes. "I'm to purchase items for some maternity baskets."

"Maternity baskets?"

"Mrs. Vanderbilt is concerned about the health of the women living on her mountains. She wants to fill maternity baskets for them."

He stiffened. "They aren't *her* mountains."

"Yes, they are, Mack. She owns every mountain within miles and miles of the house and you know it."

"We were there first, and our women have been birthing without help for over a hundred years."

"And what's the mortality rate among the mothers and infants?"

He tightened his lips.

"Exactly. Thus the maternity baskets."

He eyed her brown skirt and cream shirtwaist. Her straw hat and wool shawl. "So, these clothes you're wearing. Are they worth all the headaches you went through over the last three weeks? Did you find it more enjoyable to scrub the bathtub, iron the bedsheets, and darn Miss DePriest's clothes when you were wearing a skirt and shirtwaist?"

The train gently rocked her from side to side. "Yes."

Amusement tugged at his mouth. "Are you being facetious, or are you lying to yourself?"

"I meant it, actually."

He stretched his legs in front of him, crossing his ankles. "And the long hours? Were they worth it?"

"Yes."

"And putting up with Miss DePriest's selfishness?"

"That won't be an issue if I become Mrs. Vanderbilt's lady's maid."

He studied the toes of his boots. "I'll buy you ten skirts and shirtwaists just like the ones you have on now if you'll quit and marry me."

She whipped her head around to look at him, then pressed her fingers against each temple. "Don't tease me."

"I'm dead serious."

"Really? And if we both lose our jobs, just how is it you expect to buy ten skirts and shirtwaists? For that matter, how is it you expect to support me?"

He eyed her, wondering if she might finally be considering it. "I plan to build furniture and sell it on consignment. Woodworking was the one good thing my grandfather taught me, and Rudolf's Mercantile has already agreed to put out anything I make."

"I thought you wanted to move back to your mountain."

"I do. I will. Once my business is on its feet."

"Then why are you even at Biltmore? Why not do that now?"

"I need to buy more tools and build up some inventory. I can't do that until my siblings are back together and well provided for. But make no mistake, as soon as I have the funds I need, I'm leaving Biltmore."

Her eyes were a deeper violet today, though her skin had a distinct greenish hue. "Then you'd best not be buying me any skirts and shirtwaists."

He slowly straightened. "Is that a yes?"

"Absolutely not. I'm just pointing out you can't provide what you are offering."

"I will if that's what you want. I'll find a way. Maybe stay longer at Biltmore. Something."

She shook her head. "No, thank you. Besides, if I ever marry, it will be for reasons much more romantic than skirts and shirtwaists."

Leaning on the armrest between them, he reached over and grabbed the one on the opposite side of her, boxing her in. "I'll be glad to give you romance, if it's romance you're needing."

Her face was inches from his. The scent that was hers alone filled him. The pulse in her neck played a rapid beat.

She kept her eyes forward. "No, thank you."

They were sitting in the last seat of a nearly vacant car. He glanced at the other three occupants. Toward the front, an older man slept, his chin bobbing. A few rows behind him, a child laid her head on her mother's lap while the mother looked out the window.

He turned back to Tillie and nipped her jaw.

She jumped and leaned away from him. "Stop that," she hissed.

"Last night you said you loved me."

"I said I was *thinking* about it, then promptly emptied the contents of my stomach."

He grinned. "You love me, Tillie. You know it and I know it."

"Not enough to quit my job. At least, not yet."

"So you do plan to leave Biltmore eventually?"

She resituated herself in her seat. "Oh yes. When I'm in my late thirties."

Stunned, he could only stare. "And how old are you now?"

"Eighteen."

Anger surged through him. He tightened his grip on the armrest. "Why would you waste all those years on a job? Why? Give me one good reason."

"It's not just a job, it's an opportunity. How else would a girl like me ever get to travel or see the world?"

"See the world?" he scoffed. "Earl had to stop the wagon for you two times between the house and the train station. Just how exactly do you expect to see the world when that would require hours in carriages, days on trains, and months aboard ships on the rolling high seas?"

She crossed her arms. "I'll get to attend wondrous events that would never be open to me otherwise."

"You won't be *attending*, you'll be watching from the back. And only until someone snaps their fingers and sends you off on some errand. The rest of the time you'll be expected to be invisible."

She lifted her chin. "I'll get to meet important, influential, famous people."

"You won't meet anyone. If you even dare to look at them

from anything other than the corner of your eye, you'll be sent packing."

Turning, she looked him straight in the eye. "I'll be able to help the poor and the downtrodden in ways I could never do as a parlormaid. And the maternity baskets are a perfect example."

If he weren't so annoyed, he'd actually feel sorry for her. "That's Mrs. Vanderbilt's act of benevolence, not yours. You are merely collecting the items for her."

"It is no different than if I were collecting items for the church. Someone has to be the hands and feet."

He gentled his voice. "You're getting paid for it, Tillie."

"That's right. And I'll get paid a lot more as a lady's maid. Enough to help my family and the orphans, too."

He threw himself back into his seat. There was no talking to her. She refused to see reality.

"It's what I want," she added. "What I believe God wants."

How was he supposed to fight that? If it were another man, at least his enemy would be tangible. But a conviction? He was at a total loss. Leaning back, he glared out the window as the train pulled into Asheville.

Nineteen

Tillie stepped into The Montville, a bell tied to the door heralding her arrival with Mack. Wooden crates, burlap sacks, stoneware kegs, and barrels of all sizes crowded the mercantile. The section of shelves crammed with colorful fabrics drew her immediate attention, appealing to a deep-rooted desire for pretty, feminine fripperies. From the back of the store familiar smells of chewing tobacco and freshly ground coffee beans blended into a unique potpourri of scents.

A middle-aged man with a shiny bald spot and yellowed apron climbed down from a step stool. "Good morning, folks. Anything I can help you with?"

Neither she nor Mack were wearing uniforms, and they'd come by train rather than coach, so they had yet to be identified as Biltmore staff. The anonymity was a nice change.

"We'd like to see the nursery department, please," she said.

Glancing between the two of them, the clerk smiled broadly and clapped Mack on the shoulder. "Well, congratulations. This your first?"

Heat rushed to her cheeks, but Mack merely nodded. "This will be my first visit to the nursery department, sir."

The clerk chuckled. "Well, you've come to the right place. We have one of the best in the state."

"That's why we're here." Mack swept his hand in an after-you gesture, making no effort to correct the man's impression.

They followed as he wove between a table of dry goods, a stack of washtubs, and two barrels of crackers. "Here we are. Now, was there anything in particular you were interested in?"

"Several things, actually." Tillie ran her gaze over the shelves of baby paraphernalia. "For now, though, I'd like to look a little."

"Sure, sure. You take your time. The name's Tarwater. Just let me know when you're ready."

He returned to his step stool, leaving the two of them in the quiet corner. Big overhead fans circulated with a rhythmic click, brushing them with a subtle breeze.

"What all do we need?" Mack asked.

She fished a folded piece of paper from her pocket and handed it to him. While he perused the list, she reached for a pair of crocheted booties. They were tiny. No longer than the length of her finger. She'd only been six when the first batch of little brothers and sisters had come along. By the time the second batch was born, she'd already left home.

Had her siblings ever been this small? She ran her thumb over the tiny instep. She couldn't recall for certain.

The thought of having her own babies rose in her mind. She quickly calculated how old her mother had been when this last batch was born. Thirty-two. And by that time Mama had had eight babies already.

At thirty-two Tillie would still be working for Mrs. Vanderbilt. She'd be a full-fledged spinster. Her opportunity for babies—and even marriage—long past.

"You thinking what I'm thinking?" His voice was soft.

Yes. "I was wondering if we should purchase white, blue, or pink booties for the baskets. What do you think?" She lifted her gaze to his.

His brown eyes were dark. Intense. "I think I'd like you to have my babies."

Her lips parted. An all-too-familiar longing tugged at her vitals. "You mustn't say things like that."

He took the booties from her, cradling them. Examining them. The fragile, teeny slippers flopped over, lost within his big, callused, wonderful hands. Hands which had hefted trunks, splintered ice, and cradled her cheek.

"Marry me, Tillie."

She dragged her gaze away. "I think all three colors. If we only buy the white, there won't be enough for all the baskets."

"I don't understand."

"I know you don't, Mack. And I'm sorry." She retrieved the booties from him. "Why don't you go see what kind of baskets Mr. Tarwater can round up for us while I finish making our selections."

Sighing, he turned and did her bidding.

She collected booties, bibs, caps, diaper pins, teething rings, talcum powder, and white castile soap. Next, she needed flannel for cloths and cambric for infant slips.

The bell on the door jingled. A thin, wiry man who looked to have lived a hundred years stepped inside. A long beard as snarled as uncarded wool hung to his trousers. Unwashed hair stuck out below a hat which had seen nearly as many years as he had. He surveyed the store, his beady-eyed gaze touching on her, then stalling completely on Mack.

"Be right with you, Mr. McKelvy," the clerk said. "Coffee's warm at the back."

Mack whipped his head around, then stiffened. He held an armful of market baskets, while Mr. Tarwater stood on his stool and handed more down from a high shelf.

The old man took off his hat, jammed it on a rack, then shuffled toward a potbellied stove in the corner. Mack followed the man with his gaze.

"I'm afraid that's all the baskets we have, sir," Mr. Tarwater said, climbing down.

"These'll do fine."

"Well, let me take them up front for you, then I'll see to your wife."

"She's not my wife."

He paused. "Oh. I'm sorry. I didn't . . . I thought . . ."

Mack handed him the rest of the baskets. "Excuse me."

Hiding her embarrassment, Tillie placed her back to the storekeeper and grazed a bolt of fabric with her fingertips. From the corner of her eye she watched Mack join the old man.

"Grandpa."

She looked up sharply, losing all pretense of nonchalance. That was his grandfather? The one who'd taught him wood-working?

The tall but stooped old man looked Mack up and down. Worn and ragged clothing hung on his bony frame. "Ain't you all feisty and brigetty in yer fine cloth."

Mack self-consciously adjusted his collar. Tillie stiffened. It wasn't as if Mack were in full livery. He wore no more than neat trousers, the white shirt she'd sewn, and a brown jacket.

"What're ya thinkin' to work fer them sorry fellers up there? I couldn't believe it when Ory Lou tol' me."

"Sloop and I had an upscuddle. I want Ora Lou out of there. I can earn in a month at Biltmore what would take three or four over at Battery Park."

"Why'd ya get in a jower with Sloop?"

"He's abusing the girls."

His grandfather gave a bark of laughter. "Why, that ain't no reason to take yer foot in yer hand and light out."

"I want her out of there." Mack had his back to Tillie, but there was no mistaking his rigid posture and the arms he held stiffly at his sides.

His grandfather turned up a corner of his mouth. "You ain't talkin' sense, boy. There's gotta be some other reason." He looked Tillie's way.

She turned her attention back to the shelf and pulled out a bolt of flannel.

"Who's that?"

"She's one of the maids at Biltmore. I'm toting for her."

Grandpa narrowed his eyes. "You sweetheartin' her, too?"

"I am."

Willing the blush away, she glanced at Mr. Tarwater. He was measuring out the sanitary disinfectant on their list, but there was no doubt he was hearing every word.

Grandpa squinted and gave her a more thorough looking-over.

Waving a bothersome fly from her ear, she folded back a corner of fabric and fingered its thickness.

"She ain't nothin' but a drudge. I don't think yer up there

fer her or fer Ory Lou. I think yer just like yer brother and covetin' them soft and easy ways they have up thar." He spat onto the floor. "You shame me. And you shame yer mammy. You ain't fit to have McKelvy blood running in yer veins."

She held her breath, but Mack said nothing. Did nothing. She wished she could see his face.

The old man spit again. This time on Mack's boots. Then he shuffled to the door, grabbed his hat, and slammed out of the store.

The *click, click, click* of the ceiling fan was loud in the sudden quiet. Pulling a handkerchief from his pocket, he bent over and wiped the spittle off his boot.

Anger and protectiveness surged through her. How dare that crotchety old man say and do such things to him.

Mack turned around, his face showing no emotion other than the tick at the back of his jaw. "You about finished?"

She jumped. "Oh! Yes. I need to have some of this cut and a bit of cambric. That's all."

"Well, go ahead, then. I'd like to go see Ora Lou before heading back."

"Of course. I'll only be a minute." Hustling to the counter, she gave Mr. Tarwater the bolts of cloth. "Two yards of flannel and four of the cambric, please."

Mack waited at the door while she pointed out the cambric and reviewed with the merchant the nursery items she'd selected.

"That's fine, miss. I'll have everything wrapped and ready within an hour."

Mack opened the door. "We'll be back."

Tillie gave the clerk a quick smile, then scurried onto the boardwalk.

She had to step lively to keep up with Mack's long, angry stride. She'd hoped to stroll leisurely through town and take in the sights, but Mack didn't make any effort to slow his pace, nor glance back to see if she were keeping up.

Still, she marveled at the giant telephone poles marching down Patton Street, their wires crisscrossing the street like clotheslines gone amuck. Three- and four-story buildings housed every kind of trade imaginable. Tobacco shops, drugstores, soda fountains, cobblers, clothing emporiums, music shops, confectioneries, and lawyers' offices.

The ringing bells of the trolley car drew her gaze. She wondered where its passengers would go next. Delivery wagons and dumpcarts blocked passing carriages. Horses lining a succession of hitching posts twitched their tails and sent flies into a furious game of musical chairs. When they finally reached Black Bottom Street, she was out of breath and the soles of her feet ached.

At the top of the hill the orphanage rose up like a wart on a witch's nose. She'd been so preoccupied last time by the fight between Mack and Mr. Sloop she hadn't really paid attention to the condition of the building. But even from here she could see it was nothing short of derelict. Boarded-up windows, sagging roof, scrap in the yard, no fence, nary a blade of grass. But she'd heard Mr. Sloop was renovating the insides first in order to make sure the children were warm and comfortable.

A one-horse farm wagon sat parked out front. A giant of a man stood beside it, his golden skin and wild hair reminding her of a lion. He spoke a few words to Mr. Sloop, and then, with tears streaming down his face, lifted a pale boy of seven or eight from the wagon.

Mack slowed, then came to a stop. She stepped up next to

him. They were far enough away to offer the group privacy, but not so far that they couldn't hear every word.

The boy shook his head. "No, Pa. Please. Ya need me. With Ma gone ya won't have nobody. Please let me stay. I won't eat no more. I won't be no trouble. I'll sleep under the house and you won't even know I'm there."

The giant pulled him to his heart, trembling and shaking with emotion. The boy tried to wrap his arms and legs about the man, but he couldn't begin to reach.

Finally, the man kissed him flush on the lips and set him down. "You be good, son."

Then he climbed up into the wagon and shook the reins. "Hi-yup."

"*No!*" the boy screamed, chasing after the wagon and straight toward her and Mack.

The wagon rolled by. The boy raced down the slope, his feet getting ahead of themselves. A couple of yards in front of Mack and Tillie he tripped, lurching to the ground.

Mack jumped forward and scooped up the boy.

He kicked and screamed and pounded his fists against Mack's chest. "Lemme go! Lemme go! My pa! My pa!"

Mack's Adam's apple bobbed. "Your pa's gone, son."

The boy's green eyes clashed with Mack's. "Nooooo!" He flung himself against Mack's neck, sobbing. Begging.

Tillie didn't even know she was crying until a tear splattered against her hand. She quickly swiped her cheeks.

Mack held the boy fast until his crying began to dwindle. Then, making no move to release him, Mack continued toward the orphanage.

CHAPTER

Twenty

S loop waited for them at the top of the hill, his posture
stiff. He didn't offer Tillie a greeting, nor even a glance.
And Mack made no move to introduce them. She'd wanted
to meet him, though. Tell him of their shared passion for
the orphans. And how she hoped to offer a small donation
if she made lady's maid. Perhaps even come once a quarter
to help with the children. But with the tension between the
two men, and the heartbreak of the boy, the time just wasn't
right.

She studied the tall, immaculate director. The expensive
cut of his coat seemed oddly out of place with the pathetic
surroundings.

"What do you want, Danver?" he snapped.

"I came to see Ora Lou."

"Visiting hours aren't until four."

"I won't be here at four."

They stared at each other, the hostility palpable. Sloop's thin hair was slicked down and side-parted, emphasizing a jag in his nose. She studied the yellow skin surrounding it and wondered if Mack had broken the man's nose that day in the yard. She knew Mack was still convinced the man had hit his sister, but Tillie just couldn't believe it. Why go to all the trouble of rescuing the children only to then turn around and beat them? It just didn't make sense.

Sloop looked at the cowering boy. "Put him down. Coddling breeds weakness."

She blinked.

Mack made no move to comply. "Do you want to get Ora Lou or shall I?"

The door opened. A stout woman in black shirtwaist and skirt stood at the threshold. Her plump cheeks were flanked with braided coils covering each ear. "What does he want?"

"Wants to talk to his sister," Sloop answered.

She strode across the yard, her skirts stirring the dirt and coating her hem. "She's indisposed. Give me the boy."

Mack tried to pry him off, but the boy clung with tenacity. "Let go, son. Show Mrs. Sloop your manners and give her a proper greeting."

He buried his face in Mack's neck and shook his head. "I want my pa. I wanna go home."

"Well, your pa doesn't want you," she snapped. "Now, quit blubbering and come along or you'll do without your supper."

Tillie gasped.

Mack tensed. "Cover your ears, boy."

The boy pressed one ear against Mack's shoulder. The other he covered with a dirty hand. Mack set his lips against his teeth and let out a loud, piercing whistle, which slid up the scale, down and then up again.

Jumping, Tillie slammed her hands against her own ears.

A window on the second floor wheeled open. "Mack!" A girl on the cusp of adulthood leaned out. "I'll be right there!"

Mrs. Sloop pointed her finger at the girl. "You will stay inside and finish your work."

She looked at the woman, then at Mack. He winked.

A smile bloomed on her face and she disappeared, then burst out the door running full tilt. "What are you doing here in the middle of the week!" She flung her arms about his waist, sandwiching the boy between them. "Have you come to get me? Are you taking me with you?"

Her faded brown cheviot dress with an oversized epaulet collar suited a ten-year-old. Its short length barely reached her calves, threatening to be just this side of indecent. A thick shock of dark blond hair was gathered at her neck in a filthy ribbon.

Mrs. Sloop pulled in her chin. "I told you to stay put."

Mack nudged his sister behind him. "I'm going to visit with Ora Lou for a few minutes. We can do it here or inside."

"No one is allowed inside except during visitation." Snapping her fingers, Mrs. Sloop reached out a hand. "Come along, Homer."

Tillie touched Mack's sleeve, afraid the woman's anger would be taken out on the boy if Mack didn't release him.

He sighed. "Homer? Is that your name?"

The boy nodded.

"This here behind me is my sister. As soon as I'm through talking to her, she'll come back inside and check on you."

Ora Lou's face fell with disappointment.

"Until then, you need to go with Mr. and Mrs. Sloop." He tried to peel the boy off of him, but Homer tightened his hold.

"No, no! I won't go in. I *won't*."

Tillie stepped toward Mrs. Sloop and introduced herself. When people found out she was part of Biltmore's upper staff, they often catered to her as if she were a Vanderbilt herself.

Mrs. Sloop was no different. "Danver is carrying parcels for you, then? You're not . . . *with* him."

"That's correct," Tillie answered. "And I'm wondering if perhaps Homer could stay out here with us until Ora Lou and Mr. Danver are finished? Maybe by then he will have calmed a bit."

The woman clearly didn't care for the idea, but was unwilling to upset Biltmore's head parlormaid. She turned to Ora Lou. "Put him in with Artie when you come inside. And don't linger."

Spinning around, she commandeered her husband's arm, and the two of them disappeared through the front door.

Mack turned to Ora Lou. "You all right?"

She nodded. "They still stay clear of me. Ever since you lit into him."

"You weren't so confident last time I was here."

She cocked her head. "No? Well, it was probably because of Irene. She's not a very strong person. She needs someone to look out for her."

"And you've decided to take on the job?"

She smiled. "I guess I have."

While the two of them talked, Tillie watched the boy. The moment he made eye contact with her, she ducked her face behind Mack's shoulder in a game of peekaboo. She'd drawn many of her own siblings out of their doldrums with the universal game.

Slowly, she peered back around him. As she'd hoped, the boy's eyes were wide and watchful. She ducked out of sight again.

"Where have you been?" Ora Lou asked Mack. "I expected you a week and a half ago."

He absently patted the boy's back. "The Vanderbilts had a house party and no one got their day off. But since I was in town today, I wanted to come tell you I'd saved enough money to get you out, but I want to earn a little more in case it takes you some time to find a job. Give me a couple more weeks, all right?"

Tillie looked at him, forgetting about the game. Mack had said that as soon as he had the funds he needed for his siblings, he'd leave Biltmore. She had no idea he was so close to his goal.

Panic began to well up until she remembered he'd said siblings. Plural. Was there another Danver in the orphanage? Did that mean he'd have to work longer at Biltmore to support more children?

Ora Lou's face lit up. "Do you mean it, Mack? Just two more weeks?"

"I said so, didn't I?"

She flung her arms about his neck, again sandwiching the boy between them. Homer locked eyes with Tillie. She held out her arms and he came without hesitation.

She'd intended to put him on the ground and hold his hand, but before she could, he latched on to her the way he had Mack. The precious feel of his thin, bony frame hugging her tight cut right to her heart.

She wrapped her arms around him, rocking him, patting

him, shushing him, all while she tried to suppress memories of her mother doing the same for her. And if she were a mother, she would surely do the same for her child. But not if she stayed at Biltmore. For if she stayed until her late thirties, she would, most likely, never be a wife, much less a mother.

She looked up at Mack. He and Ora Lou had quit talking and were watching her. Homer tucked his thumb in his mouth. He was way too old to still be sucking his thumb, but no one said a thing.

Melancholy touched Ora Lou's eyes. "Reminds me of when we had to leave Ikey, Otis, and John-John with those families on the mountain."

Tillie frowned. "Who are Ikey, Otis, and John-John?"

"Our little brothers." Ora Lou looked at her. "So you're Biltmore's head parlormaid?"

She blinked. "Your little brothers? You, you have *three* little brothers?"

Ora Lou raised a brow. "Who is this, Mack?"

"Tillie Reese. We're getting married soon."

Tillie gasped. "We are not."

"Yes, we are." He turned back to Ora Lou. "We have to go. Our train will be coming in a bit and we still need to pick up our parcels. Here, you take him."

"We are *not* getting married." She tried to transfer Homer into Ora Lou's arms, but her sharp tone frightened him and he would not let go.

Mack placed a hand on the boy's back. "Listen, Homer. I'll be back on Sunday. So you go on with Ora Lou. She'll take care of you."

Homer clung even tighter with arms, legs, and desperation.

"Why don't you carry him to Artie's room," Ora Lou suggested. "That may be quicker."

Tillie glanced between them. "But no one's allowed inside right now. Only during visitation hours."

"Then make him get down," Mack said. "We need to go."

A tear from Homer's cheek dropped to her neck.

She sighed. "Show me where Artie's room is."

Instead of going through the front, they went round back. Tillie was so used to Biltmore's efficiency, the primitive kitchen took her by surprise. Only one stove for all those children?

But she didn't have time to linger. Ora Lou looked both ways, placed a finger against her lips, then led them tiptoeing down a dim hallway and into a stairwell. The condition of the building surprised Tillie. Clearly, Sloop's renovations had yet to touch this section.

With one hand, she lifted her skirt, with the other, she supported Homer—leaving none with which to hold the railing. But she'd carried many a load more cumbersome than this up and down the steps of Biltmore. Still, Mack placed a steady hand against her waist.

She had no doubt he felt the tremors scuttle up her spine. She only hoped he attributed them to the fear of being caught rather than a reaction to his touch.

Forcing herself to the task at hand, she captured brief impressions between the floors. Moldy, wet smells. Filth and cobwebs. Loose balusters. A hole in the wall. And flies everywhere.

At the third floor, Ora Lou paused. "It's right down this hall."

About halfway down, she opened a door for Tillie. The tiny room held nothing but two cots, a chamber pot, and a peg for clothes. No pitcher, no lantern, not even a candle. The walls were papered with years of grime. The floor, bare and gritty. The cots offered no bedding other than a blanket apiece—neither of which looked as if they'd been washed in a month of Sundays. Surely this wasn't where the children slept.

"Where's Artie's room?" Tillie whispered.

"This is it."

She tried to hold in her shock. "Where's Artie?"

"He's locked in the basement for bad behavior."

She gasped. Mack stiffened. Homer tightened his hold.

Locked in the basement? She looked up at Mack, his eyes as troubled as hers. How could they leave this child here? But what other choice did they have?

Carefully, she lowered herself to the edge of the cot and pulled Homer's feet to one side. "Listen to me. Ora Lou will stay here with you and show you where you need to go. I imagine it will be suppertime soon and you'll want to wash up like a good boy, so you make a nice impression on Mr. and Mrs. Sloop."

Once more, she scanned the room, wondering how he would wash up without pitcher and basin. "Mr. Danver will be back on Sunday." She looked up to double-check with Mack.

He nodded.

"Perhaps when he comes you can accompany Ora Lou during her visit." Again she checked with Mack.

Again, he gave her an affirmative.

"For now, though, I need you to let go."

"Will you come back?" It was the first words he'd uttered since his refusal to go with Mrs. Sloop.

"Absolutely. If not this Sunday, then the next one I have off."

"You promise?"

She smoothed his hair. "I promise. Now, come. Be a good boy and let Ora Lou show you what you need to do."

He slowly loosened his grip, then paused and kissed her right on the lips, their noses bumping, before sliding off her lap.

Tears clogged her throat. She'd barely whispered good-bye when Mack drew her up by the hand, whisked her down the hall, down the stairs, and then out the back door.

∞

Tillie sat on her parents' porch sewing an infant slip. Though it was her day off, the maternity baskets could not be delivered until the slips were completed. So instead of going to the orphanage with Mack, she had to stay behind to stitch. She told him to tell Homer she'd come next time. She hoped the boy wouldn't be too disappointed.

Finishing off a seam, she scanned the yard dotted with trees of light and dark green. Tucked into the corner, an impatient ash clothed in reddish violet leaves offered a premature peek at fall colors.

Her mother rocked beside her, helping to sew yet another slip. "There's been some talk about you and the useful man."

Tillie looked at her sharply. "What are they saying?"

"That you're romantically involved."

She tightened her shawl, warding off a bite in the afternoon breeze. "Says who?"

"Does it matter?"

"I suppose not. I was just curious, is all."

"A woman's reputation is not in her own keeping, Tillie, but at the mercy of others. The only control you have is to be completely aboveboard." Her mother looked over the wire glasses propped on her nose. "Something's going on. What is it?"

Tillie plucked a collar facing from her sack, then matched it against the slip's neckline. "Nothing is going on."

Mama's needle stilled. "Are you attracted to him?"

She felt a blush creep up her neck. "Mama, please."

After a moment, her mother once again set the chair to rocking and took up her sewing. "Oh, he's a handsome one, I'll give you that. And he appears to have more character than his brother. I can see how he'd turn a girl's head."

Tillie offered no reply.

"But with all that's at stake, you can't afford so much as a whisper of gossip."

"I know." She tugged on the thread, tightening her stitch.

"Lucy Lewers's mistress gave her a solid gold thimble as a token of her appreciation."

Tillie sucked in her breath.

"Did Miss DePriest leave you anything?"

She stared at her mother, until the two locked gazes.

"You know she didn't."

Mama nodded. "Then I suggest you end whatever it is between you and Mack Danver, or before you blink you'll have handed over the opportunity of a lifetime to Lucy."

Tillie studied her mother's face. The face which had seen thirty-seven years of life. Twenty-one years of marriage. The birth of ten babies. The death of one.

Subtle creases fanned the corners of her eyes and lined her lips like a button stitch. A touch of gray threaded through her hair.

"If I'm awarded the lady's maid position, I'll be the age you are now when they ask me to step down and allow some younger, prettier girl to replace me."

"And think of all you'll have seen and experienced. Think

of the money you'll have earned and saved. Think of all the good you will have done for your family and those in need."

What about the loneliness? What about all the childbearing years I'll have lost? What about Mack?

Gathering her courage, Tillie swallowed. "I think I love him, Mama."

She braced for an explosion, but instead her mother simply lowered the slip to her lap, secured the needle to its side, then removed her glasses. "How far has it gone?"

"He's asked me to marry him more times than I count."

"And you said?"

"Absolutely not."

Mama's shoulders relaxed a fraction. "Good. Remember, Tillie, this is your chance. To spread your wings. To see the world beyond these mountains. Why would you give it up to marry? To be a wife and mother and work your fingers to the bone with nothing to show for it? Don't throw away your best chance at happiness before you've grasped it. Have you forgotten how hard you've worked toward becoming a lady's maid? Why, you've spent your entire life preparing for it."

She had, but for the first time she wondered at whose behest. Throughout the years her mother had spent many an hour telling Tillie stories of the Englishwomen who had visited her hometown of Charleston. She told of their glorious gowns and beautiful ladies' maids. Of the travel and privilege those women experienced. She'd wanted to be a lady's maid herself but had neither the know-how nor the opportunity. When she married Pa and moved to Asheville, all hope was dashed.

Still, she began reading books, magazines, and training manuals describing the duties of house servants. As soon as Tillie was old enough, her mother started grooming her for the position of lady's maid, thinking to send her to Newport or some exotic location for employment. When the wealthy set began to make Asheville their home, Mama was ecstatic. But when George Vanderbilt built a veritable castle not six miles away, Mama was sure it had been predestined.

Mrs. Vanderbilt's French maid had been a setback. But now that the woman was leaving, Mama had no doubt God was opening doors for Tillie. And all she had to do was walk through them.

"Have you let him kiss you?" Mama asked.

The temptation to lie was great. Instead, Tillie slowly nodded.

"Anything else?"

Her breath caught. "No, Mama. Only kisses."

She reached over and gripped Tillie's arm. "You must put him out of your mind. And not just because it could rob you of this opportunity. But because he's a hillbilly, for heaven's sake. A man from the back settlements of the Unakas who believes a woman is less important than his hunting dog. Why, those men walk into their homes and hang their hat on the floor. Do you understand what I'm saying? It'd be nothing but drudgery. Seven days a week. Twenty-four hours a day. No evenings off. No second Sundays off. Why would you do that when you could have a life of privilege and ease as Mrs. Vanderbilt's maid?"

"Mack's not like that. He's educated. And he cares about women. That's the whole reason he's at Biltmore. To make enough money to put his sister up and support her."

For the first time, a hint of alarm touched Mama's eyes. "And then what? Back to his home somewhere on Hazel Creek? You'd be in the middle of nowhere with illiterate neighbors, no church, and no gas in the house. Why, you'd not even have a house, but a hovel."

Tillie had never been to the Southern Unakas, but her mother's sister had married a highlander. Mama had gone to visit her many times. And she knew of what she spoke.

Mama scooted to the edge of her rocker. "Those Hazel Creek men think nothing of taking off on some journey without laying wood in the stove or hearth. They fully expect their wives and children to drag the hillsides for whatever dead timber they can find and then chop it themselves with a dull ax."

Tillie shook her head. "Mack would never do that. I'm sure of it."

Mama paled. "Oh, honey. It's not the same up there as it is here. Southern highlanders don't tip their hats, they don't open your doors, they don't take your elbow. Why, at supper, the woman isn't even afforded a seat. She's expected to stand and serve the man. And many, many of the men think nothing of raising a hand to a woman in violence."

Tillie pictured all the times Mack had used his fists—and at other times threatened to. But it was always in defense of someone helpless. He would never be violent toward her. Yet he could be domineering at times.

She thought of how he'd dragged her across the barn by the hand, rather than guiding her by her elbow. Of how dictatorial he'd been about her acceptance of his proposal. As if she had no say in the decision at all. She thought of his grandfather scolding him for wasting his time at Biltmore on account of his sister, a mere female.

She looked at her mother, tears springing to her eyes. "I just get so confused when I'm with him. He's, I . . . he takes my breath away, Mama."

She patted Tillie's hand. "He's a very attractive man, dear, but you must stay focused on the prize. And at all costs, avoid being alone with him. Even if it means no more barn gatherings. These rumors about the two of you must cease immediately."

Tillie nodded. "Yes, Mama. I'll stay clear of him. I promise."

Twenty-one

From a fourth-floor window of the "Virgins' Wing," Tillie watched Earl pull the carriage away. Inside it were Mrs. Vanderbilt, Lucy, and the maternity baskets. Baskets filled with items Tillie had shopped for, had cut and folded and sewn for. She had lovingly assembled each basket, picturing the women her mother had described.

She had looked forward to seeing those women for herself. The conditions of their homes. The attitude of their men. The remoteness of their locations. Maybe even meeting her aunt for the first time.

But she hadn't been invited to accompany Mrs. Vanderbilt. Lucy had.

Tillie swallowed. After all that work, to be robbed of performing the actual good deed rocked her newfound resolve.

What if Mack was right? What if this "good work" she

was doing really was a benevolent act on Mrs. Vanderbilt's part and nothing more than menial labor on her part?

She returned to her room, lit a lantern, and sat on her bed. A decorative pillow made from dishcloths flopped over. It had been a gift from her mother when Tillie was twelve and had left home for the first time to work as a step-girl in a wealthy Asheville household. Picking it up, she ran a finger over the verse her mother had stitched onto it.

"Whatever you do, do it heartily, as to the Lord and not to men, knowing that from the Lord you will receive the reward of the inheritance, for you serve the Lord Christ." Col. 3:23–24

Tears stacked up in her throat. She had worked heartily on the baskets, and had done it with a special thrill, knowing she'd be helping the less fortunate.

Lying down on the bed, shoes and all, she hugged the pillow to her. It wasn't that she was unappreciative of whatever reward the Lord had in mind for the afterlife. It was just that she wanted to take the task to completion here on earth.

But it wasn't her task to complete. It was Mrs. Vanderbilt's. So at the end of the day, when she stood before Christ and He asked what she'd done to further His kingdom, who would get to claim the maternity baskets? She or Mrs. Vanderbilt?

She closed her eyes and listened, but no answer was forthcoming.

∞

Tillie stood uncertainly at the edge of the orphanage's property. As soon as church in Biltmore Village had released, she'd accepted a wagon ride with the Hatch family, who were bound for Asheville to visit relatives. She was determined to make good on her promise to Homer. Not only that, but she'd decided even if she didn't have the funds to contribute to the cause, she could at least give of her time. After seeing the squalor of the place, she knew she had a set of skills which could be put to good use.

Yet now that she'd arrived, she didn't quite know how to proceed. Did she simply knock on the door and say, "I'm here to see Homer and to clean up that disgusting mess in the back"?

Before she could decide, the front door opened. Ora Lou stepped out, a comforting arm around a shorter girl. Both were crying. Behind them, a harassed Mack.

"Don't go, Ora Lou," the slight girl sobbed. "Don't leave me alone with them. Please."

Ora Lou shot a look of anger at Mack. "I don't see why she can't come, too."

"I told you, it's a boardinghouse. You pay per person."

"We could sneak her in."

"Not without lying to the landlord."

"Well, what am I supposed to do? I can't just leave her here."

Tillie could see Mack's temper rising. They hadn't seen her yet and she purposefully didn't interfere, if for no other reason than to prove that no matter what Mama said, Mack was not a violent man.

"Well, we can't take her, either." He looked askance at the other girl. "I'm sorry, Irene. I just don't have the money for both of you."

Pulling in a choppy breath, Irene swiped her eyes. "I un . . . un . . . derstand."

Ora Lou grabbed both the girl's hands. "Listen, Mack says he found me a scullery job at a café uptown. Maybe they need more than one girl. I'll find out, and if they do, I'll come get you myself."

Mack threw up his hands in a gesture of frustration. "Ora Lou, she can't just leave without a place to stay."

His sister stomped her foot. "Would you quit butting in? I'm not even talking to you."

"But you're giving her false hope."

"It's better than *no* hope."

They glared at each other. Mack locked his jaw. Ora Lou thrust her chin forward.

Irene pulled her hands from Ora Lou's and took a step back. "Don't worry, I'll make do. And your brother's right. I ain't never leaving this place. But that don't mean you can't."

Huge tears began to gather in Ora Lou's eyes. "I can't leave her, Mack."

His eyes bugged out. "It's all set. Money's exchanged hands. Promises have been made. The New York Café is expecting you in the morning."

"No. If she stays, I stay."

Red filled his face. "Ora Lou Danver, you are not staying in this place one more minute."

She crossed her arms. A tremor ran through him. Tillie held her breath. Seconds ticked by.

Finally, Irene tucked her chin. "You go on, Ora Lou. I'd never forgive myself if ya didn't and then somethin' were to happen."

Tillie frowned. *If something were to happen?* Like what?

With a cry of anguish, Ora Lou pitched forward, clasping the girl to her in a fierce hug. Then she whirled around, raced across the yard, passed Tillie, and continued on down the hill.

"Ora Lou!" Face stricken, Mack gave Irene's shoulder a squeeze. "If things get bad, you send word, you hear?"

Lips quivering, she nodded.

He raced after Ora Lou, glancing at Tillie with a baffled look, as if he couldn't quite figure out what she was doing there.

She watched him eat up the distance between himself and his sister. Poor Mack. This wasn't the happy departure he'd expected or hoped for, she was certain.

He spoke rapidly, gesturing, but Ora Lou did no more than continue stomping down the walkway. Then they rounded the bend and were out of sight.

She turned to ask Irene what he'd meant by "if things get bad," but the yard was empty. Making her way across it, she knocked. No answer.

She knocked again. Just as she was about to go around back, Mrs. Sloop answered. "Oh, hello, Miss Reese." She looked over Tillie's shoulder as if expecting to see the Vanderbilts within the vicinity.

"Good afternoon, Mrs. Sloop. I was wondering if I could visit with Homer and Irene, please?"

The woman hesitated. "Irene is indisposed and Homer is napping."

"I see. Well . . ." She moistened her lips. "Perhaps I could, um, wait?"

"I'm afraid it will be quite some time yet."

"I don't mind." She cleared her throat. "As a matter of fact, I thought perhaps you might have some work you'd like me to do? Like, um, I could clean the back corridor? Or the stairwell? Or maybe wash some linens?"

Mrs. Sloop's eyes narrowed. "We rest on the Sabbath."

"Oh. I see." She swallowed. "Well, when do you think Homer will be awake and Irene will be able to take callers?"

"Come back in four hours."

Four hours? She couldn't wait that long. Not if she was going to catch a ride back to Biltmore with the Hatch family. "I'm afraid that will be too late for me. Do you think you could wake up Homer? I promised him I'd come."

"I'm sorry, but I'll be sure to tell him you came by. Now if you'll excuse me."

The large, solid door closed. Tillie stood for a moment, confused, disappointed, hurt. And worried about Homer. When Mrs. Sloop gave him the message, the boy wouldn't even know who Miss Reese was.

And if she wouldn't be allowed to volunteer her services on Sundays, then she'd never be able to, for they were her only full days off. And why was Ora Lou so worried about leaving her friend behind?

With a heavy heart, Tillie pulled her cloak more tightly about her shoulders, then headed back toward town to wait for the Hatches.

∞

Tillie carried bucket and brush to the first landing of the grand staircase. Crouching onto her knees, she began to scrub the limestone steps which protruded from the wall in a vast spiral that started on the main floor and continued clear up to the top floor.

Smartly polished boots stopped next to her. "What's going on between you and Mack?"

She didn't have to look up to recognize her brother's voice. Fortunately, no one else was around to hear the question. The hour was still early and the other maids had made their way to rooms well out of hearing.

"Nothing is happening," she said. "Why does everyone keep asking me that?"

"Because where there's smoke . . ."

"Well, believe me. There's no fire."

"Not from where I'm standing. The two of you can't get within yards of each other without sparks flying. Now, what's going on?"

She dipped her brush into the water and moved down one step.

He squatted to better see her, his knees popping. "Is he bothering you, Till?"

You have no idea. Swiping a piece of hair from her face, she sat back. Allan's dark eyes didn't hold censure like Mama's, but concern. Trust. Affection.

She glanced around. "I'm in love with him," she whispered.

There. She'd said it out loud. But it didn't change anything. Not her sense of responsibility. Nor her dreams. And certainly not the rules about the marital status of house servants.

Allan's brows lifted a fraction. "Does he love you?"

She nodded.

"Are you going to quit?"

Swallowing, she shook her head.

Flipping the tails of his jacket behind him, he sat on the landing—something he never, ever did while on duty—showing her just exactly how concerned he was.

"Why won't you quit?" he asked.

"You, of all people, should know."

"Humor me."

"I'm up for lady's maid."

"A position which, as I've said before, will rob you of your youth."

She huffed. "According to Mama, so does being a wife."

"Mama said that?" His voice rose in surprise.

"Not in so many words, but yes."

"Well, I'm sure she didn't mean it. So if you really do love Mack, I say you quit and marry the man."

Tempting as it sounded, she shook her head. "I need the position, Allan. I need it so I can help put food on our family's table. I mean, how many more things can Mr. Vanderbilt possibly want his insignia painted on? What if he runs out of them? What if Pa's joints start getting stiff all the time instead of just during the cold weather?"

He frowned. "So you're giving up the man you love on the chance that Pa might get arthritis and Mr. Vanderbilt might run out of . . . *things?*"

"Don't forget Mama," she added. "She's got all her hopes pinned on me becoming a lady's maid and she's worked so hard."

"Exactly. *She's* worked hard. But she loves you, Till. She wouldn't want you to give up a lifetime of love for a lifetime of servitude."

She raised a brow.

"Okay. Maybe she would. But Pa wouldn't. He'd be the first to say Ma's happiness ought to come from her family and her Lord. Not from trying to live vicariously through you. And it's not always about the position we hold or the money we make."

Sighing, she returned to her scrubbing. "It's not just Mama."

"I didn't think so. What is it really?"

"I want to do the kinds of things Mrs. Vanderbilt does."

He crossed his arms. "You want to live above your station?"

"No. I want to make something of my life. The Vanderbilts are so charitable. If I'm lady's maid, I can help those Mrs. Vanderbilt helps and also take on projects of my own. Like Sloop's orphanage or something."

Allan shook his head, a sad smile on his lips. "You're eighteen, Till. Do you really think God expects—?"

A noise from around the corner had Allan jumping to his feet. "We'll finish this later," he whispered, then hurried down the stairs, leaving her with no more answers than she had before.

Twenty-two

Smoothing her apron, Tillie fluffed the ruffles on her shoulder straps and knocked on the door.

"Come in."

The Oak Sitting Room connecting Mr. and Mrs. Vanderbilt's bedrooms was used as a private area for the couple. Tillie had never been inside it before. She tried not to gawk at the repeating coats of arms bordering the ceiling, the carved oak paneling, and the stately furnishings.

Mrs. Vanderbilt looked up from a sturdy library table covered with papers, ledgers, and books. A bronze statue of a buck foraging for food sat on its corner.

"Tillie." Putting down her pen, she leaned back in her chair, her brown hair arranged in an elegant donutlike shape with a bun in the middle. "It's nice to see you."

Tillie was struck again by how young she was. A good ten years younger than the master and only a handful of years older than herself. She couldn't imagine becoming mistress of a manor like Biltmore at the ripe age of twenty-five.

"Ma'am."

"I was very pleased with the baskets you put together. The women were quite happy with them, though it took some finesse to convince them they were gifts and not charity. For a moment I was afraid they'd refuse them outright."

Tillie had no idea how to respond, so she remained silent.

Mrs. Vanderbilt tilted her head. "I also wanted to thank you for being so patient with Miss DePriest. I know that couldn't have been easy."

Tillie felt her cheeks warm. "Oh no, ma'am. I was happy to do it. And the baskets, too."

A shadow of a smile crossed Mrs. Vanderbilt's face, and then she rummaged through the papers on her desk. "I realize it's only mid-October, but I feel we need to go ahead and begin a project I had in mind."

Tillie started to clasp her hands, then remembered to keep them by her sides.

"Here we are." Mrs. Vanderbilt pulled several pieces of paper from a pile on her left. "Mr. Vanderbilt and I plan to invite our estate workers and their families to the Banquet Hall on Christmas Day. As part of the celebration, we are going to give each child a toy."

Tillie blinked in surprise. "Every single one?"

She nodded. "Every single one. I have completed all my visits and have a census of every child, their names and ages and what toy I think they would enjoy." She extended the list.

Accepting the papers, Tillie glanced at them. A beautiful script neatly delineated names of families and each child within them. Beside the children's names and ages were specific toys.

Marbles, tin penny whistles, kaleidoscopes, blocks, flower presses, kazoos, and many, many more.

Thumbing through the pages, she silently added up the small fortune the list represented. She stalled on the *R*s.

```
Reese, Herbert and Christine.
Emblem painter.
    Allan (22)—Head Footman
    Matilda (Tillie, 18)—Head Parlormaid
    Gertrude (Gussie, 11)—Sateen Parasol
    Richard (Ricky, 10)—Wooden Animals
    Walter (9)—Also Wooden Animals
    Martha (5)—Finger Puppets
    Ennis (4)—Stick Horse
```

She reread the list. The gifts were perfect. Mrs. Vanderbilt hadn't just jotted down random toys. She'd obviously visited with each of Tillie's brothers and sisters. Otherwise, she never would have been able to pick out such ideal presents.

She lifted her gaze to Mrs. Vanderbilt. "I don't know what to say, ma'am. It'll be the best Christmas we've ever had. Thank you."

She smiled. "I'd like you to go to Asheville and purchase the toys, wrap them, and label them, and when it comes time, place them under the tree."

"It would be my pleasure."

"Good. You'll need an early start, and the wagon to carry everything. I'll have Mrs. Winter arrange for Earl to drive you this time and the useful man to escort and carry for you."

Tillie quickly squelched her alarm at being with Mack for an entire day, but some of her apprehension must have shown, because Mrs. Vanderbilt immediately crinkled her brows.

"Oh dear. I forgot you suffer from carriage sickness. Would you like me to have Lucy do this instead?"

"No, no, ma'am. The wagon will be no problem, and I've found that if I have a ginger cookie or two, it helps tremendously."

"Well then, we'll have Cook prepare a tin to take with you." She smiled. "You'll have to hide them from the men, though, or they might all disappear."

Tillie answered her smile. "Yes, ma'am. I'll be sure to keep some back."

"Excellent. You may take the list with you so you can familiarize yourself with it. If you have any questions or think I might need to consider a different toy for one of the children, just let Mrs. Winter know."

"Yes, ma'am. I'm sure they'll all be wonderful."

"Thank you, Tillie. You're excused."

Tillie quietly closed the door, then hugged the papers to her. This time she'd be on the project from beginning to end. From the purchasing of the toys, to putting them under the tree, to being in attendance when they were given out.

The only snag was spending the day with Mack. She'd managed to either avoid him completely or surround herself with others when he was present. Still, Earl would be going with them. Hopefully that would diffuse any intimacy which might arise.

∞

Mack sat in the back of the green farm wagon watching Earl—charm oozing from every pore—entertain Tillie. He knew his brother didn't mean anything by it. He treated all women the same, regardless of size, shape, or age.

And he didn't think Tillie's head had been turned. She'd

been working with Earl since Biltmore had opened. If she hadn't fallen for him in all that time, she wasn't likely to now.

He shifted his weight on the uneven boards. So why was he getting more and more angry as each moment passed? He'd thought about horning in on the wagon seat, but there was barely enough room for two people. There was no way it could hold three. Which meant somebody had to ride in the back. With Earl the designated coachman and Tillie a female, it wasn't even up for discussion.

Earl ran over a rut, causing Tillie to sway and Mack to be jarred off the bed and slammed back down. He glared at Earl's back, but his brother was busy flirting with Tillie and hadn't noticed.

At least they'd be in Asheville soon. He could see the outline of the town nestled in a valley of ravaged forests, which had been logged so thoroughly there was scarcely a tree left. He only hoped his grandpa wasn't there. No telling what he'd say if he found Mack riding in the bed while a woman rode up front.

He eyed her from behind. She was wearing the same outfit she'd worn last time, but had covered it up with a jacket which nipped in at her waist and flared out at her hips. She'd twisted up her hair in some kind of female poof anchored with a straw hat.

These last few weeks she'd all but ignored him. He wondered again what she'd been doing at the orphanage on Sunday. He'd rushed to town on his day off in order to get Ora Lou set up in her boardinghouse. What a debacle that had turned out to be. After all the saving he'd done and the pestering he'd put up with from her, the last thing he'd expected was resistance.

But her fear for Irene was real. Real enough to give up her longed-for freedom. Fortunately, it hadn't come to that. As soon as he'd managed to settle her down, introduce her to the landlord, and show her where her new job was, he'd hightailed it back to Biltmore just in time for the barn gathering. Only Tillie wasn't there.

At first he'd thought she was sick, for she never missed the dances. But Allan had merely shrugged and said she'd wanted to read instead.

Mack knew better. It wasn't a book that kept her away—it was he himself and those infernal parlor games.

He sighed. She wouldn't be able to avoid him today. And once he had her alone, he'd find out what was what. But Earl never left them alone. Not even to wet his whistle. He was enjoying the Christmas shopping as much as she was.

"Hey, look at this, Till!" Earl picked up a stereoscope and slipped a picture card into its brackets.

She peeked through the lenses. "Oh, my word!"

Earl waved Mack over. "Take a look. It's some fellow in the Dells of Wisconsin leaping across a nine-foot chasm, sixty feet up."

Mack joined them and the three passed each other cards of Niagara Falls, New York Harbor, the Yosemite Valley, and a banana plantation in Hawaii.

"Hey, here's one of you, Tillie." Chuckling, Earl handed her a photo of a woman leaning over a fence, hand on her stomach, looking extremely ill.

Tillie gave him a pointed look. "Very funny."

Others showed a young girl giving a cat a haircut, an outdoor painter accidentally swiping his brush across a man in a window, and a tightrope walker who'd done an act outside a courthouse in 1876. They perused a collection of children and adults in humorous predicaments, laughing at their preposterousness.

A touch of mischief in his eye, Earl dropped another card into place and passed the viewer to Tillie.

She jerked her head back, cheeks turning bright, eyes colliding with Mack's.

He took the stereoscope. The card was entitled "Texas Train Robber Holding Up a Train." But the only train the man held up was the train of a woman's gown, her ankles and calves clearly showing beneath.

What was this doing out where anyone could pick it up? He returned his gaze to her, but she'd busied herself with the list of children.

"This is for a dairy farmer's son," she said. "I think perhaps we'll stick with the pictures of a more daring nature."

Earl gave a wicked chuckle. "I'd say this one is pretty daring."

Her blush intensified. "I meant the tightrope walker and the man jumping that chasm."

"He knew what you meant." Mack placed the stereoscope on the table and grabbed Earl's arm. "I'll be right back, Tillie."

Mack propelled him through a side door which led to a back poolroom. Smoke hung over the area like a morning fog. A crowd gathered around a billiard table in the corner as a man leaned down, propping a long pool stick against his fingers.

"Right pocket," he said, followed by the clack of two balls.

Mack released his brother. "What's the matter with you?"

"Aw, come on, Mack. It was funny. You know, holding up the train?" He laughed again.

Mack caught him by the shirtfront. "I've told you to treat her with respect."

Earl frowned. "You used to think that kind of thing was funny."

"Well, I don't anymore. It embarrasses her and I want you to stop."

They stood toe to toe, each the mirror image of the other.

"Let go of me, Mack, before I lose my temper."

"I'll have your word you'll be nothing less than a gentleman when you're around her."

Earl grabbed Mack's wrists and jerked them down. "And you'll not get it, big brother." He curled his lip. "You know, you get more and more like Pa every day. It disgusts me. What would Grandpa say?"

"Hey, Danver? That you?"

They turned as a young man broke away from the crowd and headed toward them.

Earl smiled and released Mack's wrists. "Hey, Burton. You remember my brother?"

"Sure." He looked between them. "Everything okay?"

"Yeah. Mack just gets a little uptight sometimes."

Mack forced himself to take a deep breath. "You stay here while Tillie finishes up. I'll come get you when we're ready to leave."

Earl nodded. "Sure thing, *Pa*."

Ignoring him, Mack returned to the shop only to be shooed out of the way while Tillie and the store owner continued down her list.

It seemed to Mack as if she bought one of every toy Louis Blomberg had in stock. Mack remembered when the place had been nothing more than a tobacco emporium and Mr. Blomberg would sleep on the floor behind the counter so he'd be handy at any hour of the day. Since then he'd married, had kids, and expanded his place to include sporting goods, a huge selection of children's toys, and a pool hall in the back.

Two middle-aged women entered the store and went straight to a Spalding bicycle on display. "Oh, Sally. Twenty-five dollars. I just don't know."

Her friend took off a glove and ran it across the saddle. "What if we share the cost?"

"But we'd still need knickerbockers and bicycle boots and a bicycle bell."

The jingling door interrupted their conversation. Sloop and the chief of police walked through on their way to the billiard room. Mack stepped farther back into the shadows and pulled the bill of his hat down, pretending absorption with a tobacco pouch for sale.

The men tipped their hats to Tillie and the bicycle women, greeted the proprietor, then disappeared into the pool hall, a snatch of laughter and male voices slipping out as the door opened and closed.

One of the bicycle women stared at the closed door. "I do declare, that Mr. Sloop is surely earning jewels in his heavenly crown."

Her friend looked up. "I know what you mean. Taking care of all those poor indigents day after day. And his wife, too. What a trial it must be."

"I overheard my Charles say Mr. Sloop was hoping to represent Buncombe County in the state's legislature come election time."

Mack stiffened. The state legislature? Sloop was going to run against Leonard Vaughan?

"Well, I shall put in a good word for him to Woodrow. If anyone deserves it, Mr. Sloop does."

Mr. Blomberg approached the women, asking if they had any questions about the bicycle.

Tamping down his irritation, Mack made his way to Tillie, who was flipping through her list. "You find everything?" he asked.

She angled the pages toward him. "I still need three pull toys, a set of tabletop ninepins, a doll, and a collection of wooden animals. Mr. Blomberg's all out of them."

Mack scanned the pages. "I can't help you with the doll, but I can make those other things. Assuming Mrs. Vanderbilt wouldn't mind."

Her eyes lit up. "Can you really?"

"Sure. We'll have to stop by the lumberyard, though."

She smiled, her violet eyes bright, her cheeks flushed, a tiny curl of hair teasing her neck. "Thank you, Mack. We'll go there right after we visit the bookshop."

The bicycle ladies left and Mr. Blomberg rejoined them.

"I guess we have everything," Tillie said, looking at the vast collection covering the counter and a table behind it.

Mr. Blomberg nodded. "It'll take me a little while to pack all this up. Can you come back in a couple of hours?"

"Sure." Mack took her elbow. "Thanks for your help, Louis. We'll be back."

"Happy to do it, Earl. It's good to see you and your brother."

Mack touched his hat, not bothering to correct the man, then led Tillie out the door.

"What about Earl?" she asked.

"He saw some friends and is going to wait here until it's time to go home."

She didn't move.

He offered his arm. "Is the bookstore next?"

Sighing, she gave a longing glance at the mercantile, then took his arm. They strolled down the walkway in silence. Outside the barbershop an old-timer sat beside a couple of other gents, his face holding as many lines as the figure he was whittling. Mack gave him a nod, then continued past.

A fancy surrey with *Noland-Brown Mortuary* emblazoned on its door wheeled down the middle of the street. The turned-out driver in black suit and high celluloid collar looked neither left nor right, but kept his eyes trained on his high-stepping bay. Propped up in the rear seat was a distinguished-looking corpse with a neatly trimmed Vandyke beard and a jaunty hat perched atop his head.

Tillie ground to a halt. "Mack!"

"That's the duke. He's drumming up some business for the undertaker."

She stood rooted, staring in shock. "Good heavens."

He smiled. At least the surprise of the duke had jolted her out of her reserve.

"What were you doing at the orphanage last Sunday?" he asked.

"I'd wanted to see Homer, but he was taking a nap and wasn't going to be finished until almost dark." She glanced at him. "Doesn't that seem like an awfully long nap?"

"My guess is he was wide awake and they just didn't want you to see him."

"But why not?"

"They don't much care for visitors."

She shook her head. "Oh, Mack. I wish you'd not be so judgmental about them. I'm sure they're doing the best they can."

"He beats the girls, Tillie. Why do you defend him?"

She looked up quickly. "You don't know that."

"Are you saying my sister is lying?"

She stopped. "She's said that? She's said those very words?"

"What? That Sloop beats them? Yes. And not only that, she has firsthand knowledge of it. That's why she didn't want to leave her friend. For some reason, he wouldn't bother Irene while Ora Lou was around. But that won't be the case now that she's left."

Tillie paled. "But it doesn't make any sense. I mean, he's gone to such lengths to make a home for the children."

"I know. But facts are facts, and in my experience, men who abuse their power in one area often abuse it in others. I'm not only worried about Irene. I'm worried about all the rest of them, too." What he didn't mention was the concern he held for the older girls. He'd questioned Ora Lou as delicately as he could, and though he was certain the man had left his sister alone, he wasn't as confident about Irene.

Someone jostled Mack from behind, prompting the two of them to continue toward the bookshop.

"If it's really true," she said, "then the police must be notified."

"They have been. I went to them way back in August before I ever even started working at Biltmore."

"What'd they say?"

"They didn't believe me."

She shook her head. "No, I don't suppose they would. They'll have to hear it from someone more important than you or me." She squeezed his arm. "Do you really think he locked that boy in the basement? The one who was supposed to share a room with Homer?"

"I do."

"I just can't believe it." They stopped in front of Bedford's

Books. "We have to do something, Mack. We have to get Homer out of there."

"I've gone over it a thousand times in my head, and I can't think of a single thing to do for him or Irene."

"I hate to think of them up there with a monster like that."

"Me too." He opened the shop door and waited while Tillie made her selections from the list. They were the only patrons in the shop, so he was able to watch her full-on without pretending he wasn't. When her purchases were completed, he picked up the wrapped books, and they headed toward the lumberyard.

"You weren't at the barn gathering," he said.

They moved to the side to let another couple pass. When she didn't answer, he tried again. "Was it because of the parlor games?"

"Partly."

"What's the other part?"

She looked down. "You know why, Mack."

Deciding the middle of the walkway was not the best place to pursue the discussion, he let it go. But they were by no means finished with the subject.

Twenty-three

Mack strode up a tree-bordered carriage road leading to great granite steps which fronted the home of Buncombe County's state representative. Mack had not had a chance to stop in on his father's friend since he'd started at Biltmore. But between the rumor he'd heard about Sloop running for office and the conditions he'd seen at the orphanage, a visit could no longer be put off.

A footman Mack didn't recognize opened the door. He was fairly young and had a chin which went on forever. He looked Mack up and down. "Deliveries go to the back."

He started to close the door, but Mack wedged a foot into the opening. "I'm here to see Leonard Vaughan."

The servant pinched his lips together. "I'm afraid that's impossible."

Mack shoved the door open, forcing the servant back, and stepped inside. A corridor with marble busts, a grandfather clock, two side chairs, and a gas chandelier led to the home's interior.

"You tell him Mackenzie Danver is here. Where do you want me to wait?"

"I'll do nothing of the kind. Now—"

Mack squared his shoulders and took a step forward. "You have to the count of five. Then I'll go find him myself."

The footman straightened his spine. "Over my dead body."

"Have it your way." Mack pushed his way past and followed the sounds of quiet conversation and clinking glasses.

"Here! How dare you!" The footman grabbed his arm.

Mack checked his stride. "I wouldn't advise it. Valuables will break in the scuffle, and your master will be displeased about you refusing entrance to the son of his best friend."

They eyeballed each other. The footman let go, then pointed to a chair in the entryway. "There."

Mack sat. The moment the footman disappeared through a side door, Mack jumped back up and headed down the vast hallway. If he didn't find Mr. Vaughan fast, the servant would return with more footmen—the biggest and the meanest.

He found the representative and his family in the dining room. It was just as he remembered. Though a tiny fraction of the size of Vanderbilt's banquet hall, it was no less opulent. Gilded walls, marble fireplace, thronelike chairs, and stuffed footrests he and Earl had used for pillow fights a lifetime ago.

For a split second, everyone in the room stared at Mack. Mr. and Mrs. Vaughan, their two daughters who'd blossomed into young ladies, and three liveried footmen.

Mack whipped off his hat. "Forgive the intrusion, Mr. Vaughan, but I—"

The footmen sprang to life and immediately caught Mack's arms. He tried to throw them off but could not.

"Stop!" Mr. Vaughan's sharp command caused all to freeze as if they were playing a game of Statues in the parlor. "It's all right. Mr. Danver is a friend."

The footmen released him and Mack tugged his jacket into place.

"Phillip, bring another plate, please."

Mack shook his head. "No, sir. I couldn't intrude. I'll just wait until you're done with your meal."

"Nonsense."

"I insist." He nodded to Mrs. Vaughan and the girls. "Please forgive me. I'm sorry to have disturbed you."

"We won't be much longer, Mr. Danver." The lady of the house, with a warm expression, turned to a waiter. "Show him to the smoking room, Phillip."

Mack stepped into the hallway, anticipation running high at the prospect of entering the smoking room again.

The footman lit three lanterns while Mack stood at the threshold, breathing deeply, enjoying the smell of cigars which clung to the room. A series of images flashed through his mind. His father and Mr. Vaughan surrounded by the leather wall coverings and animal trophies, playing chess at the game table, reclining in the angular armchairs, debating politics over brandy and cigars.

He crossed to the bookshelves to peruse the volumes lined up according to height and color. He'd spent many an hour in this room as a boy—and paid much more attention to the older men's discussions than they'd realized.

"May I pour you a brandy, sir?"

Mack glanced at the footman. "No, thank you. And

I'm sorry about that out there. I know you were just doing your job."

"Sir." Remaining expressionless, the footman backed out of the room.

Moments later, Leonard Vaughan joined him, arm outstretched. "What a wonderful surprise."

Mack clasped his hand. "I'm sorry to have intruded on a Sunday, and in such an abrupt way, but it's my only day off."

"I was happy for an excuse to retire. The women have been talking of nothing but ball gowns and boys. It's enough to drive a man mad."

"They've certainly grown up."

"It's a bit astounding, isn't it? Even to me." Chuckling, he moved to the brandy decanter and splashed brandy into two crystal glasses, then handed one to Mack. "Have a seat and tell me how things are progressing."

Sinking into a brown leather chair, Mack told him of his job at Biltmore. Of Ora Lou's trials at the orphanage. Of Homer's heartrending arrival. Of the squalor. The beatings. The locking-up in the basement. The sparseness of the rooms. And, last, of the fears he held for the older girls.

Vaughan leaned back with legs crossed, elbow on an armrest, his mouth resting on his fist. "Are you sure? As you requested, I myself have been by. The parlor was pristine, as well as Sloop's study. The children looked like what you'd expect."

"Did you venture into the back areas or upstairs? Talk to any of the children without Sloop present?"

"I did not."

Mack didn't say anything.

Vaughan pinched the bridge of his nose. "So what are you suggesting?"

"That Sloop dresses pretty well for an orphanage director."

Vaughan slowly lowered his hand. "You think he's embezzling funds?"

"I don't know. What if we raided the place? Confiscated the ledgers? It'd be pretty clear then what was going on."

"The police would never go along with that. Nor would the townsfolk. Sloop's a hero in their eyes. And with him running against me in the election now, I can't make any accusations without it looking like sour grapes—particularly when I have no proof."

Setting the brandy on the table beside him, Mack voiced what he'd been thinking for a while now. "He needs to be replaced. The only way to completely secure the children's safety is to oust Sloop. But I have no idea who would be willing to take the directorship on. I was hoping maybe you would."

Swinging his foot, Vaughan pursed his lips. "What about you?"

Mack stilled. "Me?"

"Why not?"

"Because, I, well, I wouldn't know the first thing about taking care of all those kids."

"Of course you would. You've been taking care of your siblings since your father died."

"But that's different. I had Ma's help. And then Ora Lou's. Besides, I was planning to build furniture for a living."

"Why?"

He blinked. "Why?"

"Yes. Do you have some grand passion for building furniture?"

"Not at all. It just happens to be the only way I can make a living while simultaneously living on the mountain. Which is another thing—I don't want to live in town."

"What about your brothers?"

"What about them?"

"You just told me watching that boy's father drop him off made you realize leaving Ikey, Otis, and John-John with other families was not the best decision you'd ever made." Breathing deeply, Vaughan looked Mack in the eye. "If you were director of the orphanage, you could go get them and bring them back. Then you'd all be together again."

The idea was so new, so far outside the plans he had, he could hardly even think. "What about living on the mountain?"

Vaughan uncrossed his legs. "You'd have to give that up."

Mack pulled back. "It's my home. I think about it all the time. It's the only place where I have enough room to expand, be my own man . . ." He shrugged. "Breathe."

His father's friend said nothing. And even as Mack said the words, he knew how selfish they sounded. Would he leave Homer, Irene, any of them, to Sloop simply because he wanted elbow room? And what about his own brothers?

He dragged a hand down his face. "I need to think. Pray. Can I get back to you on it?"

"Of course."

They sat in silence as Mack continued to gather his equilibrium. "Do you even think I have a chance at it? Why would they replace Sloop with some highlander like me?"

"Because even though the chief and Sloop are close friends, when the cards are down, the chief is a good, honest man. He won't take the welfare of those kids lightly—orphans or no."

Vaughan swirled the brandy in his glass. "No, the biggest hurdle I see is you aren't married. Right?"

"Not yet."

He raised his brows. "You've someone in mind?"

"She's a maid at Biltmore. Right now, she's a bit resistant to the idea of leaving. I expect her to come around, though."

"Well, directors have to be married. How long before she'll agree, do you think?"

"I don't know."

Finishing off his drink, Vaughan set the glass down. "Well, see what you can do to speed that up. Meanwhile, we need someone to keep a closer eye on Sloop." He shifted his gaze to a corner of the room and stared unseeing at a collection of antique firearms inside a glass case. "What if in the interim, I arranged for you to be a useful man at the orphanage?"

Mack straightened. "Do you think you could?"

"I know I could. The building is an eyesore, and I made sure it was discussed at length at the last county meeting, though mostly because I've been trying to draw attention to the place since you and I talked back in August."

"Sloop would never agree to having me there."

"Sloop won't have a choice. We appoint the positions, not him. We can't pay you anything near what you're making at Biltmore, though."

"That's all right. Now that Ora Lou has work, it's eased much of the burden. And if this really happens and the boys can join me, well, then, I don't really need the kind of income I make there."

Vaughan nodded. "I'll get the ball rolling first thing tomorrow. When's your next day off?"

"Two weeks from today."

"Come back then. But this time, I insist you join us for dinner."

Mack stood. "Thank you, sir."

"My pleasure. Now, tell me what you've done with Ora Lou."

"She's at Mrs. Getty's Boarding House and does scullery at the New York Café."

"Well, you bring her and your little lady along to dinner, as well."

"I'll do my best, sir, and thank you again."

∞

"I won't allow it. Absolutely not."

Vaughan sat in the parlor of the orphanage with Chief Pilkerton and watched Sloop pace, his eyes furious, his cheeks mottled.

"The man broke my nose, Zachary. You can't seriously expect me to have him underfoot all the time."

Pilkerton held up his hands. "There's nothing I can do, Forbus. The council appointed the position."

"Under whose recommendation?"

Vaughan leaned back in his chair. "Mine."

Sloop seared him with his gaze. "Why?"

"Because I've known him since he was a boy, and he's as fine a man as they come."

"He broke my nose!"

"Which I find very troubling—particularly since I know Mackenzie to be a bit overprotective of the underdog. Just what was it you did, I wonder, to provoke such a reaction out of him, Mr. Sloop?"

The director exploded. "How should I know? The man's a loose cannon."

"Perhaps we should invite him and his sister here to tell the three of us just exactly what that fight was about."

A touch of caution entered Sloop's eye.

"What was it about?" the chief asked. "Vaughan claims Danver was protecting his sister."

"Preposterous! Do you see what I mean? The man's touched." Sloop tapped the side of his head as if to demonstrate Mack's lack of mental capabilities.

"Either way, there's nothing you or I can do." Pilkerton sighed. "The council has appointed Danver useful man for the orphanage. But he'll be under your authority, Forbus. I did see to that."

Though Sloop was still clearly upset, the idea of having Mack under his thumb mollified him somewhat.

Rising, Vaughan shook Sloop's hand. "I have another appointment at the moment, but next time I believe I'd like a tour of the back portion of the facilities."

Sloop sputtered and started to protest.

Vaughan quickly put on his hat, cutting the director off. "Good day, Sloop. I'll be in touch."

Twenty-four

Tillie wrapped a piece of twine around a bouquet of tea roses and maidenhair fern. Bringing it to her nose, she inhaled, the aroma reminding her of a freshly opened box of the choicest tea.

Arranging flowers was one of her favorite parts of being head parlormaid. Once the gardeners found Mrs. Vanderbilt was partial to tea roses, they began appearing with much more frequency.

Tillie tucked the cluster into a larger arrangement, then stood back to eye it critically. The delicate blooms blended together like the first rays of dawn with tones of gold, warm pink, and rose. Grabbing scissors from the worktable, she trimmed a fern that was poking out a little too far.

"Mr. Sterling said you needed help carrying the flowers upstairs."

She spun around. Mack filled the entire doorway. He'd

loosened his collar, rolled up his sleeves, and unbuttoned the first two buttons of his shirt. Try as they might, no one could convince him to wear his clothes the proper way.

"You can't go upstairs looking like that," she said, hoping he couldn't see the hubbub he'd created within her simply by appearing at her work door.

He rolled down a sleeve. "I'm leaving, Tillie."

"I hadn't heard Mrs. Vanderbilt was going out. Where are you going?"

"No, I mean I'm quitting."

She slowly placed the scissors on the table. "Quitting? You mean, Biltmore? You're quitting Biltmore?"

"Yes." Lifting his chin, he buttoned his shirt and adjusted his collar.

"But why?"

"I'm going to be useful man for the orphanage."

She shook her head. "I don't . . . what about . . . where will . . ." She looked around the workroom at the wire, twine, and five arrangements she'd been working on for the past hour.

"I'd like you to come with me," he said.

Her gaze flew back to his. "Go with you?"

Stepping inside, he closed the door.

"What are you doing? Open that back up. We can't be in here alone."

He skirted the table. She scuffled backward. But there was nowhere to run.

When she'd backed herself into the corner, he braced his hands on either side of her head. "Marry me."

The smell of man, starch, and determination enveloped her.

"I've already told you, I—"

He kissed her. Not a hard, demanding kiss, but one as soft and delicate as one of her tea roses.

"Marry me."

"I—"

He kissed her again, his knuckles grazing her jaw, her neck, her collarbone. He allowed a hairsbreadth of space between them, but only long enough to repeat his entreaty. "Marry me."

He again sought her lips with gentle, persuasive touches, which she found much more devastating than when he released his full passion upon her.

Groping for her hand, he found it and brought it to his cheek. "Marry me."

He angled his head, continuing to coax a response from her.

Breathless and confused, she rested her other hand on his shoulder, then crinkled his shirt with her fist. "You can't leave. Please don't leave."

He spoke against her lips. "Come with me."

"But I—"

He kissed her more urgently, his body tight against hers, then pulled his head back. "Don't say no. You can't say no. Because I'm really leaving. Today. And I want to leave knowing you'll be mine, just as soon as we can arrange it."

An ache, deep and sharp, gripped her beneath the rib cage. "Why, why?"

"Because I love you." He drew her to him, running his hands along her back and shoulders and arms, every allowable inch. "Do you love me? Do you?"

She squeezed his shoulders. *Yes. Yes.*

But she didn't answer.

He tipped up her chin with his thumbs. "Do you, Tillie? Do you love me even a little?"

Tears rose swiftly, threatening to spill. "You know I do," she whispered.

"Then marry me." He bracketed her face, kissing the moisture from one eye and then the other, before lifting her to him like a seedling bursting from the soil in search of the sun's warming gaze.

She molded herself against him, encircling his neck, kissing him back with all the love and passion she felt. Because she knew this would be the very last time they'd ever share this sweet, wonderful, breathtaking intimacy.

She drove her fingers into his hair. Ah, that thick, wonderful hair. She pressed her body against his, trying to absorb him, trying to steal some of his very essence and keep it stored within her heart.

He flipped them around, so he was in the corner and she was on the outside. He broke the kiss. "Does that mean yes? Are you saying—?"

She silenced him with her mouth, taking full advantage of her new position as she freely ran her hands along his face, his neck, his shoulders, his arms, his chest, his waist, wishing now he hadn't buttoned himself all up.

He let her have her way, then suddenly squeezed her in a vise grip she thought would surely break her in two.

And that's when her tears began to flow, salting their kisses.

He lifted his face. "Why are you crying?"

She looked into the brown eyes she'd come to care for so very, very much. She ran her fingers along his eyebrows and nose. She outlined his lips. Cataloging, memorizing, archiving.

He circled her wrist, then kissed her palm. "Why are you crying?"

Her throat wouldn't work.

A look of wariness entered his eyes. "Why are you crying, Tillie?"

"I can't marry you."

He increased the pressure on her waist. "You can. How can you even think of walking away from this?"

"I'm not the one walking away. *You* are."

He stared at her, shock and hurt slowly turning into anger. "What do you expect me to do? Continue to steal kisses? For what? The next twenty years? Is that what you expect?"

She shook her head, sobbing now. "Yes. No. I don't know."

He took her by both arms, his eyes impaling hers. "Listen to me. I'm leaving. I'm going to do what I can to ease the lives of those orphans. I want you to come with me. But whether you do or you don't, I'm going." He held her at arms' length.

She couldn't see him clearly, so blurred was her vision. She swiped her eyes, then wished she hadn't. His expression was fierce.

Gathering her emotions and courage, she stepped free of him. "Good-bye, Mack. I'm sorry."

He stiffened. A deep, horrible hurt flashed briefly in his eyes, before it was replaced with barely banked fury.

Reaching into his pocket, he withdrew a pouch of coins and plunked it onto the table. "Here's the money Winter docked from your pay for the crystal I broke."

"No, Mack. I don't—"

He wrenched open the door. "Carry your own flowers."

And then, he was gone.

∞

Nothing was the same without him. Not the mornings without his quiet presence on the terrace, his thoughtfulness in moving the furniture without being asked, his economy of movement as he swept the vestibule with quick, sure strokes.

Not the afternoons when she used to discover him repairing or tinkering with some stuck window or a machine that didn't run. Or his uncanny ability to know which fires needed tending before the November air made the rooms uncomfortable.

Not even the sorting and wrapping of Christmas toys lifted her spirits, for every one reminded her of the day they'd spent buying them. She wondered now where she would get the wooden toys he'd not yet made. He'd completed the pull toys and the ninepins, but not the collection of wooden animals her little brothers were to receive.

Last evening she'd caught sight of Earl from behind, and for the flicker of a second, before she realized it wasn't Mack, her heart took wing. Then he turned, and her misery was even worse than it had been before.

She sat now in the seamstress's room inserting fresh ribbons into a corset cover of Mrs. Vanderbilt's. Beside her was a carefully folded stack of lingerie that had loose buttons or ripped edges of lace. She no longer felt the awe she once did at handling such fine underwear trimmed with French needlework and exquisite embellishments, marveling that such beauty would be all covered up where no one would even see.

Instead it became more like work. Less and less like a privilege. The never-ending pile of repairs multiplied with each new day. The constant brushing and making over of Mrs. Vanderbilt's garments required more hours than would ever be available.

Worst of all, the monotony of the tasks failed to challenge or occupy her mind. Which left far too many hours for her to mull over the what-ifs, the what-had-beens, and the what-could-bes.

She wondered what Mack was doing and which project he'd taken on first at the orphanage. If he butted heads with the Sloops. If he interacted with the children. If he'd collected his little brothers. If Irene was all right. If Mack's presence tempered the beatings. If Homer was adjusting. If Mack thought of her as much as she thought of him.

Pulling the ribbon through the last insert, she cut the end, tied it into a delicate bow, folded the corset cover, and then began repairing frilly trim that edged a pair of drawers.

One by one, she reviewed the warnings her mother had given her about Hazel Creek men. Reminded herself of all the good she could do for her family and the less fortunate. All the things she could accomplish and see. Recalled how long she'd prepared for this opportunity. And tried to convince herself she'd made the right decision.

Twenty-five

The first thing Mack did was clean up the yard. He left the larger pieces of rusted farm equipment, hauled off the smaller stuff, and built a fire to burn everything else. But no matter how hard he worked, how busy he stayed, he could not erase thoughts of Tillie.

Like a miser recounting his money, he meticulously reviewed every conversation they'd had on the terrace. Her expression of regret at not being able to finish school. Her desire to make her parents proud and to be the big toad. Her yawns when she'd stayed up late reading. Her rants over footmen being paid higher wages for less work. Her passion for those in need. Her refusal to give up her job.

Humiliation welled up inside him. He'd been thrown over for a job. A job which looked glamorous from the outside, but was a life of toil from the inside. Why couldn't she see that?

But he knew it was more than the job. It was a dream, too. Something her mother had always wanted for her. And Tillie genuinely felt responsible for her family, the poor, the world at large. How was he supposed to fight that?

He couldn't. So he'd let her go. He'd given her over to the only One who could open her eyes and make her see. If He wanted the two of them together, He could make it happen. In the meanwhile, Mack had no choice but to move on.

Since he'd only worked outside the building, he'd yet to have much contact with the orphans or even Sloop. But this evening, when supper was over, a handful of children trickled out, drawn by the blaze. By the time full dark had set in, they'd circled round like a hunting party seeking the comfort of a campfire.

Settling himself on a giant log, he pulled out his knife and began to whittle.

"Whatcha doin'?" Homer rested his little hands on Mack's thigh and peered over his arm. The boy was normally quiet and withdrawn, but he had an insatiable curiosity. And the bond he and Mack had shared that first day had broken down some of the barriers Homer still kept between himself and the others.

"I'm whittling."

"Whittlin' what?"

"A horse."

He pressed closer. "Who's it fer?"

"A lady asked me to make it." Mack glanced up, assuring himself no one crept too close to the fire.

Out by a monkey cigar tree a group of older boys snapped off the ends of its long beanlike pods and lit them, then pretended to smoke. Two girls around ten years of age sat on the ground to the right of Mack, their knees tucked beneath their dresses.

The fire baked their young faces and turned their blond braids to the color of dried wheat. They took turns reciting each chapter from Matthew in preparation for an exam on the morrow. They were on the twentieth chapter.

A pebble sailed out of the darkness, striking one of them on the shoulder.

The girl didn't flinch or turn around but merely rubbed the offending spot. "Stop it, Clyde . . . 'Now as they went out of Jericho, a great multitude followed Him. . . .' "

A few minutes later, another rock breezed past her ear.

Mack scanned the shadows. The culprit made no effort to hide himself. Once he found a suitable missile, he brought it to his lips, then sent it flying. This one caught her in the middle of the back.

With a great sigh, she twisted to look over her shoulder. "I don't like you, Clyde. I'll never like you. No matter how many of those rocks you kiss and throw at me. Now leave me alone . . . 'So Jesus had compassion and touched their eyes. And immediately . . .' "

Clyde's shoulders wilted. Kicking the ground, he shuffled away. A well of empathy for the boy sprung up in Mack.

He pulled his attention back to his carving. "Have you memorized the book of Matthew?" he asked Homer.

"Not all of it. And I've gotten two whuppin's so far."

"Because you didn't know your verses?"

"Yep." Homer scratched his leg. "But that ain't nothin' compared to Irene. She gets the most outta ever'body. Mr. Sloop picks on her somethin' fierce."

Mack scanned the circle. "Where is Irene?"

"Doing her prayer book. Only the ones what didn't get whupped today got to come outside."

Mack counted the children. Five by the tree. Six around the fire. One sulking in the shadows. About half of the boarders. He sighed. There must have been a lot of whippings today.

The door opened and Sloop headed toward them, a coiled rope on his shoulder. Homer skittered off. The girls froze. The boys extinguished their fake cigars.

Sloop had treated Mack with barely restrained tolerance. He'd warned Mack to steer clear or he'd go to whatever lengths were needed to see that Mack lost his job.

Mack had no doubt the man meant it. And from what Vaughan told him, it wouldn't take much. The council had taken a great deal of convincing, and Mack's appointment had been passed by the narrowest of margins.

"You cannot touch Sloop," Vaughan had cautioned. "No matter what he does."

"But even the Scriptures are on my side," Mack had argued. "I can cite verse after verse where we're commanded to defend the fatherless and save them from the hand of the wicked."

"That may be so, but you have to remember neither the council nor the townspeople view Sloop as 'wicked.' Quite the contrary. And your fisticuffs are actually hindering your cause rather than helping."

Mack stared at him, aghast. "So I'm just supposed to stand there and do nothing?"

"That's not what I said, son. I said you can't use your fists. Besides, for every Scripture you could recite on defending the fatherless, I could respond with a verse on pursuing peace."

"Peace," Mack scoffed. "While he's beating defenseless children?"

"I'm just saying, when you attack Sloop it appears *you* are the problem, not him."

"So just what do you suggest I do?"

Vaughan's expression gentled. "Recognize that the problem is much deeper and bigger than you or even Sloop. And give God a little credit. He doesn't need your fists to bring Sloop down. He needs your cooperation. So intercede with prayer and petition, trust in the Lord, and keep your eyes open and your hands behind your back."

Sloop plunked the rope at Mack's feet, recapturing his attention.

"This is all I could find, Danver. Now that you have it, see to it you clear the rest of the property by close of day tomorrow."

Closing his pocketknife, Mack set it and the wooden animal aside, then picked up an end of the rope. It was twisted manila hemp. Strong, sturdy, and plenty long. The ends were unraveled, but that was easily fixed.

Sloop looked over the children. "Just a few more minutes, then it will be time for roll to be called, prayers to be read, and preparations for bed to be made."

"Yes, Mr. Sloop," they singsonged.

He returned to the building.

Mack fingered the rope, then separated its three unraveled strands and tied a crown knot.

"Whatcha doin'?" Homer asked, returning to the position he'd taken up earlier.

"I'm finishing off the end so it'll quit unraveling." Mack turned the cord so the boy could see. "You start off with a knot like this and snug it down, then you take a strand and go over and under."

He wove a couple through, then offered it to Homer. "You want to try?"

Eyes widening, the boy glanced at the door Sloop had disappeared behind, then took the rope in his hands.

Mack lifted a strand. "Okay now, take this end and tuck it under that coil."

Homer needed help loosing the twisted skeins, but was then able to tuck the strand under and pull it through on his own.

"That's the way. Do the same thing with the next strand. Over and under."

"Which one?"

"Doesn't matter which order."

Again, the boy didn't have the strength to separate the coil.

"Here, Homer. I'll help ya." The boy who'd thrown rocks wedged his finger in between two tight twists and made an opening.

Mack glanced up. All the boys had gathered to watch.

"Can I try it?" It was one of the pretend smokers.

Homer handed him the rope.

"How many times do we weave it through?"

"Three times," Mack answered. "Then we'll need to split the ends in half and make one more pass."

The boys each took turns, some with tongues held tight between their teeth, others with frowns between their brows. When the back splicing was complete, they ran their fingers over the rope, marveling at the tidy ends.

Such a simple thing. Something as second nature to Mack as walking. Yet none of these boys had ever been taught.

He let them do the other end, then taught them how to tie a figure eight knot. "Once you learn this one, you can use it for more complicated knots."

Before they all had a chance to practice it, Mrs. Sloop rang the bell. The children jumped, dropped everything, and hurried to do her bidding.

"Night, mister!" they hollered.

Watching them go, he realized they didn't even know his name, nor he theirs.

Cool temperatures reminded Mack that Christmas wouldn't be too long in coming. The sharp, heavy smell of coal fires from chimneys throughout town mingled with the wood fires from the orphanage.

Mack handed out fly swatters and empty jelly jars to the boys in the yard. "Now I want you to go all through the building and kill as many flies as you can, then put them in your jar. Whoever kills the most by the end of the week will get a licorice stick."

Thus armed, the boys charged inside to fulfill their mission, Artie in the lead. Mack hadn't known what to expect from the teener who shared a room with Homer and had been locked in the basement, but never did he imagine the boy's zest for life. He had a bent for practical jokes and often acted as the Pied Piper for the rest of the crew, leading them into all kinds of mischief.

Though his face was youthful, his arms and legs had out-grown the rest of him. He'd be as tall as Mack in a few more years. What had endeared him to Mack the most, though, was the youth's dogged determination to take Homer under his wing. Unfortunately, the thing which never failed to draw Homer out was the participation in a bit of tomfoolery.

Mack had followed their sound of laughter one afternoon only to find the two of them sitting in the washroom spitting at the ceiling. Artie was quite proficient and could make his spittle stick to the ceiling. But when Homer tried, he ended up with a mess all over his face and shoulders. One look at Homer's sparkling eyes, though, and the scolding on Mack's lips died a sudden death.

Another time, Mack had been repairing the roof when he saw Artie creep into the yard below the schoolroom's window, smear strawberry jam on his face and chest, then lie down as if he'd just been shot on a battlefield and had the blood to prove it.

As Mack had prepared to holler down and ask him what the blazes he was doing, pandemonium broke out in the school-room. "Mrs. Sloop! Mrs. Sloop!" Homer had hollered. "Artie's done jumped out the winder!"

Chuckling at the memory and marveling at how far Homer had come, Mack listened to the cries of victory inside as the boys hit their buzzing targets. The back door opened and little Becca, a thin ten-year-old with dull red braids and freckles, shuffled toward the outhouse.

His smile faded. The boys might find themselves the recipi-ents of a swat or two during the course of a day, but the girls silently suffered Sloop's fists. Never when Mack was around. Only in the after-work hours. It was Artie who'd confirmed Mack's suspicion.

"You two are awfully subdued this morning," Mack had told the boy yesterday as he pumped water for the pail he and Becca were filling.

"Sloop was prowling last night."

"Prowling? What do you mean?"

"Show Mr. Danver yer knee, Becca."

Setting down her pail, Becca hitched up her hem and pulled down her ragged stocking to reveal a swollen and severely bruised knee.

Artie tightened his lips. "She gots lots more, don't ya?"

Drawing up her stocking without the least show of modesty, she nodded, picked up her pail, and finished filling it with water.

The sound of a carriage pulled Mack back into the present. Glancing down the street, he saw the Vanderbilt landau making its way up the hill, Earl in the driver's seat. Its top had been folded down, making no allowance for the nip in the air.

Chest tightening, Mack scanned the interior of the vehicle for Tillie but could only see Mr. Vanderbilt. A moment more and it was clear the owner of Biltmore was traveling alone.

Earl pulled into the packed-dirt yard, then jumped down to open the door for his master.

Mack had rarely seen Vanderbilt up close and had never spoken to him. He was a tall, thin, unassuming man with ordinary hair and ordinary features. He wore a simple clay worsted coat. If it hadn't been for the landau, no one would ever suspect he was worth millions.

Vanderbilt smiled and offered Mack a hand. "Danver. Good to see you."

Mack clasped it. "Sir."

"My wife was sorely disappointed to lose you."

"Thank you, sir."

Vanderbilt ran his gaze over the property. "I hear you've been hard at it. The place is really coming along."

"Thank you, sir."

He gave him a sideways glance. "I don't suppose I could talk you into coming back?"

"I'm needed here, sir."

"Of course you are." He tugged his gloves on more tightly. "The reason I came by is Mrs. Vanderbilt asked me to see if you would still carve the wooden animals she was hoping to give the Reese boys at Christmas."

Mack nodded. "I haven't forgotten. I've made a few already, but it will be a while before I finish them all."

"Excellent, excellent. I brought you some tools, just to make sure you had everything you needed."

Earl removed a box from the landau.

Releasing its latch, Vanderbilt lifted the lid. "Since I had Earl with me, I was able to find a knife that would fit your hand."

Fit his hand? He'd bought a knife specifically for Mack? He glanced at his brother, then the box. Inside was not only a knife, but five different blades, a sharpening block, a strop, a set of palm chisels, and an assortment of gouges, rasps, and sanding sticks.

He picked up the knife. Its walnut handle was well balanced and comfortable. Never had he used one so fine. "Thank you, sir. I'll take good care of these and be sure to return everything when I'm done."

"No need for that. It would just sit on some shelf collecting dust. Besides, I thought you might want to teach the boys here how to whittle."

Mack blinked. "I imagine I could."

"And so you should." He again assessed the newly replaced

windows and repaired roof, then clapped Mack on the shoulder. "It's a good thing you're doing. And if you take time to share your knowledge with the boys, it'll give them much more than a skill. It'll give them hope."

Mack stared at him, somewhat abashed to realize it hadn't occurred to him to tutor the boys. Yet there was so much he could teach them. Not just whittling and knot tying, but how to use a hammer. How to dovetail wood. How to clean a chimney. Repair a fence. The possibilities were endless.

Closing the lid, Vanderbilt handed him the box. "Just send the bill to me for the toys and we'll square up."

"These tools are payment plenty, sir."

"The tools are a gift, Danver. You send that bill when—"

The front door burst open, then slammed behind Homer. "Lookit, Mr. Danver! Lookit here!"

He raced toward them, fly swatter in one hand, jar in another. "Look how many I done killed already!"

Mack steadied the boy with a hand on the shoulder. "Say hello to Mr. Vanderbilt, Homer."

The boy glanced up at Vanderbilt, then eased into Mack's side a bit. "How do, sir." When he saw Earl, his eyes widened. "Mr. Danver," he whispered, tugging on Mack's jacket. "That feller done stole yer looks."

"This is my twin brother."

Homer stared at Earl as if he were the two-headed man at a circus act.

"What have you got there, young man?" Vanderbilt asked, drawing the boy's attention.

Homer's excitement over the contest made him forget his shyness. He held up his jar, littered with a layer of dead flies. "Mr. Danver's havin' a Swat That Fly contest. Whoever kills the most gets a licorice stick! Want me to get ya a swatter and jar so you can have a chance?"

Before Vanderbilt could answer, the door opened and Sloop hurried out. "Homer Nash, get to your lessons."

Starting, the boy hid the swatter and jar behind his back. "Yes, sir."

He made a wide circle around Sloop, then raced inside.

"Mr. Vanderbilt, I'm so sorry you were kept waiting. I didn't know you were coming." Sloop scowled at Mack. "See to your business, Danver."

He gave a nod, then turned to Vanderbilt. "Thank you again, sir."

"Any time. Just let me know if you need anything else. Paint, perhaps? Would you like some paint?"

"That would finish them off nicely, sir."

"Consider it done."

Sloop adjusted the cuffs of his jacket. "Actually, Mr. Vanderbilt, I handle all the acquisitions."

Vanderbilt held out a hand to the director. "Good to see you, Sloop. I came to ask Danver if he would do a little side job for me. I hope that is acceptable to you?"

"Certainly, certainly." He waved a hand toward the orphanage. "Do you have time for a drink?"

After a slight hesitation, Vanderbilt accompanied Sloop inside.

"Swat That Fly?" Earl asked, as soon as the door had closed behind them.

"It's as bad as a biblical plague in there. Blomberg over at the emporium donated the swatters and the licorice stick."

Earl surveyed the yard and building. "How're you liking it here?"

"I'm going crazy, Earl."

"Already? You've not even been back in town a month."

Removing his hat, Mack tunneled a hand through his hair. "I know, but I'm feeling hemmed in anyway, wishing I was back on the mountain. Biltmore was bad enough, but at least it was out in open country. But here . . ." He looked at the vacant buildings crowding the street and the gray smoke hovering like a cloud over town. "It's enough to drive a man to Bedlam."

"So quit. Go home. There's nothing to stop you. Ora Lou has a job, so she can take care of herself now."

Mack sighed. "I know, but it feels almost irresponsible to leave these kids here with Sloop. And the missus is just as bad, if not worse."

"They're just orphans."

Mack tightened his jaw. "So are we."

"And we're doing just fine."

"Just fine?" Mack huffed. "We pawned off our flesh and blood to neighbors we hardly know and never see. How is that just fine?"

Earl cocked his head. "What's the matter with you?"

Mack again scanned the buildings on the street, cursing civilization and man's desire to make his mark. What was wrong with looking out your window and seeing nothing but God's green earth?

"I'm feeling guilty about Ikey, Otis, and John-John," Mack said finally. "But at least they're still on the mountain with individual families. They'll do for the time being. But these kids?" He waved a hand toward the orphanage. "I'm finding I can't simply walk off and leave them."

"You're just one person, Mack. You can't take on the whole world."

Mack turned a steady gaze onto his brother. "No, but I can take on one orphanage."

∞

Tillie pulled her jacket tighter about her, though it wasn't the chill in the air that had her shivering. It was the prospect of seeing Mack. She'd been sent to town on errands, one of which was to take him paints for the wooden toys he was carving. If Earl had been driving, she would've had him deliver the paints.

But Charlie, the coachman who'd broken his arm, had healed. Today's jaunt to Asheville was his first trip since returning to duty and the cold air had made his bones ache. The man was in so much pain, he insisted on staying in the driver's seat, forcing her to enter the orphanage unescorted.

The closer she drew, the more anxious she became. She wanted to see Mack. Had missed him more than she thought possible. Yet nothing had changed. She wasn't going to quit her job, or marry him.

Regardless of what he'd said, the things she did served the greater good. She didn't owe him or anyone else justifications for her decision.

Squeals of laughter drew her attention to the side yard of the orphanage. The children were lined up beside a merry-go-round of sorts.

A tall pole had been sunk into the ground. A large wagon wheel lay secured on top, like an umbrella. Attached to the wheel's rim were ropes of varying lengths. The children took hold of the ropes and ran around the pole, causing the wheel to rotate. Before long the wheel turned so fast, the ropes lifted them clean off their feet, swinging them in the air.

She scanned the crowd and spotted Homer, but not Mack.

The yard was immaculate. The building in good repair. The windows set to rights. The roof held spots of bright new shingles.

She veered toward the children. None wore coats. A few of the boys were barefoot. She stopped next to a young girl standing at the end of the line. Her cheeks were sunken. Her red braids lackluster.

"Excuse me."

The girl looked up, then edged closer to the boy beside her. He glanced over his shoulder at Tillie. "Who're you?"

"I'm looking for the useful man. Do you know where I might find him?"

"Mr. Danver?" he asked. "He's in the shed."

She started to ask where that was when she spotted Homer again. Smiling, she caught up to him. "Hello. Remember me?"

A wide smile crossed his face. "You came. I didn't think ya would."

He looked wonderful, though she could still see a bit of melancholy in his eyes. Squatting down, she took his hand. "I came the very next Sunday, but Mrs. Sloop said you were napping and wouldn't be up until dark."

"Napping?" He shook his head. "Nobody naps round here. Not even on Sundays."

"You don't?" So Mack was right. "What about the babies?"

"Ain't no babies here. Mrs. Sloop don't allow 'em. Says they're too much trouble." He tilted his head. "How come you didn't come see me all them other Sundays?"

She swallowed. "I only get every other Sunday off, and lately I've had a lot of extra work and wasn't able to make it to town."

Mack's prediction about the lack of freedom she would

have as lady's maid rang in her head. She pushed it aside. Things would settle down after Christmas.

"I see you have a new merry-go-round," she said.

"Yep. Mr. Danver let us help him build it. We used a bunch o' stuff he collected from the yard. But he only had one rope and wouldn't let us use it."

The group at the swings lifted into the air, shrieking with delight.

"Where did you get the ropes, then?" she asked.

"From the graveyard. They had some old ones they used fer lowerin' the pine boxes with, but they don't need 'em no more on account as they always have to have new ones. Folks don't like it if they drop the dead people into the holes. They want 'em lowered real slow-like."

She bit her cheek. "I imagine they do. Where's Mr. Danver?"

"In the shed round back."

The wheel slowed to a stop, the children let go of the ropes, and the next bunch rushed in.

"That's me!" Homer said. "Gotta go."

She watched for a moment until his little legs lifted off the ground, his grin wide, revealing a missing lower tooth.

Waving good-bye, she headed to the backyard.

The newly constructed shed was not much bigger than a side-by-side outhouse. The door stood open, soft lantern light glowing within.

She caught sight of Mack polishing something small with a rag. A rush of feelings ran through her, not the least of which was her reaction to the final kiss they'd shared.

Gathering herself together, she stepped up to the entryway. "Hello."

He swung around, flinging whatever it was he'd been

polishing across the room and bumping his hip into the edge of the table. It teetered, then settled back onto its feet.

The two of them stood, he inside, she at the threshold, doing no more than absorbing the sight of the other. His skin had taken on a golden hue only hours in the sun could cause. His hair needed cutting. His shirt, ironing.

She lifted the bag in her hand. "I brought you some paint and an assortment of brushes."

He made no move to take them.

She stepped inside and set them on the table, the glass bottles clinking. "The place looks nice. You've been busy."

Still he said nothing, so she allowed her gaze to wander the shed, noting how everything had a proper place. A rake with a few prongs missing. A shovel with a rusted spade. A coiled rope with backspliced ends.

Her eyes returned to his big brown ones.

"Homer says you helped them build that merry-go-round out there," she said.

Snapping out of his daze, he glanced toward the front yard as if he could see through the walls. "Yeah. I've, um, I've shown them how to do a lot of things, actually."

"Have you?" She smiled. "They must love that."

"The boys do, but the girls . . ." A pained expression crossed his face. "I'm of no help at all to the girls."

"I'm sure Mrs. Sloop sees to them."

"She doesn't." He tossed the cloth on the table. "You'd think she'd have them cook and clean and sew and all that stuff. But they don't do any of those things. They just do lesson after lesson, spend hours on their knees saying prayers and memorizing their Bibles, then start all over again the next day."

"Then who cooks and sews and cleans for them?"

"Nobody."

She frowned. "They have to eat, Mack."

"Well, yes, of course. There's an old gal who comes in and cooks and the girls do scullery for her. But nobody cleans their bedding or darns or any of that stuff."

The filth she'd glimpsed before flashed through her mind. She pictured Homer's room without so much as a pitcher or washbasin. "How's Ora Lou? Have you seen her?"

"I've seen her, and she's fine." His lips thinned. "I can't say the same for Irene, though. Whatever Sloop's doing to her and the other girls, he does it when I'm gone at night."

She pulled back. "You aren't suggesting he . . ."

"If he is, no one's talking. But he's definitely beating them. Sometimes with straps. Sometimes with switches. Sometimes with his fists. But never when I'm around to catch him. And he refuses to let me sleep here."

"Is Irene doing anything to anger him?"

"Hardly." He scoffed. "The girl's afraid of her own shadow. And it's not just her, it's most all the girls."

She crossed her arms, hugging them close. "Isn't there something that can be done? Someone to go to?"

"There's only one thing I know of."

"What?"

"Replace him."

"With who?"

"With me."

Slowly straightening, her mouth fell open. "Can you? Will they let you?"

"Yes. Under one condition."

"What?"

"That I have a wife."

Her breath caught. "A wife?"

"The director is required to be married. If I don't have a

wife, then I can't replace him. And I'm the only man in town who wants the job. So unless I marry, there is nothing that can be done."

She lowered her gaze, looking at the tips of her scuffed shoes peeking from beneath her skirt. His boots stepped into her vision. The smell of wood and hard work assailed her.

"If we were married," he said softly, "we could oust him and clean this pigsty and stop the beatings and grow a garden and get some chickens and teach the children skills and give them a chance to make something of themselves before they leave."

Her heart hammered within her breast. She didn't dare look up.

"We could also go get my little brothers and bring them and Ora Lou here. Then my family would be back together. All except for Earl, that is."

She lifted her gaze then. "You'd give up the mountain to live in the city?"

"I would."

She didn't know what to say.

Slowly, the intensity in his eyes dimmed, replaced instead with resignation. "You'd better run, Tillie. Run back to Biltmore. To the dangling carrot of pretty dresses, world travel, and a room with a fire."

Stumbling back a step, she frowned. "That's not fair. It's more than that and you know it."

He leaned a hip against the table. "Maybe. But do you honestly believe you can do more good at Biltmore than here at the orphanage with me?"

"Don't judge what I do, Mack. Every part of Christ's body has its job. Don't belittle mine simply because it's not yours."

Sighing, he looked around, picked up a hinge off the floor, and started to polish it. "Thanks for the paints. I'll have those toys for you to wrap by a week from Friday."

"Mack—"

"Good-bye, Tillie."

Stung, she spun around and hurried from the shed.

Twenty-seven

Tillie stepped into the Oak Sitting Room surprised to see Mrs. Winter at the table alongside their mistress.

"Come in, Tillie," Mrs. Vanderbilt said. "Mrs. Winter and I were just talking about you."

She recognized the morning dress Mrs. Vanderbilt wore. It was a simple but elegant cut of wool, and Tillie had replaced some buttons along the back and reinforced its side seams.

Mrs. Vanderbilt slipped her pen into a holder. "We've both been suitably pleased and impressed with your performance. Bénédicte will be leaving come the new year and so I will need to make a decision soon. The two of us thought it would be a good idea for you to take over my morning toilet for a while and see how you do."

A thrill rushed through her. "Thank you, ma'am."

"It would mean giving up your morning parlormaid duties

on the first floor. Who would you recommend to step into your place as head parlormaid during those hours?"

"Alice Breeding would do very nicely, I think, ma'am."

"Very well. I'll take her into consideration." She straightened a stack of papers in front of her. "How are the Christmas gifts coming along?"

"Everything is purchased, wrapped, and labeled except for the wooden animals from Mack Danver. He expects to have those finished a week from Friday."

"Very good. You'll need to pick them up when they are ready."

Tillie kept her expression carefully blank. "Yes, ma'am."

"Mr. Vanderbilt and I will select a Christmas tree this week. I'd like you to oversee the decorating of it, along with all the holiday decorations throughout the house."

Tillie sucked in a quick breath. Mr. Vanderbilt always set a towering Fraser fir in the Banquet Hall. She'd long admired the exquisite ornaments and trim but had never handled them before. "It would be my pleasure, ma'am."

"Excellent. Just let Mrs. Winter know what members of the staff you would like to help you, and all will be arranged."

"Thank you, ma'am."

"You're welcome." She gave a nod of dismissal.

Tillie hesitated.

Mrs. Vanderbilt lifted her brows. "Was there something on your mind?"

"Actually, ma'am, there was."

"What is it?"

"When I delivered those paints to Mack Danver last week, it came to my attention that the orphan girls are not being taught any skills which will help them acquire jobs once they reach adulthood." She moistened her lips. "It made me think a wonderful opportunity was being passed up. I mean, what if those girls—and even the boys—were to receive classes in domestic science? As often as I go to town, it would be quite simple to stop by and take an hour to teach them some domestic skills."

Mrs. Winter straightened, her cheeks turning florid.

Clasping her hands on top of the table, Mrs. Vanderbilt leaned forward. "That's a very noble suggestion, Tillie. But Asheville is a bit far, especially when there are so many families right here on our mountains who are in need. Thank you for bringing it to my attention, though."

Tillie dropped her gaze. She knew her request had been brazen, but as philanthropic as Mrs. Vanderbilt was, Tillie really thought she would take the situation into consideration. To be refused outright shook her more than she wanted to admit.

Bobbing a curtsy, she thanked her mistress and quietly left the room.

∞

Tillie crossed the empty yard of the orphanage. The ropes on the merry-go-round hung forlornly in the cold breeze, as desolate as the trees without their leaves. She scanned the building, wondering where Mack was. Smoke swirled out of its two chimneys, adding more gray to the already cloudy day.

Picking her way to the shed, she avoided muddy patches left behind by a fierce afternoon thunderstorm. She wiggled the door, but it was locked and bolted. He must be in the house.

Her breath came out in a cloud of vapor as she made her way to the back stoop, wondering if this would be the last time she'd see him. Once she collected these toys, she'd have no more reason to seek him out. She would come see Homer, of course, but so long as the Sloops refused her help, her visits would be restricted to the parlor. There wouldn't be much chance of seeing Mack there. Tightening the scarf about her head, she knocked.

A bowed woman with a soiled apron and dirty mop cap answered. Her wrists were tiny, her fingers bent, and her gray hair frizzed.

"Good afternoon. I'm Tillie Reese from Biltmore. I need to see the useful man, please."

"Well, come on 'fore you let all the cold air in."

Warmth from the kitchen immediately embraced Tillie. She scanned the area. Two giant pots of water sat atop the stove, and another kettle hung inside a huge, crackling fireplace. A young girl sat perched on a stool plucking feathers from a chicken. Another knelt on the floor scrubbing dishes in a tin tub. The woman shuffled to a table and began chopping carrots.

Unfurling her scarf, Tillie hooked it and her coat on a peg by the door. Mack's jacket hung on the peg next to it. "Do you know where I can find Mr. Danver?"

"In Irene's room doing some repairs," the cook said, waving her knife toward the upper floors.

"Do you know which room is hers?"

"The girls are on the top floor."

Tillie nodded. "What about the Sloops? Are they in?"

"The missus is. She's up yonder schooling the kids." The knife pointed to the front of the building.

"Thank you. I'll just go see if I can find Mr. Danver, then."

"Suit yerself."

Now that she wasn't dashing through the building on a clandestine mission, she had a better chance to see how badly the place needed scrubbing. Cobwebs crisscrossed every corner like fishnets. A few had fallen loose, only to be snagged by the plastered walls, leaving filmy webs dangling like tinsel.

She walked toward the stairwell, her boots loud in the quiet of the hall. On the top floor, the girls' rooms were similar to Homer's, only with one cot instead of two. Each was covered with dingy, moth-eaten blankets. No personal belongings. Nothing to indicate anything about the occupants.

She rubbed her arms against the chill in the air. Where in the world was Mack? Turning around, she headed back up the hall, then spotted a closed door with a light coming from beneath. Muffled voices came from within.

She gave a light tap.

The voices stopped.

"Come in."

She swallowed. It was Mack. Slowly turning the knob, she pushed the door open.

Irene sat slumped on the edge of her cot, her eyes red and swollen. She cradled her arm—splinted and wrapped with newspapers—against her stomach. A large hole in the ceiling exposed wooden beams and joists. Below it, chunks of debris lay in a puddle of water.

Mack knelt at Irene's feet, his face grave. He rose when he saw Tillie. "I guess you're here to collect the wooden pieces?"

Something was terribly wrong.

"What happened?" she asked.

"Irene broke her arm. Mrs. Sloop sent me up here to wrap it."

Her gaze flew to the girl. "How?"

His lips tightened. "She says the ceiling caved in during the storm and struck her arm."

"But I thought you'd repaired the roof."

"I must have missed a spot."

She looked again at the girl's splint. "Has the doctor seen her?"

"Sloop says no doctor is needed."

"Is she going to be all right?"

"The arm will heal, if that's what you mean." The tension emanating from him was palpable.

"What else, then?" she asked. "What else is wrong?"

He jammed his hands into his pockets. "Seems Irene has a birthday coming up in January. After that, Sloop says she'll be too old to stay. That she'll have to leave."

And go where? Tillie thought. From what Mack had told her, the girl had no skills, was in a constant state of fear, and had hardly any meat on her bones.

He took a deep breath. "Seems that when this occurs, Sloop puts a bug in Daphne Devine's ear."

"Who?"

"Daphne Devine. The owner of a brothel out on Saloon Row."

Tillie sucked in her breath. "No."

"Daphne has already been by to offer Irene a place in her establishment."

Shivers scuttled up Tillie's spine. Smoothing her skirts beneath her, she sat on the filthy cot next to Irene. "I'm Tillie Reese. A friend of Mr. Danver's and head parlormaid at Biltmore."

Irene's eyes widened. "You are?"

As Tillie had hoped, working for the Vanderbilts gave her special status in the girl's eyes.

"I certainly am. And you must not do this . . . thing."

Irene sniffled, then whispered. "She says I can have chocolate cake any time I want."

Tillie squeezed her hands together. "I can teach you how to make chocolate cake. There is no need to go to that . . . that *place* for cake."

Irene said nothing.

Completely out of her element, Tillie prayed for guidance, then raised her gaze to Mack. "Would you excuse us, please?"

Swallowing, he knelt back down. "Irene, you can speak freely with Miss Reese. She's my special friend and she'll keep what you tell her to herself. Now I'm going to fix that roof." He looked at Tillie. "I'll have those wooden pieces for you whenever you're done here."

He slipped out the door, clicking it shut behind him.

Tillie sat in silence, continuing to pray and gather her thoughts. Finally, she turned toward Irene until their knees bumped. "Do you know what you would have to do if you went to Mrs. Devine's establishment?"

Tears welled up in the girl's eyes. She nodded.

"Then you see why you cannot go there."

Irene's chin quivered.

"You mustn't go," Tillie implored. "Promise me you won't go."

They sat in silence for so long, she was afraid the girl wouldn't answer.

Finally she whispered, "Then where would I go?"

"Anywhere. Anywhere but there."

"There is nowhere else."

Tillie smoothed a piece of hair behind the girl's ear. "You could do scullery work like Ora Lou."

"Miz Devine says anywheres I go, the man what gives me the job'll use me. At least at her place I'll get paid fer it and not have to do no scullery."

It was a veritable speech, indicating the girl's level of distress. Tillie's heart squeezed. She still couldn't believe Sloop had given that Devine woman access to Irene.

Pushing aside her fury, she concentrated on the task at hand. "That's just not true. There are many, many respectable men you could work for."

"Doin' what? I ain't no good at nothing. And Mrs. Devine says she won't let the fellers hit me none."

Tillie took Irene's good hand and folded it into hers. "Listen to me. You are much too special to work for that woman. I can teach you the skills you need to get good, honest work. I will come every day off I have and show you how to stitch and iron and clean and style hair."

Irene's shoulders slumped. "It ain't no good. How can I do all that with a gimp arm?"

Glancing at the girl's arm, she noted it was the left that was broken. "Which hand do you hold your pencil with?"

"My right."

"Then there's plenty you can learn to do." She squeezed Irene's hand. "What do you say? I can come this very Sunday."

"Won't do no good. There ain't enough time."

"You just wait and see." She rose. If she received a Christmas bonus this year, perhaps she could save some back for the girl rather than giving it all to her father. "This Sunday, then?"

Irene shrugged.

The door burst open. Tillie jumped. Irene scrambled back to the corner of the bed, protecting her arm behind updrawn knees.

Mrs. Sloop's gaze darted between them, her eyes narrowing. "What's going on? What are you doing here?"

Tillie lifted her chin. "I came to arrange a time when I could give Irene a sewing lesson."

"Sewing lesson?" She humphed. "Well, these aren't visiting hours, and all guests are to wait in the parlor. Besides, Irene can't do any sewing, not with that arm of hers."

"So I see. Has she been looked at by a doctor?"

"The useful man wrapped it up good and tight. That's all it needs."

"I'm afraid I don't agree."

The woman took a step forward. "What has Irene been telling you?"

The girl pressed herself even farther into the corner.

"You better not be making up lies, girl," Mrs. Sloop said, then turned to Tillie. "Did she say something about my husband?"

"We were simply discussing when would be the best time to schedule a sewing lesson."

"Well, Irene won't be receiving lessons anytime soon."

"On the contrary, I plan to be back Sunday." Tillie gave her a penetrating look. "And make no mistake, I will expect to see her."

Pulling her skirts to the side, Tillie swept from the room.

∞

Tillie sat cross-legged on the floor of the pantry, sorting and counting soiled table linens from supper. Eleven napkins. Picking up her notebook, she carefully recorded the number, knowing the head laundress would do the same in her book. The job required quiet concentration, because when these items were cleaned and sent from the laundry to Mrs. Winter, the two books would be compared with each other to ensure all articles were accounted for.

Dropping the napkins into the hamper, she started on the doilies.

"Here you are," Allan said, stepping over a pile of large tablecloths.

"*Shhh.*" *Five, six, seven.* She recorded the number, dropped the doilies into the hamper, then looked up at her brother. "What are you doing down here?"

"Looking for you. I thought this was your day off."

She scrunched up her nose. "I made the mistake of coming back too early. So don't ask me to do anything else. As soon as I'm done here, I'm disappearing up to my room with a copy of *Ivanhoe.*"

"You've read that thing a hundred times. Don't you get tired of it? It's not like it's going to end differently this time around."

She smiled. "I know. I still enjoy it, though."

Settling across from her, he leaned against the wall. "So how are things going?"

She cocked her head. "You mean with my new morning duties for Mrs. Vanderbilt?"

"No, I meant how are things going without Mack?" He was still wearing his formal serving livery, the maroon jacket handsome across his broad shoulders.

"Not so good," she whispered, her shoulders wilting.

"Having second thoughts?"

"I can't afford second thoughts."

"Why not?"

"Too many people would be impacted."

He stretched his legs out in front of him. "Like who?"

"Well, you for one."

"Me?"

"Yes. Think about the impact it would have on you if I

left Biltmore. It would mean you'd feel more of the financial burden for Mama and Pa."

Crossing his ankles, he tapped the toes of his boots together. "I've already talked to Pa about the finances."

"What? You have?"

He nodded. "Pa says they're doing fine. Gussie will be getting a job next year, and the boys won't be far behind her. That'll mean less mouths to feed and more money coming in."

She sighed. "I hate to think of Gussie having to do all that."

"Why? You did. I did." He shrugged. "That's just the way it is. And it'll only be until she marries."

"I suppose."

"You know what Pa told me?"

She shook her head.

"He never really believed you'd actually find a lady's maid position, no matter what Ma's ambitions for you were. Those spots are just too few and far between. And Pa sure never expected you to forgo a husband and family of your own to help them."

"Did he really say that?" Standing, she gathered up the tablecloths one at a time, dropped them in the hamper, then recorded a *three* in her book.

"Yes. So you see, you *can* quit."

"No, I can't. Regardless of what Pa says, Mama would never recover." She tried to smile, but her lip trembled. "Besides, if I left, I'd hardly ever see you."

Pushing himself up, he tweaked her chin. "If you marry Danver, I have a feeling he'd keep you so busy with babies you wouldn't have time to miss your ol' big brother."

Blushing, she shooed him away with her hands. "Go on. I've got work to do, unlike footmen who get paid ridiculous sums of money for looking pretty while we females work to the bone for a fraction of the wages."

Preening, he ran his hands down his lapels. "You've got to admit, though. I do make a handsome sight."

Rolling her eyes, she threw a serving towel at him. He dodged, then scurried out the door.

∞

Mack arrived at the orphanage after breakfast had been cleared and the children were already in the schoolroom. He'd managed to repair the roof yesterday, but he wanted to fix Irene's ceiling first thing. Her room must have been freezing last night with only a layer of shingles to keep the cold air from pouring through that gaping hole.

Unlocking the shed, he grabbed a ladder and pry bar. He couldn't do anything until he figured out how many laths needed replacing.

A touch of snow swirled in the air but immediately melted upon making contact. Stomping the mud off his boots as best he could, he entered the kitchen. "Mornin', Mrs. Gleaves. Looks like we might have us a white Christmas if this keeps up."

Flour covered her arms up to her elbows as she kneaded a huge glob of dough. "We might, at that."

Leaving his jacket on a peg, he made his way to the stairwell. He'd lain awake a good part of the night trying to figure what he could do to keep Irene out of Daphne's place. And every scenario involved money he didn't have. Right now, his all went to Ora Lou. He couldn't even afford a room for himself. He'd been bunking down in the loft of McGhee's livery in exchange for adding on new stalls. He sure didn't have the wherewithal to put up Irene.

Tillie's offer to tutor the girl had come as a pleasant surprise, but it was too little too late. She'd only have two Sundays off before Irene was kicked out. Not nearly enough time to teach the girl what she needed to know.

Stepping into the hallway, he noted all the bedroom doors were propped open except for Irene's. Frowning, he knocked.

No answer. He knocked again. Nothing.

Finally, he pushed it open, then stumbled back in shock. Ladder and crowbar crashed to the ground as he rushed forward.

A rope had been slung over the exposed beam and secured to the bedrail. At its other end hung Irene.

Twenty-eight

Irene's tiny room couldn't hold all the people gathered, forcing Vaughan and the police captain out into the hall. Mack, however, refused to budge. He stood in the corner, arms crossed, legs spread, watching and listening. His anger and remorse and suspicions were way too close to the surface. He needed to calm down before he said or did anything.

Old Doc Kuppenheimer arrived, black bag in hand. He was as old as Moses with a head wrinkled like a coconut and covered with straggly hair. The police chief made room for him to pass to the cot, where Mack had laid Irene after freeing her lifeless body from the rope.

Sloop held his wife by the shoulder, patting her as she cried into her handkerchief. Chief Pilkerton picked up Irene's prayer book, which had been open to yesterday's date. Scrawled across the top, in choppy letters was: *I aint no gud fer nothin. I wish I wer ded.*

Setting the book back down, the police chief looked every one of his fifty years, though he'd not grown soft in the middle like his captain. The chief's salt-and-pepper hair made a horseshoe around his head, leaving the top as bare as a baby's bottom. He fingered the noose and studied the trajectory of the rope.

Are you thinking what I'm thinking, Pilkerton?

But Mack kept his thoughts to himself. For now.

"Tell me again the last time you saw her?" Chief Pilkerton asked the Sloops.

Mrs. Sloop blew her nose. "From six to seven we call roll. Then the children read their prayers and prepare for bed. Lights are to be extinguished at half past seven."

Pilkerton lifted his brows. "So early?"

She stiffened. "Only from November to May. In the summer we let them stay up until eight."

The chief took a moment to let that settle in. "And Irene was accounted for during that time?"

"I've already told you, yes, yes, and yes." Her eyes teared up again.

Sloop shushed her and gave Pilkerton a slight frown.

The chief turned to Mack. "When did you leave yesterday?"

"I didn't finish patching the roof until it was almost too dark to see. The last contact I had with Irene was when I splinted her arm late in the afternoon."

"So the break was new?" Doc Kuppenheimer asked from the bed, cutting the newspaper from Irene's arm.

"Yes, sir. She claimed it broke when the ceiling fell through."

"Claimed?" Pilkerton asked. "Interesting choice of words."

Mack tucked his hands beneath the pits of his arms. "I just found it strange she would've been up here during the storm. She should've been in school during that time."

"She wasn't feeling well," Mrs. Sloop said. "So I had her come up and lie down for a spell."

Mack lifted a brow but made no further comment.

"What was wrong with her?" the chief asked.

Mrs. Sloop looked at her husband, then back at the chief. "Well, she's been very glum lately. She hadn't been participating in class discussions. She wasn't playing with the other children. And she was eating less and less. Just before classes yesterday, she complained of a stomach ailment. When I touched her forehead, it was a bit warm, so I sent her up here to rest." Bringing her handkerchief to her mouth, she cast red-rimmed eyes at Irene's body. "If I'd known, had any idea, she was contemplating . . ." She turned into Sloop's shoulder and sobbed.

"There, there, dear." Sloop frowned at Pilkerton. "I think I'll take my wife to our room, where she can rest."

Mack cleared his throat. "I'd rather you didn't do that just yet."

All but the doctor turned to him. Even Mrs. Sloop's sobs ended as she stared at him in shock.

Mack stepped to the rope and gave it a slight tug. "There's just a lot of things that don't seem to add up. I was thinking the Sloops might be able to clarify them for me."

"Your puzzlement doesn't concern us, Danver." Sloop slipped his arm around his wife. "Now, if you'll excuse us."

Pilkerton held up a hand. "Let's hear what he has to say, Forbus."

"But—"

"I was wondering about this rope," Mack began.

The chief slipped his hands into his pockets. "We're listening."

"Well, it's just that this is my rope. The one I keep locked up in my shed. I'm wondering how Irene got it. I mean, the only people who have keys to the shed are me and the Sloops."

Sloop stiffened. "You just said yourself you were working on the roof all afternoon. She could have slipped into your shed at any time and gotten the rope."

"No, it was there when I locked up last night."

"You can't be sure of that."

"I'm positive. It was in my way, so I moved it to a higher peg."

The chief pursed his lips. "How do you know this is your rope?"

Mack showed him the ends. "Because it's backspliced. It's the only backspliced rope on the property. Besides, I went and checked the shed while we were waiting for you to arrive. My rope's gone."

"This is ridiculous." Sloop turned to his friend. "I'm not staying here for this."

"That's not all," Mack said, stalling them. "I'm also trying to figure out exactly how Irene managed to tie this knot. This isn't a simple overhand knot and neither is the one on the bed."

The chief twisted the rope so he could see.

"It's a fisherman's loop." Mack pointed to it. "And to make it, you have to first form a slipped overhand before securing it with a regular overhand." He pointed to the bed. "That one over there's a cow hitch. I never knew any girl who could tie one of those. Especially not with this big old heavy rope."

"Are you suggesting this isn't a suicide, Danver?" the chief asked.

"I'm not suggesting it. I'm positive it's not."

"Because of the knots?" he asked.

"Because of the knots. Because it would take a good deal of height and muscle to pitch this rope up over that beam. Because it would've been a lot simpler for her to take a stool out to the yard and use one of those ropes on the merry-go-round. Those are already hanging and ready to go."

No one moved or made a sound.

The doctor snapped his bag shut. "I don't know anything about knots, but he's right about one thing. It would have been impossible for this girl, with this broken arm, to throw that rope up over the beam or to tighten the knots once they were formed. This is no small fracture here. Both bones in her arm were broken."

Mack turned to him. "You think a few pieces of debris from the ceiling could cause a break like that?"

"If she was right under it when it fell. And if she covered her head with her arm. Yes, I think that's possible."

"What if she was covering her head to protect herself from getting a beating? Could that cause a break like hers?"

Mrs. Sloop sucked in her breath.

The doctor slowly stood. "Depends on what instrument was used."

Mack nodded. "According to what the children tell me, Sloop beats the girls with whatever's handy."

"That is preposterous!" Sloop took a step toward him, his face mottled.

"Is it? Then how do you explain all the abrasions the kids keep carefully hidden from view?"

"I don't know what you're talking about."

"No? Why don't we ask one of them and find out, then?"

Sloop swung a fist, hitting Mack clean in the jaw and knocking him back into the corner.

Mack caught himself, but forced his hands to stay put. If he fought back, they might never get to the bottom of what happened to Irene or what was happening with the others.

Mack gave Pilkerton a searing look. "Go get one of the girls. See for yourself."

The chief looked at Vaughan out in the hall. Nodding, Vaughan headed to the stairwell.

Sloop swirled toward the chief. "You can't seriously think—"

"Shut up, Forbus. Just *shut up*."

Sloop exchanged a glance with his wife. She'd gone pale. Even her lips held no color.

"Let's move into the hall so the children aren't exposed to this . . . tragedy." Pilkerton herded them out of the room and closed the door behind them.

A minute later, Vaughan returned with Artie and Becca. The hem of her stained brown dress hung loose on the right side.

Artie ran his gaze over the crowd, then settled it on Mack. "Irene?"

Swallowing, Mack shook his head. "I'm sorry."

Artie pressed his lips together, his Adam's apple bobbing. "It weren't no accident, were it?"

The chief cleared his throat. "What's your name, son?"

"Artie Alsup, sir. And this here's Becca."

"Hello there, Rebecca. Arthur. I'm Chief Pilkerton."

"I knows who ya are."

The chief nodded. "Well, I just had a couple of questions for you. The doctor tells us Irene's arm was broken. Would you know how that happened?"

Artie flicked a glance at Sloop, clearly struggling with

whether or not to tell the truth. Mack wanted to reassure him, but the fact was, he couldn't. He couldn't protect Artie or Becca or any of the rest of them. Irene had made that fact crystal clear.

Finally, Artie squared his shoulders. "Sloop broke it."

"Why, you—"

Artie shoved Becca behind him and raised his fists. "I done tol' ya last time, ol' man. You ever lay a hand on me again and I'll give ya back as good as I git."

Sloop lifted his chin. "The child is lying. He's been nothing but a troublemaker since the day he arrived."

"Show them, Artie," Mack said quietly.

Sloop whipped his head around. "Stay out of this, Danver."

"Show the chief what you showed me," Mack repeated.

Artie pulled Becca beside him. "Show 'em yer knee."

She grabbed Artie's sleeve. "Ain't nothin' wrong with my knee. It's just a knee like ever'body else's."

Artie patted her hand. "She's scared. Sloop cuffs us boys now and again. But he done whales on the girls."

"I will not stand here and listen to this." Sloop made to move around them.

Vaughan stopped him. "You'd best stay right where you are, Mr. Sloop, until the chief says differently."

Pilkerton gentled his voice. "No one will hurt you, Rebecca. I give you my word. Now, is what Arthur says true? Has Mr. Sloop struck you before?"

Biting her lower lip, she gave a negative shake of her head.

"See there." Sloop adjusted his cuffs.

"I cain't blame her fer not wantin' to talk," Artie said. "It don't take much to set the ol' man off. And when ya do, why, he'll grab just about anything. A stick o' stove wood, a shoe, a skillet, or he'll just use his fists. Ain't that right, Becca?"

She said nothing, but Mack could see her shivering.

Sloop forced a laugh. "The boy's trying to seek revenge. He's been angry with me ever since he had to do extra chores after pulling a prank. Rebecca here has told you the truth. Why are we wasting our time?"

Pilkerton rubbed a hand against his jaw. "Show me your knee, Rebecca."

She looked at Sloop, then Mrs. Sloop. "It's just a knee. Ain't nothin' special 'bout it."

The doctor stepped forward. "Miss Rebecca, I'm Dr. Kuppenheimer. I've seen all kinds of knees in my day. Some young, some old. Some ordinary, some not so ordinary. Why don't you come with me for just a minute. I'll be able to determine right quick what kind of knee you have."

She considered him. "Yer a doc?"

"I am."

She chewed her lip. "Can Artie come, too?"

"Arthur can come, too."

He led the children into one of the available bedrooms and closed the door. In the hall, Sloop exchanged an anxious glance with his wife. Vaughan rubbed his forehead. Pilkerton stared at his boots. Mack held himself perfectly still.

The door opened.

Doc Kuppenheimer's expression gave no hint to his thoughts, but Artie was consumed with fury. He speared Sloop with his glare.

The doctor guided the boy to the other side of the hallway. "You and Rebecca return to the classroom now."

When their footfalls could no longer be heard, Kuppenheimer cleared his throat. "That child is black and blue. She's clearly received a recent beating. The knee is scarred from a previous one."

"I know nothing about that!" Sloop yelled.

Mack curled his fists. "Just like you know nothing about Irene? Or that rope? Or those knots?"

"I think *you* killed Irene!" Sloop screeched. "It's your rope. You're the one who's the knot expert. You killed her!"

"I wasn't even here. And I have absolutely no reason to kill that girl. I'm not the one who was selling her to Daphne Devine this January. You were. What happened? Were you afraid she'd tell someone what you were planning to do with her? Or did she tell you she wouldn't go? And that made you mad because you'd lose your kickback from Daphne?"

Sloop lunged.

Pilkerton caught him, then shoved him toward the captain. "Get him out of here."

"I don't know what he's talking about!" Sloop jerked within the officer's hold. "Surely you don't believe him over me."

When they reached the door leading to the stairwell, Sloop braced his hands and feet against the doorframe. "Okay! Okay! I'll tell you the truth."

The captain slowly relinquished his hold.

Mack held his breath.

"It was an accident. She was speaking with disrespect, so I . . . I struck her. I used a bit more force than I'd intended and she fell back, cracking her head against the floor. There was no blood, she just . . ." He darted his gaze between Pilkerton and Vaughan. "She just convulsed, then died. So, you see, it was an accident."

Sorrow tugged on the police chief's face. "That doesn't explain the rope, Forbus."

Eyes wild, Sloop pointed at his wife. "That was her idea! She hung the girl."

Mrs. Sloop gasped. "Forbus!"

"It's true. She said if we made it look like the chit took her own life, then no one would be the wiser. She got the rope. She put it around the girl's neck. She pushed her off the chair."

"He's lying!" She looked at the chief, clearly horrified. "You've got to believe me."

Pilkerton sighed. "Better take her in, too."

Tillie expected the hike to Asheville to be cold and miserable. Instead, she found her heart buoyant and her steps lively. The sun made its first appearance in days, having burned off the stubborn fog sometime during church.

A little gray bird with a small body and long legs raced across her path, its tail tipped up. She smiled, well remembering the days she, Allan, Clarence, and R.W. would chase after them. Try as they might, her brothers could never catch one.

But she could. She'd scoop one up and put it in her apron. Before she could catch another, the captured bird would have long since run out the side. Still, it was one of the few times she could best the boys, making her one step closer to being the big toad.

The king of all songbirds swept into view, cawing and heckling, cooing and croaking. She watched the raven dive toward her, then swoop back up, filing a saw with its throat.

Poor Noah, she thought. No wonder he let the raven out first chance he had. There'd be no peace with that show-off on board.

She enjoyed the evergreen trees and surveyed the bare branches of the deciduous ones, longing already for spring and summer, when the forest would once again be garbed in a profusion of colored blossoms and budding trees.

The closer she came to town, the more evidence there was of loggers. They'd descended like grasshoppers, consumed all within sight, and left devastation in their wake.

She didn't even bother going through town but headed straight for the southern edge, Sloop's orphanage, and Irene. She couldn't wait to give the girl her first sewing lesson. Had been looking forward to it since her visit on Friday.

She'd brought a basket of sewing supplies to leave behind with the girl. Her first lesson would be a straight stitch and a hem stitch. If she happened to see Mack, well, that would be an extra bonus.

She hoped Mrs. Sloop wouldn't give her any difficulty in spending time with Irene. Surely with it being Sunday, the children would have more freedom than on school days.

The orphanage came into view, and to her surprise, its yard was filled with boiling pots, washtubs, clotheslines, cots, and children. Every door was flung wide, every window open.

She walked through a labyrinth of clotheslines hung with blankets. Girls with baskets and clothespins added more to the lines, their chatter gay. Laughter rang out as boys disassembled cots and piled the bedding in a heap by boiling pots of water. Mack's sister, Ora Lou, oversaw those cauldrons and the girls who stirred them.

Younger girls knelt over washtubs scrubbing blankets against washboards. Homer and a few of his friends wrung

out the wash, making no effort to keep from saturating themselves, even though the air was nippy. She looked for Irene but
couldn't spot her in the confusion. Mack's deep voice came
from behind the orphanage.

She circled the building, then paused. He wore no hat,
no jacket, and no collar. Red long johns peeked through
his unbuttoned shirt. Dark suspenders crisscrossed his blue
shirt.

A boy stood beside him. With an ax in hand, Mack showed
him how to grip the handle while using shoulders and legs to
arc the ax into the wood. His hair fell across his forehead and
curled along the back of his neck.

Propping a log end-up on a stump, he caught sight of
her out of the corner of his eye and straightened, his face
sobering.

He was still angry with her, she supposed. For refusing to
leave Biltmore. She girded her heart, preparing to ask about
Irene's whereabouts, then retreat as gracefully as possible.

Saying something to the boy, he set down the ax and headed
toward her.

"I'm here to tutor Irene." She lifted her sewing basket.
"But I couldn't find her amidst all the activity."

His brows drew together.

She sighed. "If you'll just point me to where Irene is, I'll
leave you to your business."

Swallowing, he cupped her elbow. "This way."

He led her to the front door and escorted her into the
parlor. She'd never been in this part of the orphanage. It was
a far cry from the back.

Clean and cozy, the upholstered furniture grouped about
the fireplace evoked warmth and intimacy. To Tillie's keen eye,
she saw immediately that the floor and the legs of the chairs

had not been properly polished. Still, they'd been dusted. She wondered who took care of the room. Mrs. Sloop?

Mack guided her to a settee upholstered in gold and green cotton tapestry.

"Is it all right for us to be in here?" she whispered.

Nodding, he seated her, then lowered himself beside her.

She glanced at the arched entryway. "I don't think the Sloops will like it, Mack. Can't you just tell me where Irene is? I don't mind fetching her myself. And you shouldn't be sitting there. You're getting the couch dirty."

He took the basket from her lap and placed it at her feet. So grave.

"I'm afraid I have some bad news."

"Bad news?"

Taking both her hands into his, he rubbed her knuckles with his thumb. "Irene's dead, Tillie."

She jerked back.

He squeezed her fingers. "I'm sorry."

"What?" She looked about the room. Heavily fringed draperies of the same fabric as the couch hung over two front-facing windows. Beyond them, children filled the yard. Laughing. Chattering. Working.

"But that's impossible. I just saw her two days ago. I'm giving her a sewing lesson today. We were going to do the straight st—"

"Tillie."

Her chin began to quiver. "You're mistaken."

"I'm sorry."

She shook her head, scooting back. "I don't understand. How could . . . it was just a broken bone."

He said nothing.

Tears filled her eyes. "Are you sure? Are you absolutely positive?"

Lifting one hip off the couch, he withdrew a handkerchief and handed it to her. "I saw her myself."

She dabbed at her eyes. "What happened?"

He heaved a great sigh, propped his elbows on his knees, and hung his head. His hair tipped forward, the ticking in his jaw outpacing the mantel clock. "She was killed."

"What!" She pressed the handkerchief to her mouth, the smell of burnt wood and lye soap strong against her nose. "How?"

His Adam's apple bobbed. "They're trying to determine that now, but when I found her she'd been hung by the neck."

An involuntary moan keened from her throat. Surging to her feet, she skirted around the couch as if placing the piece of furniture between him and her would shield her from his words. "I don't believe you. We're in Asheville, not some Wild West town. And who would do such a thing, anyway?"

He lifted his gaze. "The Sloops."

The blood plummeted from her head straight to her toes. She could feel it. Actually feel it draining. The room began to fade. Black spots appeared in her vision.

"Easy." Mack jumped to his feet and encircled her waist, leading her back to the couch. "I'm sorry, Tillie. I didn't know how else to say it other than straight out."

Helping her stretch out, he grabbed a throw pillow from a nearby chair and placed it beneath her head.

She resisted and tried to sit up. "I can't. My shoes will get the cushion dirty."

She heard how ridiculous that sounded compared to what he'd told her, but her body had a will of its own.

"Hush. Just close your eyes." He pressed her back down, then removed her hat.

She lowered her lids, but it was as if they were somehow attached to her knees the way the call buttons were attached to the old annunciator boxes. When one was lowered, the other rose.

Her knees drew up to her chest. Her back curled. And her tears began to flow.

Kneeling beside her, he tucked her skirts about her legs, then wrapped her in his arms and pulled her against his chest. He rocked her. Kissed her hair. Murmured words of comfort.

The mantel clock struck three. Then the quarter hour.

Her tears slowed. "Tell me," she whispered.

He told her all he knew. About Irene. About the abuse. About Sloop's story of an accident. About the couple being in the county jail. "Several of the older girls have come forward now. If they didn't comply with Sloop's demands, he'd beat them. Sometimes he beat them anyway." He shook his head. "It sounds as if the only thing protecting them was an agreement Sloop had with the brothel owner, of all people. Seems the madam wanted chaste girls. But there was plenty Sloop could do without endangering that."

Tillie moaned. "No, Mack. No."

"I'm sorry." He rubbed her arm.

"Ora Lou?" she asked.

"He left her alone, thank God. But she's devastated about Irene and has some misplaced guilt over it."

Tillie's heart broke for Ora Lou and the other girls. She thought of her own sister, Gussie. The same age as the girls Sloop targeted. She could not conceive how anyone could do such a vile, nefarious thing.

"I just don't understand."

He took a deep breath. "I'm afraid that's not all. There might be some embezzlement of funds, as well, but I haven't had time to look at the ledgers because I've been appointed interim director until they can find a married couple to replace the Sloops."

Opening her eyes, she kept her face pressed into his shoulder. Her eyelashes brushed against his shirt. The feel of him, the smell of him, the whisper of his breath against her cheek brought comfort and strength.

"That's why the place is being cleaned out," she said. "Because you're in charge."

"Yes."

"And that's why the children are so happy. Because the Sloops arc gone."

"Yes."

"Do they know about Irene?"

"Only that she died. They were already in the schoolroom when I found her." He pulled away, smoothing back her hair. "You all right?"

Tears spurted to her eyes again. "When is the funeral?"

"Tomorrow."

"I need to go home. I need to ask for time off." She started to rise.

He held her in place. "Shhhhh. Let's take it slow, okay?"

Drawing in a choppy breath, she nodded.

He continued to stroke her. His fingers ran along her hairline. His knuckles down her cheeks. His thumb across her lips.

I love him, she thought. *I love him still.*

It was too much to contemplate all at once.

"I want to go home." She pushed into a sitting position. This time he let her up.

"How did you get here?" he asked.

"I walked."

"From Biltmore?"

Nodding, she felt her hair, pulled out the pins, and stuck them in her mouth.

"I don't want you walking back alone."

"Awl be fawn."

He removed the pins from her mouth and handed them to her one at a time.

"I'll be fine," she repeated.

"Let me walk you."

Reaching for her hat, she secured it to her head. "You can't, Mack. You have to stay with the children."

"Then let me send Artie with you."

"Who's Artie?"

"One of the older boys here."

She stood and shook out her skirts. "Don't be silly. Besides, I'd like to be alone. I have a lot to think about."

He hovered like a bird at a feeder, afraid to get too close, afraid to get too far. "Are you sure?"

She placed a hand on his cheek.

He immediately stilled and covered it with his.

"I'm sure, but thank you." Slipping from his grasp, she picked up her basket and walked out the door.

Mack watched her leave, comforted that he'd see her tomorrow at the funeral. Bereft because he didn't know if he'd see her after that.

He'd accepted the position as interim director without hesitation, even though he'd be giving up his freedom. More and more the prospect of living on his mountain seemed lonely without the orphans. Without his siblings. Without Tillie.

Yet already the restrictions of the job were making themselves felt. He wanted to walk her home. Hated the thought of her going all that way after receiving such a shock. But he didn't have the freedom to follow her. To pursue her. To do for her. His obligations were here now.

He stood at the door. Watched her weave through the yard. Stop and speak to Homer. Introduce herself to his helper.

His feelings for her ballooned. Pushing and pushing and pushing against his skin.

A burst of laughter from a group of girls hanging blankets drew his attention. They looked at each other, covering their mouths as their shoulders shook and their eyes sparkled. It was a sight to behold. He smiled just watching them.

Then the realization hit him. Came to him as he leaned with one shoulder propped against the doorframe and his ankle crossed over his foot. As if God himself had dropped down from heaven and spoken directly to him.

Freedom didn't always equate with coming and going as he pleased. Or to living out in the open. Or to doing whatever he wanted.

Sometimes, it was simply a matter of being free to laugh. Free to help others. Free to fulfill his calling.

After the girls had long since returned to their laundry and Tillie was but a speck in the distance, he pushed away from the door and headed to the chopping block. Ah, but it felt good to be free.

Mrs. Winter would not allow Tillie to go to Irene's funeral. Now that Tillie was performing Mrs. Vanderbilt's morning toilet, nothing else—in the housekeeper's mind—was more important. So Tillie examined the clothes worn by Mrs. Vanderbilt the evening before, removed the mud from the hem, beat the skirt lightly with a handkerchief, arranged the toilet table, lit the fire, swept the hearth, placed the linen before the fire to air, and laid out fresh articles of dress.

All the while she wondered if the children would be attending Irene's funeral, and if they were, who in the world would help Mack get them ready? What would they wear? Who would comfort them? Answer their questions?

And if the children weren't going to the cemetery, who would watch them while he was gone?

Tillie answered Mrs. Vanderbilt's summons and quietly laced her lady's stays and adjusted her linen.

If Mack were director, who would teach the girls to repair a seam, to cook a meal, to mix up furniture polish, to perform a toilet, to practice hygiene?

She brushed and frizzed Mrs. Vanderbilt's hair. Applied pomade to it with her own hands, then dipped a brush in bandoline and smoothed the hair down. She rolled it over frizettes the same brown as her mistress's hair and finished it behind with a plait.

Every task, every gesture was done efficiently and decorously. But her heart was not in her duties. Her heart was with those orphans. And Irene. And Mack.

By the time the toilet was complete, Tillie could barely bank her distress. Mrs. Vanderbilt thanked her and left the room.

Tillie stood in the middle of the shimmering gold and purple suite with its fancily trimmed mirrors and cut-velvet draperies, then sank onto the ivory Savonnerie rug, pressed her skirt to her face, and cried. Unsure if she cried for Irene, for herself, or for the doubts that pressed against her chest.

∞

With all that had happened, Tillie hadn't so much as looked at the wooden pieces she'd picked up from Mack last week. But before tomorrow afternoon, when every family and child on Biltmore Estate would celebrate Christmas with the master and lady of the manor, Tillie needed to wrap this one last gift, which her brothers would share.

Letting herself into the closet she'd used to store the presents, she turned on the light. Packages of all sizes and shapes filled the tiny room. Their red, green, and white wrappings were in stark contrast to Mack's brown parcel lying on a stool.

Making a space on the table, she cut the twine and folded

back the brown paper, then touched her throat. Instead of carving a few wooden animals, he'd constructed an entire Noah's ark complete with flat-bottom boat and a house on the deck. He'd painted faux wooden slats along the side, paned windows, and topped it off with a bright red roof. The base of the boat had a wide access hatch along its side.

She slipped its latch free, lowering the hinged cutout, which folded down into a broad ramp. Tucked inside were a variety of animals. Nothing was to scale; the ducks were as big as the cows. But they were easily distinguishable and intricately painted.

She removed each and every one. Pairs of zebras, pigs, goats, raccoons, skunks, squirrels, frogs, deer, sheep, and . . .

She examined an oblong shape which arched up in the middle, a snicker escaping before she could stop it. A worm. He'd made her little brothers a pair of *worms*.

She arranged all the animals on the table, imagining the hours and hours Ricky and Walter would spend with the toy. She touched a pesky raven perched on the roof. Mr. and Mrs. Noah on the deck. A dove on the railing.

Her heart filled. Her vision blurred. He'd done this not for the Vanderbilts, nor even for her brothers, but for her. And, maybe, for Christ.

Even though Mack wouldn't be at the celebration to see the boys open their gift, even though he had nothing to do with the Vanderbilts' mission, his time and care were just as much an offering as the Vanderbilts' sharing of their abundance.

She looked at the tissue-wrapped presents filling every available space on the shelves. Overflowing onto tables, stools, and even the floor. She considered the thought behind each gift. The tremendous effort her mistress had gone to—to not only meet each child, but to become acquainted with them. Learn their likes and dislikes.

She thought of her Father in heaven who knew all there was to know about her brothers and the rest of the children. Every triumph. Every fall. Every hair on their heads. Every hair on *her* head.

She swallowed. Regardless of what Mack said, she knew the tasks she performed on Mrs. Vanderbilt's behalf were worthy and important. That they would please and honor God.

So why was she so miserable? So empty?

Could it be that just because there was a door of opportunity, it didn't necessarily mean it was God's will for her to step through it? Had she allowed favorable circumstances and the chance for a better position to drag her places God had not designed for her?

She slowly lowered herself onto the stool.

"He calls his own sheep by name . . . he goes before them; and the sheep follow him, for they know his voice."

Swiping her eyes, she returned the animals to the hatch, lingering over each before carefully stowing them away.

I'm listening, Lord. Call to me. Just like the sheep. Just like these animals that you called to the ark. Call to me and I will follow.

∞

ASHEVILLE SPECIAL

Hundreds of employees of Vanderbilt's estate were given a most elaborate Christmas entertainment in the banquet hall of Biltmore House. In the center of the hall was the largest Fraser fir

to be found on the estate, a mammoth tree that
towered to the ceiling of the immense room. It
was lighted by innumerable wax tapers and glit-
tered with tinsel.

Beneath the Christmas tree were stacked presents of every conceivable nature. There was a
gift for every person who worked or lived on
the estate. Mr. and Mrs. Vanderbilt, with their
own hands, distributed gifts to the assembled
guests and wished all a merry Christmas and a
happy New Year.

Tillie smiled. The article didn't come close to capturing yesterday's excitement. The expression on the children's faces as they received an apple and an orange, then opened their gift. The delight of the estate workers, some of whom had never set foot inside the house. The staff's astonishment at the envelope containing a ten-dollar bonus from Mr. Vanderbilt. The children's awe at his reading of A *Christmas Carol* in front of the crackling fire.

As much as she had enjoyed the day, though, her mind had continued to drift to Mack and the children at the orphanage. How had they spent their Christmas? Had anyone thought to provide them with apples?

She recalled Ricky's and Walter's squeals when they'd unwrapped their Noah's ark. If only Mack had been able to see them at that moment.

What had Mack's little brothers opened? she wondered. It was, after all, their first Christmas without their mother. Without their family.

"Tillie?"

Putting the newspaper back on the table of the servants' hall, she looked up.

A hint of a smile touched the corners of Mrs. Winter's lips. "Mrs. Vanderbilt would like to see you in her sitting room."

Tillie's eyes went automatically to the telephone that was normally used when the housekeeper summoned. It hadn't rung. Which meant that, for whatever reason, Mrs. Winter wanted to deliver the message personally.

"Yes, ma'am." Tillie tried to keep a serene expression. This was her time off—a mere two hours. She'd hoped to have a cup of tea and rest her feet.

Moving past the housekeeper, she headed to the stairs. Moments later, she knocked on the door of the Oak Sitting Room.

"Come in."

Tillie approached the library table Mrs. Vanderbilt worked behind. After a moment, the mistress put her pen in the holder. "Thank you for coming."

"It was no trouble, ma'am."

She smiled. "The gifts were a wonderful success, I thought. Didn't you?"

"The children loved them, ma'am. My brothers and sisters chattered and played all evening when we returned home. They'll not forget the day for a long time to come."

"And it was in no small measure because of you."

A spurt of pleasure rushed through her. "I really enjoyed it, ma'am."

"I did, too." She leaned onto the table. "I called you in because Bénédicte will be leaving for France next week and it is time I come to a decision. It hasn't been easy, but I must say you have been quick to learn my likes and dislikes, eager to please, thorough in every task I've assigned, proficient with hair and wardrobe, and, well, I just simply like you." She smiled again. "I'd like you to be my lady's maid."

Such simple words. Words Tillie had longed to hear. Words that would change her life forever were she to simply answer yes.

She shifted her weight from one foot to the other. "I . . . I don't know what to say."

"I think we're going to get along very well. Congratulations."

Tillie placed a hand against her waist, then covered it with her other hand. "Mrs. Vanderbilt, I . . . I don't know how to say this, but . . ."

Mrs. Vanderbilt tilted her head, giving Tillie time to formulate her words.

"I'm afraid I can't accept."

Her lips parted. "Did you not find the job to your liking?"

"No, no. It wasn't that at all. It's just . . ." She looked down, then back up and took a deep breath. "The truth is, I've decided to go work at Sloop's orphanage. Except it isn't Mr. Sloop's anymore, of course. It's Mack's. But he's trying to handle it all by himself and the girls need someone to teach them some domestic skills and he certainly can't do that. And you should see the condition of the place. It's a mess inside and there's only one cook, who's a bit unimaginative. There's no garden. No henhouse. No cows. No—"

Mrs. Vanderbilt held up her hand, palm out. "I thought Mack was only an interim director. I thought he had to be married to stay on."

Tillie felt her cheeks warm.

Mrs. Vanderbilt raised her brows. "Are you and Mack . . . ?"

Tillie swallowed. "I love him, ma'am."

"Good heavens." She fell back against her chair. "Why had I not heard of this?"

Tillie moistened her lips. "I've been fighting it, ma'am. As a matter of fact, I haven't even discussed any of this with him. But I plan to. Just as soon as I can be released from my duties here."

Placing an elbow on the armrest, Mrs. Vanderbilt curled her fingers against her mouth. "Maybe you'd better start at the beginning."

"About Mack and me?" she squeaked.

A slight smile. "About the orphanage."

∽

Tillie slipped in the back door, knowing Mama would have already tucked the children in for the night. The kitchen was dark, other than a soft glow radiating from the last of the burning embers in the fireplace. Retrieving a candle from the mantel, she lit it, then made her way upstairs.

All was quiet except for the soft murmurings of her parents from inside their bedroom. Light seeped beneath their closed door, touching Tillie's hem as she softly knocked.

Her father opened the door, hooking his suspenders up over his long underwear. Surprise touched his face. "Tillie-girl! What are you doing here?"

"I know it's late, Pa, but I needed to talk to Mama. And to you, too."

He widened the door, a frown beginning to form between his brows. "Everything all right?"

Instead of answering, she stepped inside the cozy warmth of a room she'd always associated with love and heartache. For it was this room her parents always retreated to when they needed privacy with one of their children. Whether it was for comforting a broken heart or scolding a misdeed or discussing things which were too private to be discussed elsewhere, this was the room it was done in. Tonight would be no different.

Woodsmoke touched the air and her nose, drawing her gaze to the robust fire, whose heat she could already feel. The oak bed had been turned down, the brown, red, and blue spread she and Mama had crocheted folded neatly at its foot. Her father's gifted hand had painted intricate scrolls on the headboard, matching dresser, and vanity.

Mama put her brush down and slowly stood. Her long hair hadn't thinned a bit since the days when Tillie used to dress it, though its deep brown had been frosted with threads of gray. "They've made a decision."

Tillie nodded.

Mama scanned her face, then gripped the top of the vanity. "They gave it to Lucy?" Her voice was thin and rose in disbelief.

Tillie nodded.

"No!" Mama pressed a fist to her chest, causing her white nightdress to bow out. "Why? I was so sure!"

It would be so easy to let her mother assume Lucy had been their first choice. No one but Allan and Dixie knew it had even been offered to Tillie. But she didn't want Mama to think it was due to lack of training or something she had or hadn't done. Mama had worked too hard to be lied to now.

Pa closed the door. "I'm so sorry, honey."

Tillie offered him a fleeting smile, then returned her attention to her mother. "Actually, Mrs. Vanderbilt offered me the position first, but I didn't accept it."

Mama pulled back. "Don't be ridiculous. You'd have accepted it if you'd been offered it."

"No, Mama. I was awarded the job, but I didn't take it."

She shook her head. "You're not making sense."

"I know. And I'm sorry. But I'm leaving Biltmore. I'm leaving service altogether."

Color draining from her face, Mama sucked in her breath. "It's him. It's that useful man, Mack Danver. He's compromised you, hasn't he? Oh, Tillie, how could you? I *told* you to stay away from him."

"I love him."

"Oh, for heaven's sake. We've been over this." She looked at Pa, telegraphing her distress.

He cleared his throat. "Are you in a family way, girl?"

"No! No, nothing like that. I just needed to admit to myself that I loved him. And not only that, but I've had questions about where I should be serving. Here at Biltmore or in the orphanage with Mack."

"You are to be serving at Biltmore," Mama snapped. "Never was anything more obvious. We've trained you for the service your whole entire life, and who does God drop out of the sky and into our backyard but *George Washington Vanderbilt III*! And does he build some summer getaway in town? No. He builds a castle. *A castle.* The only thing it lacked was a princess."

"Mama, I know you thought—"

"I was beside myself when his new bride had some foreign French maid, and I have been on my knees daily. Daily! And then—*poof*—the French maid decides to leave. Things like that don't just happen, Tillie. God did that. He heard my cries and He answered my prayers, and you are going to throw all that back at Him by running off with this . . . this *backwoodsman?*"

"Christine—" Papa began.

"Shut *up*, Herbert, and let the girl speak for herself."

Tillie took a fortifying breath. "It isn't just because of Mack."

"Of course it's because of him. What else could it possibly be?"

"Me, Mama. It's me. I realized I was equating money and status with achieving my calling. When all I really need to do is serve God, no matter what my income, no matter what my status, no matter where He takes me. And if that means leaving Biltmore, then I leave Biltmore."

"For Hazel Creek?" She pointed toward the Unakas. "You'll be so busy doing drudgery you'll be the one needing charity, not the other way around. You cannot convince me God wants that for you."

"I wouldn't consider it drudgery, but even still, I've no plans at the moment to go to the Unakas."

Pa cleared his throat. "Where is it you're going, honey?"

"I'm going to work in the orphanage. I'm going to teach the girls domestic science."

"Oh, for mercy's sake." Mama whirled around and faced the back wall, propping her hands on her waist.

Tillie turned pleading eyes to her father. "I long to know the children. I think about them all the time. I think of all I can do for them."

"Have you prayed about this?" he asked.

"More than you know. And the more I prayed, the more certain I became."

Mama humphed, her back still turned.

"And Mack?" Pa asked. "If he weren't at the orphanage, would you still want to go?"

"I would, though I love him, Pa. So much it hurts, deep in here." She pressed a fist up under her breasts.

Slipping his hands into his pockets, he looked at the floor. "It's an awful lot for your mother to take in all at once."

"I know. I'm sorry. I suppose I should have seen it coming, and maybe I did. But I fought it so much. I didn't want to believe it."

"And now?"

Tears filled her eyes, not of sorrow but of amazement and joy. "I'm going to marry him, Pa. Can you imagine? Me? A married woman?" She shook her head in wonder. "I never even thought to have any children, but now, why, I could be a mother by this time next year."

Mama spun around, the veins at her temples bulging. "Well, children aren't all they're purported to be, Matilda. You give and give and give of yourself and in return you get nothing. Nothing but disappointment, that is."

Tillie gasped.

Papa slashed a hand through the air. "*Enough.*" He gave Tillie a grief-stricken look. "She didn't mean that. She's just upset."

Her tears of joy quickly transformed into shock and hurt. "I'm so sorry, Mama. I am. Not for this new life I'm embarking on, but for shattering your dreams. They were mine, too. But I've been given something even better. Can you not see it?"

Mama said nothing, her face as hard as flint.

Pa slipped an arm around Tillie's shoulders and gave her a squeeze. "Of course we do, girl. But this has kinda taken the wind out of her sails. So maybe you better let me and Mama be alone now."

Devastated, she nodded. "I'm sorry, Pa. I'm so sorry."

And though he pulled her close and whispered reassuring words, she knew it would take Mama a long time to recover.

Thirty-one

M ack now understood why the Sloops had the children in bed by half past seven. It was only six and already he was exhausted. But at least he'd had Tillie's help today.

He glanced across the kitchen. She wore an old apron over her skirt and never lit in one spot for too long. She'd set the little ones to clearing the table and wiping it down. Others swept the floor. Some older boys pumped water and hauled in wood. A few girls washed and dried the dishes.

"I can't reach, Miss Tillie." A tot of about five stood on tiptoes, trying to return a clean bowl to the shelf.

Mack swept the girl up, suspending her in the air. Squealing with laughter, she set the bowl in its proper place, then ran to fetch another one as soon as her feet touched the floor.

Tillie caught his eye and they shared a smile.

Her arrival that morning had surprised him. She'd not even attended her own church, All Saints in Biltmore Village, but had shown up at the orphanage first thing to help the girls dress for services here in Asheville.

Afterward she'd helped with dinner, then gathered the girls together for a rudimentary lesson in sewing. The younger ones learned to thread needles. The middle ones practiced simple stitches. The older ones stitched up a seam.

It had given him a chance to spend the afternoon alone with the boys. They pulled up rotten baseboards along the first-floor corridor, sawed and cut new ones, then hammered them in place. It took him four times as long as it would have if he'd done it alone. But the pride and sense of accomplishment the boys displayed along with a new sense of camaraderie was well worth the delay.

Tillie draped a drying cloth across a dowel, then reached behind her back to untie her apron. "All right, everyone, let's gather in the great hall. Mr. Vanderbilt loaned us his copy of *The Prince and the Pauper*. Since we finished the dishes so quickly, we might have time to read two whole chapters before bed."

The children scurried past Mack, all jabbering at once.

Tillie hung her apron on a peg, then turned, pushing a tendril of hair from her face. The sound of the children's footfalls diminished into silence, leaving the two of them alone.

"You can't mean to stay and read to them," he said. "The sun will be setting soon."

She shrugged. "I don't mind."

"I do. I don't want you walking back to Biltmore in the dark."

"Earl will be with me."

"Earl?"

She nodded. "He said he had some business in town and he'd swing by here on his way out."

Mack could just imagine what his "business" was but refrained from commenting. He followed her to the hall, settled into a chair to listen, and found himself as disappointed as the children when she finished the second chapter and announced bedtime.

An hour later, he stood in the parlor gazing out at the merry-go-round. He wondered if the lumberyard had any old pieces they could donate for a seesaw. It'd be a simple project for the boys to make.

"A penny for your thoughts."

He looked over his shoulder. She stood in the doorway, her cheeks flushed, her skirt wrinkled, her hair askew.

"Just thinking," he said.

She clasped her hands together. "May I come in?"

"You don't need an invitation."

Strolling through the room, she centered an empty vase onto a crocheted doily. Ran her hand along the back of the gold and green settee. Angled a candlestick on the fireplace mantel.

"The girls are settled?" he asked.

"Mmmmm. The boys?"

"Yes."

Picking up a poker, she started to stoke the fire.

He gently commandeered the instrument and did it for her, even though it didn't need it. "Thank you for coming today. It was a tremendous help."

"I enjoyed it very much. They're wonderful children."

"They are at that." He stood, then propped the poker against the hearth.

She backed up, giving him room. "Anything new with the Sloops?"

"They signed a confession this week."

"Both of them?"

He nodded. "Mrs. Sloop only took part in Irene's tragedy, though. She wasn't the one who beat or abused the girls—though she certainly knew about it."

Leaning against the edge of the sofa, Tillie picked off a speck of lint. "I saw their bruises." She looked up. "When I was helping them to bed."

"They're bad?"

"They're fading." She pressed her lips together. "Still, I was very angry, but I didn't show it, of course. Just chattered away as if it were perfectly normal to be yellow and green like that."

Her pupils were large and troubled, the irises a deep violet. "Of course, those were only the bruises I could see. The other ones, the ones in here . . ." She tapped her chest. "Those will take a bit more time to heal."

He wanted to touch her. Pull her close. Comfort her. Kiss the sorrow from her eyes.

He kept his hands firmly at his sides.

Hooking a loose tendril behind her ear, she looked down at her shoes. "I was thinking."

He waited.

"If I only read two chapters of *The Prince and the Pauper* every other Sunday on my days off, it'll take me eight months to finish the book."

His breathing hitched. She wasn't coming back. He'd expected that. Tried to prepare himself for it. But when she'd shown up this morning, hope had sprung anew.

He should have known better. "I could read it to them."

Nodding, she bumped her hip against the sofa. *Thump, thump, thump.*

"I suppose you could," she said. "But it's such a treat to look up and see their rapt, wide-eyed expressions. I'd hate to miss out on that."

He frowned, unsure of what she wanted him to do. "Then we'll just wait until you can come. They'll enjoy it no matter how long it takes."

Pushing herself off the couch, she swished her hands together, as if brushing away dirt. "No, that just won't do. Eight months is entirely too long. What if the new directors won't allow me to finish? That would be awful."

He hadn't thought of that. Had purposely tried not to dwell on being asked to give up his position to someone else.

She shrugged. "I guess I'll just have to come more often."

"But you can't. You wouldn't have enough time on your weekly evening off. And you'd miss the barn gatherings."

"True. But I wouldn't be going to the barn gatherings anymore anyway."

"Because of the parlor games?"

"Because members of the swell set don't usually participate. It tends to make everyone else uncomfortable."

He sucked in his breath. The butler, chef, valet, and lady's maid were the elite who made up the swell set. "You got the lady's maid position."

It was more of a statement than a question.

She nodded. "I was offered it."

Holding himself perfectly still, he pushed his anguish

aside. But it was there. Just beneath the very surface of his skin.

She searched his eyes. "Nothing to say?"

He wasn't about to congratulate her. "It won't take eight months to finish the book, it'll take two years."

The barest of smiles flickered across her lips. "I thought the same thing."

How long before Earl came for her? he wondered. How long would he have to stand here and pretend she hadn't completely shorn his heart in two?

She ran a thumbnail along the edge of her waistband. "That's why I told them no."

It took a moment for him to absorb the words. He furrowed his brows. "What do you mean you told them no?"

"I told them no. No, thank you. I don't want the position of lady's maid."

He furrowed his brows. "But . . . I don't . . ."

"Will you marry me, Mack?"

He stared at her. Certain he'd heard her incorrectly. The silence stretched between them. The fire popped.

A shy smile began at one corner of her mouth. "Would it help if I got down on one knee?"

Giving himself a shake, he let out a quick huff of air. "No."

Her face collapsed. "*No?*"

"I mean, yes! No." He grabbed her against him. "No, you don't have to get on one knee, and yes, I would very much like to marry you."

Throwing her arms around his neck, she stretched onto tiptoes.

He crushed his mouth to hers.

The front door opened. "Knock, knock? Anybody home?"

Inwardly groaning, Mack pulled back and rested his forehead on Tillie's. "It's Earl. Maybe if we hide behind the couch he won't find us."

She giggled.

Earl strode into the parlor and quirked a brow. "Release that woman, big brother. I have to get her home before we both miss curfew."

"She is home," Mack growled softly.

Tillie stepped from his embrace. "Not just yet."

"When?" Mack asked.

"A week from Saturday?"

"I'll make arrangements for the children."

Earl grasped Tillie's hand. "Come on. We're going to be late. See you later, Mack."

Throwing Mack a kiss, she snatched her coat off the hall tree and ran to keep up with Earl as he dragged her out the door.

❦

With it being a workday at Biltmore, no one could attend the wedding. Mack and Tillie exchanged vows privately in the preacher's back office of All Saints church. Mr. Vanderbilt had loaned them his Portland cutter sleigh, and Mack drove it right down the Approach Road instead of the back road the staff usually used.

Snow sheltered the landscape with its thick, icy down, sparkling so bright it hurt his eyes. A red squirrel hopped from one barren branch to another, shaking loose a flurry of powdery flakes. He recalled the dread he'd felt when he'd first traversed this road at the end of the summer, never dreaming it was leading him to the woman he'd want to spend the rest of his days with.

Holding the reins in one hand, he placed his arm on the seatback and pulled Tillie close. She'd been quiet and stiff during the ride. But if she was having second thoughts, it was too late. They'd said their vows and as soon as he returned this sleigh, he was putting her on a horse and taking her to honeymoon in his home on the mountain.

Rubbing her arm, he glanced down at her, then frowned. Her face was pale and drawn against the dark green of her new jacket and gown.

"Are you cold?" he asked.

She gave a quick shake of her head. "Fine."

He leaned away from her. "Look at me."

Slicing him a glance, her smile was stiff.

He slowed the horse to stop. "What's the matter?"

"Nothing. I'm fine. Everything's fine."

"It's not." He wrapped the reins around the rail, then swiveled her toward him. "What is it?"

Her expression was pained. "I'm just feeling a little queasy, is all."

Relief swept through him. It wasn't second thoughts; it was carriage sickness.

"I'm all right," she said. "I just forgot to have the kitchen make up a batch of ginger cookies. We're almost there."

Scooting from beneath the blanket which lay across their laps, he hopped down and scooped up a hunk of snow.

"What are you doing?" She eyed him with suspicion.

"Next best thing to gingerbread." He climbed into the sleigh and clapped the snow against the back of her neck.

She screeched and tried to pull away.

Fortunately, the horse didn't spook but stood patient and calm.

Tillie continued to struggle. "That's *freezing*. And you're getting my collar wet. What in the world?"

"Hold still, it'll help your stomach."

"That is the most ridiculous thing." Straightening her spine, she frantically pushed against his arm. "It's going down my back!"

Finally, he released her, tossed the snow over the side of the sleigh, and handed her his handkerchief.

"I can't believe you did that." She scrubbed her neck and inside her collar. "What were you thinking?"

"Is your stomach better?"

"I'm too mad to tell."

He smiled. "Well, your face certainly has more color." Smoothing the blanket across them once more, he pulled her close.

She pushed against his chest. "Oh no. Don't think for a minute you're going to distract me. If I wasn't so worried about wetting the hem of my new dress, we'd be having the biggest snow fight of your life right now."

He tightened his arms around her. "Wouldn't do any good. I'd still win."

Her brows shot up. "Want to bet?"

"I do. But to prove your point, you'd have to get your hem wet." Leaning down, he nuzzled her neck and dropped the tenor of his voice. "Of course, if you removed your skirts and petticoats, that wouldn't be a problem."

She gasped.

He nibbled his way along her jaw. "That would give you an unfair advantage, though. I'd be way too distracted to dodge."

He trailed kisses along her cheeks and nose, then found his way to her lips.

Her enthusiastic response nearly undid him. He dragged her onto his lap and made free with his hands, claiming what was finally his.

A sigh emerged from the back of her throat.

The horse blew out a breath and shifted his weight, jostling the two of them apart.

Her eyes slowly opened, dazed and disoriented.

He gave her a wicked grin. "Bet you won't cast up your accounts after that kiss."

Jerking upright, she leapt from his lap, returned to her place on the cushion, and yanked the coverlet back into place.

Laughing, he released the reins and gave the horse a *hi-yup*. When they reached Biltmore, he pulled the sleigh into the courtyard by the servants' entrance. Stableboys rushed out to take the reins.

Allan met them at the door and helped Tillie alight. "Well, if it isn't Mrs. Danver."

Blushing, she gave her brother a peck on the cheek. "Good morning."

He swatted her back end. "Go on, brat. Everyone's anxious to see if you look any different now that you're a married woman."

She disappeared inside and Mack accepted the hand Allan offered.

"Took you longer than we were expecting," Allan said, lifting a brow.

"Tillie had carriage sickness." He hurried inside, cutting off any further questions.

Belowstairs the servants' dining hall had a wedding cake and a table of food. Tillie's parents and siblings were in attendance, and the rest of the staff popped in and out as duties permitted.

Tillie's father gave her a hug. "You look mighty pretty, Tillie-girl."

"Thanks, Pa." She pecked him on the cheek, then turned to her mother. "Hello, Mama."

The carefully hidden strain behind Mrs. Reese's composed face was only evident to Mack because Tillie had warned him to expect it.

"It's done, then?" Mrs. Reese asked.

A twinge of hurt touched Tillie's eyes, before being quickly submerged. "It is."

He tried not to feel angry with the woman's attitude, but it was difficult.

"Well." Mrs. Reese heaved a sigh. "Your father's right. You look lovely."

"Thank you."

His new mother-in-law looked him up and down. She opened her mouth as if to say something, but tears welled up and she quickly turned and walked away.

After an awkward moment, Mr. Reese held out his hand. "Welcome to the family, son."

"Thank you, sir." Mack shook hands with him.

The man turned to his daughter and squeezed her arm. "Don't worry about your mama. She'll come around. Just give her a little time to let old dreams die."

Swallowing, Tillie nodded.

"Mack!"

He turned at the youthful voice and barely had time to see who was rushing toward him before the boy squeezed Mack's legs.

"John-John? What . . . ?" Holding the boy close, Mack

looked up. Ikey and Otis raced around the corner, Earl a step behind them.

Kneeling down, Mack captured all three boys into his embrace, his heart expanding.

"Earl fetched us," John-John said, his brown eyes filled with excitement. "He says you've found a woman to do for ya."

"I did at that." Standing, Mack winked at Tillie, then clasped her hand. "These are my brothers. Ikey, Otis, and John-John."

Earl had somehow managed to make them bathe and sit still for haircuts, and had even wrestled them into proper clothing. They stood before Tillie with cheeks scrubbed and hair slicked down.

"How do you do," she said. "I'm Tillie."

"Earl made us wear shoes." Ikey stuck out a newly shod foot.

"You don't like shoes?" she asked.

"I don't see any use for 'em a'tall."

Mack started to respond, but she squeezed his hand.

"Well, do you like cake?"

His eyes lit. "Yes, ma'am. All of us like cake. Mack too."

Releasing Mack, she held out her hand to Ikey. "Well, come along, then. I'll cut you each a large slice of our wedding cake and introduce you to my brothers and sisters."

Ikey placed his hand in Tillie's, and the boys trailed after her. Mack admired the way her dark green jacket nipped her waist and her skirt swelled over her backside.

"Put your tongue back in, big brother."

Mack smiled at Earl. "When did you get the boys?"

"I left the day before yesterday." Earl watched Otis stuff a whole piece of cake into his mouth at once. "It was good to see them. I hadn't realized how much I'd missed them."

"Me too. Thanks for fetching them."

Earl shook his head. "From what I can gather, they haven't done much schooling since you dropped them with the new families. Not when there was harvesting to do. Pa's probably spinning in his grave. You're going to have your work cut out for you if you plan to get them caught up to where we were at that age."

Mack wondered at what point Earl had begun to care more about Pa's opinion than that of their grandfather's. Before he could ask, Mr. and Mrs. Vanderbilt entered the dining hall. Their presence brought an immediate buzz of excitement.

For them to have approved the celebration during working hours and to personally appear belowstairs spoke of their high regard for Tillie. They spotted her immediately. Mr. Vanderbilt squeezed her hand and said something to make her laugh. Mrs. Vanderbilt cooed over her gown.

Tillie's mother lit up when they greeted her and she offered her first smile of the day. After a few moments, Vanderbilt's gaze swept the room, then stalled on Mack and Earl. Skirting the table, he headed toward them, a long scroll of some kind in his hand.

He shook Mack's hand. "Well, I half expected you to have your collar off and your sleeves rolled up."

Smiling, Mack looked down at his Sunday-go-to-meeting clothes. "The preacher wouldn't marry us if I wasn't properly suited up."

"I imagine not." Tapping the scroll against his trouser leg, Vanderbilt gave Mack a long look. "I'm not sure whether to congratulate you or not. You're taking away a girl we think the world of around here."

"It wasn't easy, I assure you."

"Glad to hear it." He handed Mack the scroll. "Your wedding present."

Mack's brows rose. Taking the scroll, he untied the strip of leather and unrolled it. An elevation plan of a large three-story building was on the first page. He looked at Vanderbilt questioningly.

"It's the new orphanage I'm building."

"New orphanage?"

Vanderbilt turned the page, revealing a first-floor plan. "Tillie told us about the other one. I talked to our state representative, Leonard Vaughan?"

Mack nodded.

"He said the whole thing needed to be leveled. So I had my architect draw up a more modern one. But rather than build it in town, I thought the children might enjoy having a bit more room."

Mrs. Vanderbilt and Tillie joined them.

Mack rested his hand on the small of Tillie's back. "More room, sir?"

"Yes. Out on my estate. In the mountains somewhere. Not Hazel Creek, but far enough away from the city to have plenty of elbow room. I thought when you returned from your honeymoon, you might like to ride out with me to a couple of sites I had in mind. See what you thought of them."

Mack's heart started to hammer. "Why me, sir?"

Vanderbilt looked at him, surprised. "You and Tillie are going to be the new orphanage directors, right?"

"Yes, sir."

"Then it seems to me you ought to be involved in the project."

Mack glanced at Tillie, then back at Vanderbilt. "Well . . .

I don't know what to say." He clasped Vanderbilt's hand. "Thank you, sir. Thank you very much."

"You're welcome, Danver. Just make sure you take good care of our girl here."

"I can promise you, sir, it'll be my pleasure."

Tillie had always heard mountain men were extraordinary walkers and carriers of heavy burdens. She hadn't assigned that image to Mack, though. Yet he'd refused to ride up the mountain to his home, where they were to overnight.

Instead, he'd put Tillie on a horse, commandeered the reins, then slung her sack of items onto his shoulder without benefit of a pack strap. Every so often, he'd shift it to his other shoulder. He gave no more notice to the snow beneath his feet than he would have a solid wood floor.

The higher they went, the more monotonous the view became. With the forest pressing in on every side, she couldn't imagine why he considered this land open and airy. It was much more confining than the cavernous rooms of Biltmore and its sweeping panoramas.

At times the climb was so steep it seemed as if Mack could stand up straight and bite the ground. At others, they'd plunge down at such an angle she'd have felt better if he'd had hob-nails in the seat of his pants. Yet nothing winded him. And the farther from civilization they went, the more energy he seemed to have.

She wasn't able to say the same for her horse. Not only was the trek challenging for the animal, it also shied several times, making her wonder what wild beasts might be lurking in the thicket.

Scrutinizing the area, she looked for any rustling branches. Listened for a cracking of twigs. But nothing stirred. Only the steady *clomp-clomp-clomp* of her horse's hooves touched her ears.

She flipped a blanket up over her head. The sun's rays were no longer able to penetrate now that it had begun its descent. She hoped they'd arrive before it disappeared completely but bit back the question of *how much longer*.

Just before full dark, Mack led her into a clearing with the most rudimentary log cabin she'd ever seen. The logs had been hewed flat, leaving wide spaces between. She couldn't imagine how its crumbling chinking would keep cold air from whip-ping through the structure. A long, narrow porch ran along the front, flanked by a big stone chimney at one end and a lean-to at the other for a kitchen.

"Stay put," Mack said, handing her the reins.

He stomped onto the porch, knocking snow from his boots, then disappeared through a large plank door. The horse let out a shudder, his warm breath fogging the air about his muzzle.

A moment later, Mack returned without the sack and lifted his arms to her. She slid from the saddle, barely suppressing a moan. It had been a long time since she'd ridden. But how could she complain when he'd walked the entire way?

He pulled her against him, then swept an arm beneath

her knees and gave her a long kiss. It warmed her as no fire could.

"I'm going to enjoy having a lifetime of those," he said. She tightened her arms about his neck. "Me too."

He carried her across the threshold, then set her down while he tended a prelaid fire. Clearly someone had cleaned and prepared the cabin for them. It was a one-room affair without stain, varnish, or veneer. The interior walls had been hewn the same as the outside, and she realized the home must have been built while the timber was still green and unseasoned.

The wood sagged and the joints had warped, so none fit properly or sat squared. She could see dissolving daylight through exposed, curled shingles. And the floorboards had shrunk, leaving wide cracks which conducted outside air, sending it straight up her skirts.

Eight split-bottom chairs circled a homemade table holding her overnight sack. Two large beds graced the rugless room. One against the wall with no bedding. The other in front of the fireplace fully dressed with fresh linen, blankets, and fluffy pillows.

Blushing, she averted her gaze, noting a split-pole ladder leading to an empty cockloft. She tried to imagine growing up in such a place and could not.

Still, for all its archaic appearance, it held a homey, picturesque quality. The very fact that its lines were catawampus allowed it to fit in with its wild and rough surroundings. Anything more modern would have confused the senses.

The fire popped. The smell of burning wood began to permeate the room.

Mack rose and rubbed his hands against his thighs. "I'm going to tend to the horse."

He slipped out the door, leaving her to wonder exactly

what she was supposed to do or where she was supposed to sit. With the bed blocking the hearth, there was no room for her to drag any chairs close to the fire's warmth.

Moving to the table, she opened her sack, then stalled. She couldn't unpack her nightdress and lingerie. What would she do with it? Hang it on the pegs?

She gave a hysterical laugh at the thought of Mack returning to find the walls lined with her unmentionables.

Digging around, she found the foodstuffs Biltmore's chef had packed for them. But there were no cupboards. No closets.

Four large trunks lined one wall. Perhaps there would be table linens in one of them. She raised a lid, then touched her throat. It was filled to the brim with books.

She ran her hand over the thick volumes. Picking one up, she angled it toward the fire. *Payne's Business Encyclopedia and Practical Education*. Beside it, *The Little Giant Bookkeeper, Bookkeeping at a Glance*. And *Blaine's Handy Manual of Useful Information*.

Closing the lid, she raised the next one. More books. *Pictorial History of the United States. Conquest of Peru. Handbook of Pronunciation. Robert's Rules of Order. Thimm's French Self-Taught.*

All four trunks contained books. Academics, essays, poetry, dialogues, recitations, etiquette, medical, religious, fiction, atlases.

Mack's footfalls sounded on the porch. She pushed the lid closed and darted back to the table.

A cold whoosh of air and a flurry of snow entered with him before he secured the door. His gaze went first to the fire, then swept the cabin, snagging on her.

Snow dusted his hair and shoulders. He plucked off his

gloves and stuffed them into a pocket. Keeping his eyes pinned to hers, he unbuttoned his jacket, shrugged it off, and blindly hooked it on a peg.

Her stomach bounced.

"You cold?" he asked, blowing into his hands.

"No."

"You've still got the blanket on."

"Oh!" She whipped it free and shook it out. Before she could hang it up, he was there, taking it from her, doing the honors.

"Gloves?" he asked.

Flushing, she tugged on each fingertip, slipping the outdoor gloves off.

He set them on the table, noticing the food. "You hungry?"

"Not really. Not after all the food we had at Biltmore. But I could eat if you're hungry."

"I'm not hungry." Taking her hands into his, he brought them to his mouth.

"Your hands are freezing." She covered one of his with both of hers and rubbed it quickly until it warmed, marveling anew at how rough and large his hands were compared to hers. She did the same with his other.

Finishing, she released him. They stood facing each other, his eyes dark. Very dark.

She fingered a button on her jacket. His gaze followed her movement. She snatched her hand to her side.

Slowly, he reached up and pushed her coat button through its housing, then the next and the next until all were undone. Turning her by the shoulders, he helped her out of it and hung it on a peg.

She didn't move, afraid to face him, afraid not to.

Running his hands down her arms, he touched his lips to the back of her neck and left them there, his breath fanning the hairs on her nape. Tremors zipped down her spine and continued clear to her toes.

Finally, he lifted his head and slipped his arms about her waist, locking his fingers together and pulling her back against him. Swaying from side to side, he rocked her as if to a lullaby only he could hear.

Little by little, she relaxed. "Who prepared the cabin for us?"

"I did."

"When?"

"Yesterday."

"Good heavens," she sighed, unable to believe he'd made such a trek two days in a row.

With one hand he slid a hatpin from her hat.

"You grew up here?" she asked, trying to digest how eight people had shared this one area. No wonder he valued freedom, air, and elbow room.

"I did." Splaying one hand against her stomach to ensure she stayed put, he placed the pin and her hat on the table in front of them, then went back to rocking her.

"Whose books are in the trunks?" she asked.

"My father's."

A log on the fire shifted. Cold air ruffled her petticoat through the flooring.

He nuzzled her hair.

Tilting her head to the side, she gave him more access.

He nibbled her ear. Explored her neck. Kissed her shoulder through her bodice.

She shuddered.

Scooping her up, he carried her to the hearth, then placed

her on her feet between the fire and the bed. He reached for a bed warmer she hadn't noticed before and slipped it under the linens, running it along the mattress before returning it to the fire.

He tunneled his hands into her hair, tipped up her face, and kissed her. Heat pressed at her from within and without.

"Let's go to bed, Tillie."

Eyes closed, she nodded.

He removed the pins from her hair, placing them on the mantel, then took her tresses into two fists and buried his face in it, inhaling deeply.

Her knees weakened, but she remained still, allowing him all the time he wanted.

Finally, he brushed it behind her back, then dipped down to find her collar fastenings. She reached up to detach it, but he pushed her hands away.

"Tonight," he said, "I will be your lady's maid, and I will do for you what you have done countless times for others." His eyes slid to half-mast. "But this will be much, much more enjoyable."

Flushing, she stood motionless as he tenderly removed collar and cuffs, setting them next to her pins on the mantel. Kneeling before her, he untied her boots, then slipped them off.

Still on one knee, he twisted to hold his hands to the fire before slipping them blindly beneath her skirts. She jumped, bracing her fingertips against his shoulders as he whisked her garters off and rolled down her stockings.

The plank floor was cold and rough beneath her feet, giving her blessed relief from the flush overtaking her body.

Bodice, overskirt, skirt lining, skirt, petticoat, corset cover, corset, and chemise. With the removal of each layer, he whispered words of praise and awe, paid homage in the age-old way of man, and then carefully attended to the piece of clothing in his hands, shaking it out before hooking it on a peg. Finally, his breathing deep, his eyes fierce, he lifted the bed linen.

She slid beneath the covers, heart full, every nerve quivering. He made quick work of his own clothing, suspenders swinging, articles flying.

He joined her in their marriage bed, and though the cold mountain air whistled through the cabin and snow collected at its corners, neither were touched by their icy presence.

Epilogue

L et there be light.

    Tillie pressed the white button. Electric lights flared, illuminating the living hall of the Irene Martin Home for Children. The large area held several groupings of child-size chairs and tables resting on wool rugs from the Sears, Roebuck catalogue.

It was her favorite room in the new orphanage. The children gathered here to mingle, play games, or spend a lazy afternoon reading. The piano Mr. Vanderbilt ordered had finally arrived, bringing a great deal of excitement with it.

Scattered on various tables were odds and ends the children had made or collected to amuse themselves with. Buttons, flower presses, wooden blocks, scraps of fabric, yarn dolls, and toy soldiers.

Her childhood library and the trunks of books which belonged to Mack's father now lined one wall. Opposite it, a wall of windows and French doors looked out on the river, waiting for daybreak.

Mack leaned against the frame of an open door leading onto the terrace, his back to the room. He looked over his shoulder, brown eyes warm. "Can you turn off the lights? They're disturbing the quiet."

The hum of the light bulbs grew loud in her ears. She plunged the room into darkness, then stepped up beside him. It was moments before sunrise. Still too dark to see the beautiful view of the French Broad River, Mt. Pisgah, and the miles of open land surrounding the orphanage.

The only hint of illumination came from a sky stretched with black clouds against a light gray canvas. Little by little, behind a string of Carolina mountains, the edge of the horizon turned from gray to white, as if God had slathered it with a layer of whipping cream.

The clouds moved down, or maybe the white moved up, chased by a layer of pink with a light, light salmon hovering at its midpoint.

Mack slipped his arm around her, pulling her against his side. She rested her head against his shoulder. It was as if there were no one on earth but her, him, and God Almighty. Then suddenly, it was there, peeking over the mountains like the tip of a blacksmith's white poker, turning the clouds purple. The landscape gray.

Though she never saw it move, the white nucleus somehow lifted above the horizon, breaking free of the mountains, lighting the sky and gilding the clouds with fire. Its blinding rays obliterated the sight of everything in its immediate path. As if God's fingertip, so bright, so powerful, had touched the horizon and made an arc up into the sky.

Mack shifted, turning toward her, pulling her against him, his shirt soft, his chest hard.

She looked at him, amazed she had ever considered walking away from him when right here in the Irene Martin Home for Children she had been blessed with more riches than she'd ever dreamed of.

A beautiful sunrise. Purpose. Children she delighted in. A man she loved with more abundance than she could ever contain. And the freedom to enjoy it all.

She slipped her arms around his neck, glorying in the intensity of his eyes. "Good morning."

"Yes, it is." He enfolded her in his arms and lowered his mouth to hers, infusing her with a warmth and passion which could only come from the same source as the sunrise.

Author's Note

Biltmore Estate was built in 1895 by George Vanderbilt and is still owned by the family. It is open to the public and is one of America's greatest national treasures. What makes this particular historical home so unique (other than its sheer size, its grandeur, and its state-of-the-art technologies) are its furnishings and accessories. Every other historical home I have ever visited had furnishings "of the time." But never was the house fully furnished with the original pieces. Yet Biltmore holds the very items that belonged to George and Edith Vanderbilt. I can't tell you what a treat they were to see. If you haven't visited the Estate, it's not to be missed. I'm going again with my readers this fall and will be showing them behind-the-scenes settings from *Maid to Match*. If you'd like to join us, go to *GetawayWithDee.com* for more information.

Now for confession time. I had to bend a few things in order to make my novel work, and since the Vanderbilt family has gone to such lengths to preserve their history, I feel I should set the record straight. First, George and Edith were indeed married in Paris in 1898, but they didn't arrive at Biltmore until October. (I had them well ensconced in the house in August.)

Second, Edith did not bring a French lady's maid with her. George had the housekeeper hire a local before they ever arrived. So I totally made that up. (George did like to hire from the area, though.)

Third, all the servants in my book are fictitious. I didn't want to use the real names of the housekeeper, butler, or anyone else because I might have done them an injustice. So the household positions were accurate, but the characters were a figment of my imagination.

I portrayed the Vanderbilts' progressive views of the servant class and their approachability according to what I discovered in my research. At first I thought the docents were being generous because the place where they worked was still owned by the family. But my study encompassed sources well outside the influence of the Vanderbilts, and every one of them underscored the same thing: George and Edith cared about their staff and treated them with unprecedented consideration.

The maternity baskets—true. Walls of windows in the basement—true. Central heat and electricity for the servants—true. New furniture bought specifically for the servants' bedrooms—true. Indoor plumbing for the servants—true. The giving of gifts at Christmas—true. The newspaper account I included (of the Christmas celebration) was a real article and one of many that showed up, year after year, describing how Edith made her list and checked it twice. As a matter of fact, she did not send her lady's maid to do the shopping, but did all the shopping herself. She also made sure it was done locally so as to boost the economy. Then they invited all the families that worked for them and had a big Christmas morning celebration where they gave a gift to every staff member and every child. That would be impressive if done today. In 1898, it was unheard of.

If you are an expert on the servant class of the late 1800s, you might have thought I didn't do my homework. I want to assure you I did; it's just that the American servant class differed from the British servant class. For example, in Britain, the butler was at the top of the food chain, but in America, it was the housekeeper. In Britain, they called the leaders of the domestic corps the Upper Ten; in America, they were called the Swell Set. In Britain, there was no talking during staff meals. In America, they were a bit more relaxed. So if you find something that doesn't jibe with what you know to be true in England, it's likely that we backward Americans just did it a little differently.

As for the orphanage, I made that whole thing up. I could find no record of Asheville having an orphanage, nor did George Vanderbilt build one. That was merely a device on my part. (Though a local businessman did have a Swat That Fly contest in an effort to solve the fly problem the city had, and the owner of the mortuary really did parade a corpse down Main Street in an effort to drum up business.)

All in all, Biltmore was a great place to set a book. I hope you can join me live at Biltmore this coming fall. We're going to have a great time. Again, all the details are at *GetawayWith Dee.com*. See you there!

GET AWAY WITH DEE'S CIRCLE OF FRIENDS
Biltmore 2010

This fall, join bestselling author Deeanne Gist for a luxurious weekend at the beautiful Biltmore mansion in Asheville, North Carolina. Let us whisk you away to the Gilded Age in a special readers getaway! Experience the romance of history up close as you relax with Dee and go behind the scenes of the *Maid to Match* world.

Weekend includes:

- Private tour of Biltmore mansion
- Gilded Age party with Victorian parlor games and book swap
- Photos in turn-of-the-century clothing
- Author's luncheon
- Optional activities such as carriage rides
- Lots of laughs and quality time with Dee

And much, much more!

For more information, visit
GetawayWithDee.com